I0564508

MIST
AND
DIVIDE

MIST
AND
DIVIDE

M. E. SHOTWELL

CITY OWL
PRESS

MIST AND DIVIDE
Soulquake, Book One

CITY OWL PRESS
www.cityowlpress.com

Cover Design by MiblArt. All stock photos licensed appropriately.

Map Design by Agustina Elizondo.

Edited by Tee Tate.

For information on subsidiary rights, please contact the publisher at info@cityowlpress.com.

Deluxe Hardback Edition ISBN: 978-1-64898-476-1

Paperback Edition ISBN: 978-1-64898-475-4

Digital Edition ISBN: 978-1-64898-477-8

Printed in the United States of America

CITY OWL PRESS
Escape Your World ◆ Get Lost in Ours

To those fighting for better

THE TERRINS OF ELSINOR

CORALLON

IOGATON

TUSINDA

MIDMAREA

HEFRIS

SPOKIZAR

ELSINEA

DEVRENIM

North

ULOPRA

YOBROL

PROLOGUE

Coryn carried the infant in one arm, a pudgy-legged boy with big brown eyes and even bigger curiosity. He held out a hand as they passed through the market, reaching for silky soft fabrics from their lands to the west, exotic bird quills from the southern rainforests, sparkling gems from the northeast. His lips turned down in a dramatic frown at the sight of the silvery scales and agape mouths of the fish from the north.

"I know you want to see everything, but we're losing daylight," Coryn said. Not that the market didn't continue on until the late hours of the night. Many a shop owner found their largest profits after sundown, when drunken revelers' pockets loosened. Coryn didn't want to be around such company, especially with her boy. Besides, she was to see her dearest friend, and it wasn't every day that Nera had a chance to step away from the palace kitchen to see how much the boy had grown.

They waited by a grain stand, a place Nera picked. As she put it, the palace could never have too much fine meal and flour, a good excuse to be out during odd hours and happen to cross paths with Coryn and the boy.

As the aromas of perfumes and sweet delights diminished, gradually replaced by the bitterness of hops and seared meats, Coryn scanned the passersby with a frenetic energy, worried she had missed the meeting window. She turned around at the tap on her shoulder, sighing relief.

"This can't be him!" Nera's grin warmed the coldest of hearts. "He must've doubled in size since I saw you last!"

The two women kissed cheeks and exchanged the boy, Nera giving Coryn's arms respite from holding the child.

"I apologize for the lateness." Nera tickled the boy's belly. "Supper was delayed, then eventually turned down. If I had known that to begin with, I could've arrived sooner."

"It's all right. I've secured a place to stay for the night, and a cart to return in the morning. You know how he loves watching the horses."

"You do spoil him." As if knowing what she said, the boy pressed his hands on Nera's cheeks. She giggled. "Yes, I mean you, little one. But I can understand why. Too precious not to spoil."

Coryn gently squeezed the folds of his leg. "And I plan on spoiling him some more. You spoke of a toy stall?"

"Yes, around the corner. I know the wood carver. Very skilled. Come, I'll show you."

Nera carried the boy on one hip, leading Coryn through the busy crowd. The palace kitchen had its own set of noises, banging pots, boiling soups and bubbling gravies. But out here, there was life—noisy, loud life, with the cacophony of shoppers bargaining, musicians playing for coin, bleating of animals for sale. In short bursts, it made her blood excitedly race, while too long amidst the din overwhelmed her. She could only imagine what the young boy thought of it all.

She stopped before turning the corner, the boy all too happy to watch a merchant performing a slight of hand trick with an egg, and checked she hadn't lost her companion. Coryn stood a ways behind and grazed her fingers along a scarf of deep scarlet at a table. Nera gave her an approving nod. It wasn't every day that Coryn had a chance to shop for herself. She had suffered for years to have a child, finally having the boy, and spent all her time and energy on him. Nera was more than happy to give her a moment.

"Come, come. Let's see the wonderful toys." Nera weaved through the shoppers and pointed at the stall of wooden playthings. The boy's stare immediately turned from the dolls and games to the animals, simple carvings of bare wood with heads that turned or legs that swiveled to and fro. "Look at all—"

For a moment, Nera couldn't tell if her hand shook, or the stall. The lambs and snowcats wobbled, dolls tumbling over. Then she felt it. The rumble beneath her feet. Dust billowing down the buildings, roofs crumbling into pieces.

The loud grumble and crack.

Screams.

A man bumped into her shoulder, spinning her round. A woman tripped beside her. Nera bent down to help her up, then lost her footing. She cradled the boy as quickly as she could before falling to the ground, the trembling surface blurring her vision, rattling her insides. The boy whined in her arms. She held him tight to her chest, the yells piercing, overshadowed by something deeper, visceral. A growl, as if the core of the land itself let out an angry rage.

She hummed, whether to calm the boy or herself, until...stillness.

For a moment, the world was quiet.

Then groans. People stood, wiping off rubble, hugging one another. Crying for help.

She eyed the boy who looked up at her with those innocent brown eyes. "Thank the Spirits." She kissed his forehead and clutched him tight. The ground had ceased moving, but her legs shook as she stood.

Others helped those who'd fallen to their feet. Shop owners righted tables. A man screamed in pain, another tearing cloth from his tunic to wrap the gash on his arm.

"Coryn." Panic tingled her spine and flowed to her fingers, her toes. She stumbled over broken stones and bricks and lumber.

A woman limped up to her, blood dripping from a gash on her forehead. "What...where...?"

Nera twisted away, protecting the boy. She tasted metallic sourness, realizing she had bitten her tongue hard enough to bleed. It mingled with the inhaled dirt tarnishing the air.

A thick hand grabbed her ankle, the heavyset man sprawled on the ground, feet buried under a fallen cart. Nera frantically shook herself loose from his grip.

She turned the corner, making it to where the scarf stall had stood just moments ago.

"Coryn?" She turned every which way, squinting through the settling dust, trying to distinguish her friend's voice through the cries for help.

A young man came running, leaping nimbly over the wreckage on the street. He carried fruit in his cloak as if it were a sack. He briefly stopped by Nera, nabbing two scarves that lay among the debris, before running off again.

Nera looked down, red poking out of crumbled stones. She hurried to it, pulling out the deep scarlet scarf.

"No. No, no." She set the boy down at her feet. He fussed, whining and clinging to her legs, trying to pull himself up as she lifted stones, one by one, tossing them aside. "Cor—"

She froze.

Her ears muffled the shouts and pleas, the shifting of rubble. The world.

The last stone slipped slowly out of her loosened grip. She held a hand to her open mouth, as if her own soul would break free of her body.

The boy babbled and crawled forward.

Nera snapped to, scooping him up. "No."

She pressed his head on her shoulder, the exposed, lifeless face of Coryn among the debris blurring behind her tears.

19 YEARS LATER...

ONE

C old.

Just how far it ebbed its way into my chest, I wasn't sure. I blinked it away. Heard it through numb ears. Tasted it on frozen lips.

The rows of alabaster trees in Ashwan Forest didn't seem to care about the cold or the blood that had shunted to my vital organs. Two hours now and my hands and feet suffered for it.

That was the thing about the cold. It betrayed the body, no matter the amount of fabric and hides and furs. It seeped into the thinnest cracks in my armor—a snagged sleeve over my wrist, a tear in my cloak, a pinhole in my boot.

I tightened the collar of fur around my neck in aching slowness, my hair tucked between my ears and cloak. My hood lay on my shoulders, out of the way of my peripheral vision.

I had tracked the otari when the sun hit low, the time it abandoned the sea to forage for nocturnal critters as they awakened. Its tracks were easy enough to locate. Two front flipper arches, like boomerangs, etched into the snow, along with the rear hoof. The telltale signs of a mature otari, the only animal left on Corallon whose fat was dense enough to provide fuel. The meat it provided was a bonus, albeit a slightly chewy and bitter one.

Actually killing it took skill and most of all, patience. They were skittish creatures, jumping to alertness at a foot's crunch of snow, a muted cough, or sometimes what seemed like nothing audible.

Now was the hardest part. I waited for the next breeze for noise cover, then reached beneath my cloak to the pouch tied around my waist. I secured a pellet, a smooth rock amongst my collection of ammunition. In my other hand was my sling, a bit of rope with a pocket along the middle for the projectile. I secured the end's loop around my forefinger and pinched the other end's knot. I'd only get one shot.

The sling worked best by spinning it across my body, in a figure eight, then releasing. But here I had to make my best single swing and release.

I moved my hands out of the cloak's opening on my right. It made no sense to have it open in the middle, down my torso, when hunting. That was an archer's preference.

Evella, the sideways hunter, Reil would say. Then I'd tease him about his dwindling arrow supply and knock out our dinner with one try of the sling.

But he wasn't here now. He couldn't block the otari from fleeing. He couldn't share in the spoils. He couldn't comfort me, or make me laugh, or reassure me that there was still goodness to be had in this world.

There was only me.

With the rope's ends in my left hand and pellet secured in the right, I froze.

The otari perked up its tiny triangular ears for a moment, then slapped them back down.

Now.

In one fluid movement, I swung the rock pellet in an arch, releasing the rope at the right moment to fling it directly toward the animal's head.

A crack of a branch behind me snapped the animal out of its calm, my pellet nipping its hind hoof as it raced away.

Now I had two problems. The otari got away.

And someone else was near.

I wrapped my sling back into my hip satchel and unsheathed my blade from its holster. The metal was barely longer than my hand, wrist to fingertips, but it did the job well enough. These days it was hard to find metal, let alone someone who could work it into weaponry. At least on Corallon.

I crouched low and snuck right to get behind the intruder. The snow reached over my sorry excuse for boots to my calves. If it was a hunter, keeping low was the safest option, despite my frozen legs. It wasn't uncommon to have an arrow fly by from unskilled hunters who didn't see me, or the occasional one who did.

A grunt came from ahead. The breeze whirred in my face as I stood downwind, and I smelled the newness of him. No otari oil on his fingers, or ale on his breath, or wood smoke in his hair, or dirtied animal fur on his body.

He sat between two alabaster trees, like a plump flea amidst the white teeth of a comb. The summer forest, though short lived, provided tall grass between the skinny, white-barked trees, filling in the floor and offering plenty of shelter for woodland creatures. But in the winter, the grass lay dormant. The forest was spikes of white that branched into full webs of limbs and twigs in the canopy, as if stretching and searching for their long-lost leaves.

We were near the northern edge of the forest, right before the trees gave way to acres of field. If I ran out to him from behind, he could run for it in that direction. Beyond that stood my family's home. The snow-covered field in winter minimized unwanted visitors, animal, or human. I wasn't about to let him be one.

His other option would be to run west, where he'd have ten or twelve paces before reaching the cliff to the sea.

I took a final quiet step to better make out my adversary, a man on his knees catching his breath.

In a leap I wrapped one arm around him, my blade in the other at his neck.

"Don't move."

He remained still, his body thin but solid under the thick cloak. I wasn't sure if I could've overtaken him if he had snuck up on me.

"You could very well slice me," he whispered. "I do realize that. But not before I'd yell and attract those Raiders."

His breath smelled fresh, like a sprig of mint with a rich spice.

"What are you talking about?"

He turned and looked at me, his face light brown with the start of dark stubble, a contrast stark against my white skin and the barely whiter snow. He tipped his head to the bush. "Down there."

"Don't try anything." I kept the sharp end of my blade aimed at him as I released my grip and crept along the ground. He could easily run. To be honest I wasn't sure if I'd go after him. I simply wanted to make sure *he* wasn't after *me*. Running would only alleviate that concern.

The sun had long gone over the horizon, but as I reached the land's edge, I could make out a clunk of rusted metal in the moonlight. Four figures carried it through the surf, onto the sand in organized heaves. Two of them collapsed on the beach by the structure while the other two caught their breath. Their clothes were dark in color and clung to their bodies, unlike the amalgam of my pelts and furs and cloak. Every now and then someone moved just right for the moonlight to shine off something on their clothing—a clasp or buckle. Or maybe it was some strange armor.

"What are they doing here, so far north?" I whispered to the man who remained ten paces behind. It wasn't entirely surprising to see Raiders. The town reported more frequent sightings in the last several days. It was hard to know which rumors emanating from the townsfolk were true. They used gossip and conjecture as their main form of entertainment, each tale taller than the last. Apparently at least one of them was based in truth.

The stranger crept closer to me, crunching and panting.

"Are you trying to attract attention?" I whispered.

He caught my glare. "Apologies."

I pictured throwing him off the side—for the noise, for invasion of the space he occupied around me. And for making me lose the otari.

The four on the beach chatted. I looked at the young man and placed my finger over my lips, then inched as close to the edge of the cliff without hurling over, my stomach to the ground. Whatever they were doing here, it couldn't be good. If there was some plan to attack Corallon, or take more of its young inhabitants, I could warn everyone. It would give them time to collect their weapons and defenses, come up with a plan. I needed to know how many more there were, if this was their targeted landing point, anything that could help. Perhaps if I did something good for the town, for Corallon, then my past would be forgotten…

One of the Raiders looked up, and I pulled back, knocking over the man who had barely balanced himself squatting.

"Someone is up there." A voice echoed from below.

I rolled over and planted myself on top of the man, the tip of the blade near his eye. "Don't. Move." I mouthed the words, and he nodded with the smallest of movement.

The voices below continued. "It might be—"

"If we've been discovered already, our mission is compromised. We must leave."

"But what about—"

"Not tonight, son."

The other two whined, then grunting commenced as they pushed their metal ship into the sea. I waited for the splashing to cease before braving another glance.

"I think they're gone." I released the stranger entirely from my body weight. But not from my suspicion.

I dared a peek at the shore. The beach had cleared, their metal ship nowhere on the water. I stood, scanning the ripples of the water. It was rumored Raiders used enchanted steel to make underwater ships. Other hearsay highly doubtful proved true. How would steel float? What made it enchanted? It was nonsense.

But now I wasn't so sure. The moon gave up no objects floating on the sea's surface. In one moment the ship and its crew were on land, and the next, gone.

"They should call them Invisible Raiders, shouldn't they?"

I turned to my new neighbor. "What are you doing here? Who are you?"

"I could ask the very same of you." He brushed snow off his black cloak. It cried its age, that of a fresh, newer cloak. Older clothing, like what remained available in Corallon, was faded, tattered, and mended many times over. No stitch looked out of place, though the lighting was poor. As for his trousers, well, he'd get along better in the desert of Yobrol than the Corallon winter.

His indignation waned as I sized him up. "I was looking for food, if you must know."

"By the looks of it, you were sightseeing for food."

"What's that supposed to mean?"

I shook my head. Although he might get away with it more at this hour of night, a black cloak might as well have announced his arrival. Not to mention it didn't look like he had weapons on him. At least I didn't feel any when I pressed him to the ground.

"Are you traveling alone? With family?" I briefly scanned behind him, half afraid the whole ordeal was a trap laid out by a group of men.

He continued brushing off snow, having made it down to his knees. "I have no family."

I looked him in the eyes; they were deep brown, nearly black in the night. "You're a Displaced?"

He nodded once.

"From where?"

He sighed, seeming annoyed with my interrogation. I could very well just stab him instead. It wouldn't be hard seeing as I was still irritated he chased away the otari. Others out here wouldn't have hesitated to kill a stranger that chased away their prey.

"From the south."

"And how did you get here?"

"By heading north."

I drew my blade, aiming it at his chest. "I don't have the time or patience for games. I spent the better part of the evening tracking down the otari that you scared off, so I don't have much sympathy for you, either. In fact, I should ask you to pay for the loss."

He put up both hands. "Please. I apologize. I really don't have family, or shelter for tonight. I've had very little to eat besides…well, whatever it was that lady gave me yesterday morning that felt like leather and tasted worse."

There was only one food that could be described so distastefully and accurately. *Dried gunnel skin.* It wasn't animal skin at all, but a filet of gunnel smoked until it curled. They only lived along rocky shorelines and were a major food source when the waters were too cold for red sardines. Which meant he had traveled from the southern shore of Corallon to here in two days.

Which meant he was lying or, for what he lacked in survival skills, he made up for in quick feet.

"It's getting dark. I suggest we go our separate ways and try not to ever encounter each other again." I sheathed my blade and traipsed out of the forest edge into the blanketed field.

"Wait."

I stopped. *Don't turn around, Evella. You'll regret it.*

I pivoted back. Funny how my body didn't listen to my head.

"Can you at least point me in the right direction? May I walk with you until we reach a town?"

"I'm not going to town."

"Not going to town?" He nervously chuckled. "What, do you live out here in the open?"

"No, I live in a house. You may have heard of it. Walls made of stone. A roof."

"Sounds lovely."

I turned around and marched northward. This man had taken enough of my attention. And my fuel and meat. Mother and Father would be wondering about me. I wasn't to venture long past dusk. Mother would say it was because of the predatory animals and occasionally dangerous people, but I knew better. Most of the big game, save for the occasional boar or snowcat, had been hunted to extinction years ago, and as far as dangerous people, well, danger was relative.

No, I knew what she thought amid those words.

She didn't trust me. Despite being seen as too old to be living with my parents. Despite what I provided for them.

It wouldn't help my cause if I didn't show up home soon. My knees ached from all the standing, and the cold pierced my joints as I got into a steady pace. I tried ignoring the loud footsteps behind me, the stranger fighting the snow as if it took his feet hostage.

"You know I did kind of save your life back there."

I paused, foot mid-air waiting to grasp my next step.

"With the Raiders and all."

I considered his point. At least for the time it took my words to form. "Never mind that when they discovered us, they fled." I dabbed my nose on the back of my hand, the walk stirring circulation from both physical exertion and mental annoyance. "But, who knows? Maybe they would've chopped me to bits." The sarcasm oozed out my lips. That wasn't what Raiders did. At least not on land. While they had a reputation for pilfering towns and travelers for their food and supplies, Raiders preferred the more confusing crime of kidnapping, stealing away young men and women. I did fit the profile of those taken, being nineteen. But did anyone know what else they were looking for in their victims? Or what they did to those poor people?

"They could've taken you." Apparently wherever he was from, he'd heard the same.

"Then I wouldn't have to listen to you."

"That hurts."

I broke a smile, despite my efforts. He wasn't going to leave me alone unless I did kill him. Which, with the increased talking, didn't seem that implausible. I'm sure the town would love that. *Trapper Girl Murders Man Who Saved her Life*. Rolls off the gossip tongue.

However, if he was a Displaced, I couldn't leave him out for the night. A Displaced had no say, no choice in what happened. He couldn't help where or when the quakes struck. Or the why or how or who. No one knew the truth behind them.

All anyone could do was survive. To not help a Displaced was to let another person or family die.

It was Father's spoken policy—a Displaced was family. Unfortunately, not everyone felt the same.

"What's your name?"

He caught up to me through the snow, looking like a newborn deer grasping the concept of walking. "Arek. Uh, why do you ask?" His apprehension was almost endearing, half-cowered, ready to recoil as if I were a snake about to strike. I nearly felt sorry for him.

"Because I like to know the names of everyone who stays in my family's home."

"Really? You mean it?"

I sighed. "I can't let a Displaced stay out here for the night, especially not one looking as unprepared as you."

I winced despite myself. *You don't have to make the truth sound mean,* Mother had said.

Truth doesn't depend on feelings, Mother.

"Anyway, I'm Evella Trapper." I kept my hands within my cloak, hesitant to expose them to the cold and saving myself the formality of greeting customs. Elbow to elbow was too friendly, a hand to his shoulder and his on mine too formal not to mention awkward with the touching and closeness of it.

"Evella. Very well."

"Have you heard of it? My name?"

He swallowed slowly. "No. Should I have?"

I grinned, biting the inside of my cheek. "No. That's actually for the best." I began walking again, and he continued by my side.

"Why's that?"

I peeked at his oval face, his profile plain but strangely handsome in the moonlight. "Less explaining to do."

TWO

After repeatedly going through the conversation of *thank you, I really appreciate this, again thank you,* Arek finally conserved his energy for trudging through the snow.

My family home sat near the northern edge of the island, west of the town of Corallon. Father said that after The Quake, the newly split lands—ten altogether—had to decree an official name. Most chose to name their terrin after the largest town left in their jurisdiction. Such was the case with Corallon. Although after a few years Dern, a town in the south, grew more populous.

"I feel like we're on the ends of the earth."

"That's because we are." The island of Corallon was the northernmost terrin of Elsinor, what they called the unified land up to twenty years ago. The town had been a fishing village, close to the current that wrapped over the northern shorelines bringing an abundance of sea life. After the Quake, the detached terrin seemed to shift further north, subsequent quakes widening the sea's expanse. The current no longer flowed in the north, but the south. And the entire island experienced longer winters with deeper cold spells.

"How far is town?"

I pointed to the open space off to the right. "That way. Beyond the hill."

"Does anyone else live out here?"

"Sure. My parents, brother, and sister." It wasn't the answer he was looking for. "It's more strategic in terms of hunting and trapping, closer to Ashwan Forest."

While that was true, it wasn't the reason we had moved out of our two-story wooden home of my childhood. If he wanted to know that, he could ask anyone in town for the story.

As my nose began running again and fingers numbed, the point of the circular roof appeared on the dark horizon. I could barely make out the emanating smoke, and as we stepped closer, the heat of the fire warmed me, whether for real or in my head.

The circular house was made of murite, large stones stacked and sealed in place with mortar, except for the door. That was a remnant of our old home, hewn from sturdy olum wood. Yet another resource used up in my lifetime. While there were windows etched into the sides for each of the rooms—miniature swinging doors that made holes large enough to escape —they remained closed during the winter months to keep in the heat.

"Here we are." I opened the latch on the striated wooden door, the thick knots so familiar I could draw the pattern in the snow. Arek followed me in, and I closed the door behind him. "I can't tell you how many times I've told my family to keep the door locked."

"I don't suppose you get a whole lot of strangers out here."

Just the likes of you. I stomped my boots on the dirt floor, the frozen-on snow not willing to give up its grip on the exposed fur at my ankles. While the boots were made of boar leather, I additionally wrapped my feet in hare pelts tied secure with thin rope as extra insulation. I unraveled the rope and stood in my gray socks, my big right toe sticking out of the hole. It was a miracle they didn't have more holes in them. Wool was hard to come by, so we had to reuse what little we had.

Arek took off his black boots, shiny, stiff things that stood upright without his feet in them. He wiggled his toes in his red socks, not a hole to be found.

Where did he get red wool? And so recently?

There were too many questions for him, but a ruckus sounded in the kitchen, and I walked Arek through the house. It was a simple set up. The entrance hallway opened to a round room, where the fire kept ablaze during winter—and most of fall and spring. Our bedrooms branched off to the left and right, the dividing walls like spokes of a wheel. There were doors to each bedroom, yet they remained open most of the time to welcome the fire's warmth.

The kitchen lay straight ahead, and we walked around the large fire pit. I briefly nodded to the two men occupying my brother Wren's room, who chatted quietly in the candlelight. They had been here the past three nights after they approached Father when he was out trading, twenty-somethings who had been wandering most of the season through Corallon.

I led Arek through the doorway into the kitchen.

Mother stood by the stove in the corner, her back to us, while Father sat at the head of the table, completely consumed in what he was saying. Wren and my sister Tulla noticed our entrance but kept quiet, not disturbing Father.

"He said that the Midmareans are taking further steps to form their own government. They've even gone as far as asking the other terrins if they'd be allies. Can you believe that? Right under Elsinea's nose. Or should I say right over their eyes."

Elsinea remained the capital of the ten terrins, but Midmarea, the island directly north of it, argued it was more central to the terrins than Elsinea, with a larger chunk of land—over twice the size. At least from what Father had reported from other Council rumors he'd gathered in weeks past.

Even though Father did have a question in all of that, he didn't mean for it to be answered. "Now Tusinda is also getting ideas, and their Council is arguing with Midmarea's Council. They've argued enough that they're not accepting each other's currency. I can't even keep track of which terrin I can use a Corallon coin, or which ones don't take an Elsinean bill."

His thick beard twitched, a minute movement that happened

whenever he clenched his jaw. He was a formidable figure, tall, with broad shoulders. Mother said years ago he hadn't a pinch of fat on his body, with how hard he worked the fishing boats. But he lost most of that physique, a softer yet doubtfully quieter man.

"The worst part is that the king is doing nothing about it."

I swallowed hard. It was frowned upon to speak ill of King Ronin. Usually it was safe in the walls of our house, but Arek stood beside me. I didn't trust most of the answers he had given me, and who knew what his position was on the king.

Mother turned from the stove, mixing a concoction in a pot she carried to the table. Her face was flushed red from the stove heat, her graying curly hair pulled loosely in a braid down her back. "Why not be separate at this point? Would it really be that bad?"

Father made a fist on the table. "Because we rely on them!"

"For less and less." I stood frozen, the words having escaped my mouth.

"Evella, you're back." Father grinned. I wondered if it was in victory over Mother, him betting I'd come back while she postured I had run away or worse. "No otari?"

Ugh. It was nice having almost forgotten about the escaped prey. "No. Instead I brought Arek. He's a Displaced."

"Oh dear," Mother said. "How long have you been wandering?"

Good question, Mother.

Father put up a hand. "I'm sure the journey has been a tough one." He scanned the man from crown of the head to wool-covered toes. "Or not, I don't know."

I chuckled. When it came to assessing surroundings, like in hunting or trapping, Father's instincts mirrored mine.

"But we can't take another in tonight. We still have two with Wren, we can't add a third in there. Plus, we need to replenish our supplies."

Although I hadn't terribly wanted Arek to spend the night, it was irksome that Father chose when or when not to hold his word true. "What happened to *a Displaced is family?*"

"I agree with Evella." Mother met my gaze and gave a slight nod. It wasn't often Mother took my side on anything. "Maybe we should take a vote, as a family."

As much as this conversation needed to happen, it was embarrassing to have Arek, the source of contention, standing right there.

"I think we should stick with our plan," I said. "There were times I, or Tulla or Wren, even Gareg when he was here, didn't care to share our bedrooms with strangers. But we did it, for the sake of doing the honorable thing."

Father rubbed his forehead with his thick hands. "We can't do it. There's nowhere to put him."

"He can sleep in my room," I said.

Mother's jaw dropped. "Absolutely not." She composed herself, holding her throat as if it calmed down the words she wanted to say. "He can sleep in here. We can spare a blanket."

Father sighed, shoulders slumping. He was giving in.

Then Mother dug in with her dagger. "In the old house, we could take them all."

Father slapped his hand on the table. "We aren't there, are we?"

I wanted to sneak off to my room. Arek's wince said as much.

"We have all we need here. A roof, warmth, beds. Generally enough food for us all and some to spare when we can for the Displaced."

"I miss my old room." Tulla looked down at her empty bowl, her loose curls the same as Mother's, though still holding their golden hue. I couldn't blame her for saying it, yet at eight years old, perhaps I could blame her for not reading the room.

Arek stepped closer to the table, wringing his hands near his waist. "It would be temporary—for the night. Then I'll be on my way."

It was the first time I did genuinely feel sorry for him. Whoever he was, from wherever, he was in a foreign land, hadn't had food all day, and had nowhere to go tonight. Not only that, he was thrown into the world of the Trapper family.

"I owe him a debt," I said. "He saved me from being detected by Raiders. It's the least I can do."

"Raiders?" Mother placed her left hand on her right shoulder, a gesture Spiriters believed alerted their guardian spirit to strife. And non-believers like me found absolutely useless. She could slaughter an eel and jump in the air ten times while naked, for all I cared.

Because there were no spirits to call on. No help was ever coming.

"They left as quickly as they arrived, but were it not for Arek, I may have been discovered." Or they would've infiltrated deeper into Corallon with whatever their plan was. Frightening to think what could've happened. "I think it may be time to up the patrols."

The voluntary patrol unit consisted of a handful of people that covered a small fraction of the coast. No one quite believed Raiders would fully invade Corallon, if not for its climate alone, when they had nine other terrins to choose from.

"I'll tell Gareg next time I see him. Maybe he can get Penni to present it to the Council."

"And Arek?" There was a certain face I'd make—pleading eyes, pouting mouth—that broke down Father's walls. It didn't work quite as often as I've gotten older, but I gave it my all.

His steel facade melted, revealing his real squishy self. "Ahh, fine!" He threw up his hand. "But not in your room. Here in the kitchen, like your mother said."

"Very well." I turned to Arek with a grin. He reciprocated with a smile.

"Can we eat now?" Tulla asked.

"Yes, please. Let's do," Mother said.

"What about the other two?" I asked.

"They had their fill early," Mother said. "Planning on leaving first thing in the morning." She ladled out the trowroot stew. The taupe broth lacked the slightest appeal, but she did have a way with getting it to taste good enough. The warmth it provided in my stomach defrosted the rest of my body.

Arek sat next to me, sipping small mouthfuls out of the spoon. It was an acquired taste, one he obviously hadn't achieved yet.

I leaned toward him. "You'll get used to it."

He swallowed hard. "By the end of the bowl?"

I shook my head. "By the end of one hundred bowls."

Mealtimes were about the only times I learned anything from the

Displaced. It was easy to spot someone who hadn't experienced Corallon's bleak fare. You'd think with all the strangers flowing in and out of our home, I'd have learned much about the other nine terrins, or even the other corners of Corallon. Most of the time, the travelers arrived tired, scared and...lost. They didn't know where to go after here, or how they'd carry on with their lives beyond this. Many grieved the loss of loved ones and didn't want to speak, especially around a cohesive family. Some ran off in the middle of the night, some found work in town, and others roamed the rest of the disjointed lands of Elsinor.

I sipped water from my cup. Water was plentiful in winter. All one had to do was melt snow, although it took an overwhelming amount to fill a cup. That was Tulla's job, as the youngest in the family. She kept the vat in the corner of the kitchen full of water. In the short season when the snow melted, she walked to the creek east of the forest and carried the containers back.

"What's most important to get from town?" I asked. "I'll be going in the morning to trade, if my traps bring about anything."

"Lard." Mother winked. It was what she asked for every time, and with good reason. We needed fat in our diets and certainly didn't get it from root vegetables. I would've been the hero of the day if I had scored that otari. But now we were down to adding lard to everything Mother cooked.

"Father?"

He took a deep breath and let it out. As if he had been in deep thought and blew it away. "Fish, if they've got any. Otherwise—"

"Lard." I nodded, studying his face. Something worried him, the pain in his eyes. "What is it?"

He glanced at Arek, then back to me. "I received another call today for royal rations."

"We can barely feed ourselves," Mother said.

"It's not like we received anything in months here." Wren spoke with his face in the bowl, embarrassingly licking the sides. He was destined to have Father's broad shoulders, although his frame was skin and bones at the moment.

"You don't receive rations here?" Arek had stopped eating, fidgeting with the spoon on the table.

"Supposed to," I said. "But Wren is right. It's not just Corallon. The towns to the south haven't either. Which is why your red wool socks look not only comfortable but suspicious."

I glanced underneath the table, and he tucked his feet under the seat.

"I wouldn't worry about it, Father," I said. "We can't give what we don't have. Besides, didn't you say the Council reported Elsinea was taking an unfair share? That other trade agreements are being made between terrins to bypass the king?"

Arek's eyes grew wide with surprise. "Bypass the king?"

A low grumble reverberated through my feet, along the floor. The table shook, the remaining pot on the stove rattled, and the vat of water slished and sloshed.

Another one.

"Under the table!" Father yelled.

I slipped under the table as Mother helped Tulla, who counted up slowly. *One...Two...Three...*

Wren joined in on the hug, and Father looked at us as the earth shook, his head protected but the rest of his body exposed to the falling debris.

Arek crouched next to me, his shoulders against mine. My impulse to create space between us was stifled by the desire to survive. He breathed hard, his eyes wide with terror. I covered my head as if the hard table wasn't enough protection. It was more to drown out the sounds—rattling of utensils, rumbling of the ground, clinking of pots. The scream from Reil that I heard every quake, despite covering my ears.

Dust puffed off the stone walls. Wren's bowl crashed onto the floor, and Tulla yelped, sending a shrill up my spine. Not much fell these days during a quake, with most of the furniture anchored to the ground. It only took the first one in this house when the stove chased Mother to make the adjustment.

Seven...Eight...

And then it was still.

I panted, as if I had been holding my breath. Arek's white knuckles released his tight grip from the table leg.

The two men from Wren's room ran into the kitchen.

"Everyone unhurt?" Father asked.

The men nodded, followed by Mother and the rest of us as we unfolded out from under the table.

"They're getting longer," Wren said.

"And stronger," Tulla said.

Mother clutched her right shoulder, Tulla and Wren mimicking her. I turned to Arek. He too held his shoulder. Just as superstitious as Mother. I wondered if he was used to the quakes, wherever he was from. By his frightened reaction, he didn't seem used to them. But then again, quakes were the cause of Displaceds. After experiencing the death of a loved one due to a quake, they were harder to endure.

"The Raiders," Mother said. "It's because they touched down here, isn't it?"

"I'll assess any damage outside in the morning, when the sun's up," said Father. "Let me know if there's roof damage in your rooms. If they continue getting worse, we'll have to reinforce the roof when the snow thaws." He looked at Mother. "If we have the supplies by then."

Father had wanted to work on roof maintenance before winter, but supplies ran slim to non-existent over the short season. With the quakes getting worse by every measure, I worried about our safety here. I trusted in Father's skills, but the freezing and thawing cycle could wreak havoc on the best of masonry, without the added threat of quakes.

"Please reach out to Gareg too." Mother looked at me. "Or maybe you could inquire when you go into town tomorrow?"

I nodded, although what I was agreeing to was not something I could guarantee.

Arek leaned over. "Who is Gareg? He was mentioned before."

"My oldest brother."

"He doesn't live with us anymore because he is unioned." Tulla's grin suggested the fear of the earthquake had left fully with the change in conversation. A fear we learned to control over the years, until the quakes started strengthening. "Are you unioned yet?"

Arek's gaze turned down to his bowl.

"Tulla, not polite," Mother said.

"It's all right." Arek cleared his throat. "No, I'm not unioned."

"How old are you?" Tulla's face scrunched together, figuring him out.

"Tulla, that's enough." Mother shook her head.

"No, really." Arek offered Tulla a smile. "I'm nineteen."

"You're like Evella!

"Before the Quake or After?" Mom asked.

"Before."

"Oh, Evella was after," Tulla said. "But still close."

Arek shot his gaze over to me. Yes, the nineteen-year-old hag of Corallon. With the quakes intensifying, more pressure was placed on unioning by eighteen, starting families as soon as possible to carry the bloodline, the family name. Admittedly, it was surprising to meet someone else my age not unioned. Then again, meeting people wasn't a priority. Avoided, if anything.

Arek raised an eyebrow and turned to me. "Everyone hoping you're next?"

"Gareg's actually younger than me." Not that the fact answered his question.

"She was to be unioned last year," Tulla said. "But Reil died in a quake."

The sound of his name nearly brought up the stew. One year since he died. Some days already a year, others only a year.

Wren elbowed Tulla.

"Ow, that wasn't nice."

"What you spewed out of your mouth wasn't nice."

She had only stated the truth. Unfortunately the truth still hurt.

"Excuse me." I stood, leaving my scattered dinnerware at the table.

"Evella." Mother pleaded. Dad patted her hand and let me go without a fight.

I headed for my room, hasty footsteps following behind me.

Explaining to Tulla that she didn't do anything wrong was not something I had the energy to do right now.

A hand touched my elbow.

I turned around reluctantly, the pity in Arek's dark brown eyes unmistakable.

"I'm sorry about that," he said.

There was much I wanted to say. *You couldn't have known. You don't know me at all. Or my family.* But it applied to me too, about him. I didn't know his story, his tragedies, if indeed that was what led him here.

"You don't have a role in any of it." I released my elbow from his loose grip. I wanted him gone. I wanted everyone gone and to be alone. But I never got that in the house. Only on the outside. It was one of the reasons I needed to move out during the short season, make my own place. Living with my parents at nineteen, with no prospects—or desire—of unioning didn't help perceptions, either.

"Since you're staying, I'll get you a blanket." I walked a quarter of the way around the central fire and into my room, grabbing one of the quilts Mother had sewn years ago.

"Here." I met him back by the fire. "You can borrow one of mine."

"You won't catch cold on my behalf?"

"Don't worry about me."

He nodded. It wasn't his job to worry about me. Or anyone else's. I didn't need anyone's pity over Reil.

I needed them to let it go. To carry on, as I have tried to do for the past year.

I especially didn't need a stranger looking at me the way Arek did now. The fire sparkled in his sad eyes, and I wanted to push him away, out of the room, out of the house.

Instead I swallowed the ire. "Good night. Don't let them keep you up too late with their stories."

I turned into my room, hiding in the shadow behind the wall. No footsteps sounded for what felt like an eternity.

Then, the soft patter of feet diminishing, and his voice.

"Good night."

THREE

Despite my noble efforts in providing Arek with my blanket, I regretted the decision soon after the last of the family went to bed. We let the fire die down on its own at night, the murite stone walls not only keeping the heat indoors but retaining heat. In the morning they'd still be warm to the touch, a trait our old wooden house couldn't claim.

Yet diminishing my covers by one blanket was enough to keep my toes and fingers cold. I couldn't get warm, wrapping the quilt that remained over my ears. The tip of my nose froze, and I fought the impulse to move around to keep warm. It didn't help that Tulla fell sound asleep within moments of hitting the bed.

When all efforts to sleep in the room proved futile, I brought my quilt and sorry thin excuse of a pillow out in the circular room, around the fire. Not much else was housed here. Wren had placed his shoes outside his doorway, and Tulla left an empty water pitcher on the floor near the doorway to the kitchen.

I added two logs to the dying embers, enough to ignite a flash of heat in the short-term and not too much that I'd have to stay up longer to keep a watchful eye on it. The dirt floor was no worse than my shelf of a bed in terms of comfort. The hay on my bed was down to a few strands, leaving the wooden slats bumpier than if they were bare. But the dirt was worse in that it was…well, dirtier. It clung to my quilt and felt cool when my toes escaped the cover. I pulled my hair up into a quick knot after a few seconds of brushing off dirt, having been careless when I initially laid down.

All of this posed the question. Why did I go out of my way to help Arek? Maybe it was because he alerted me to the Raiders. Or the family's stance on helping Displaced peoples. Or maybe it had more to do with the sense there was more to his story. I believed he had traveled most of the day and came from the south. What I didn't believe was why. Had he really been driven from his home by a quake?

Then there was tonight's quake. Had the presence of Raiders brought it about, or was that a coincidence? Did it originate from the shoreline where they had touched down or closer to the house? Father said he'd assess in the morning but it was hard not to want to know sooner.

No wonder I couldn't sleep.

I closed my eyes, lying as still as I could. I started at number one thousand and counted backwards by seven. It helped clear my mind, and seven seemed the hardest number to deal with. It was odd, and large enough to have to think of the next number in the series—unlike five or three. And nine was too easy.

Never had I ever reached below one hundred before falling asleep.

The cold numbed my fingers, poking out of the tattered gloves. It didn't matter I couldn't feel them, or my toes, anymore. I couldn't feel anything anymore.

Not after what happened to Reil.

The square in Corallon pulsated with my feverish dizziness. I saw myself as if a bird, swooping overhead, separated from the body of that helpless young girl freezing in the snow.

There was no time to think over my decision any longer. It was tonight or never.

A soft purple light glowed from the shop's window. The rest of the town *stood quiet, everyone in their homes or inn rooms, except for a drunkard passed out at the foot of the holy house.*

I kept my hood pulled tight around my head. If anyone were to come out and recognize me—

I was inside the shop, a menagerie of powders, elixirs and potions to keep away this ailment and cure that one. A lone candle flickered in the center of the room, an eerie purple flame that lured my stare. An omen? Or trickery from the apothecary?

My jacket pocket felt heavy as I stepped away from the candle. I slipped my hand in, feeling the weight of a smooth glass bottle in my thawed fingers. My heart pounded faster than a hummingbird's wings. I had never done such a thing before. But I needed it—

I ran through the snow, my breaths short, blowing white puffy air. The apothecary shop followed me, the door an enormous mouth retching the horrible warning.

"That's not enough!" it said in an elder man's voice. "For all things living, that's not enough!"

I lay on a hard table, writhing in agony. Father's face above me, eyes pained.

Mother held my hand, tears rolling down her cheeks. "Not my Evella," she cried. "Not my Evella."

Pain flooded through my body. My organs burst, expelling poison. I screamed with all my might, but not a sound came out—

I awoke, my neck and back drenched. I sat up, throwing the quilt off my body, my clothes soaked. I didn't want to see the red again. So much red.

But no red this time.

Only sweat.

The cool air immediately washed a chill over my body.

My fingers grazed my abdomen, feeling the ridges of the scar across my lower torso. Intact. No blood. No pain.

The same as always with the nightmare. The cold snow. The apothecary shop. The table.

I longed for Reil. Just to be near him would be enough. But I wanted his arms around me, his words in my ear, his kisses on my neck. I wanted him to tell me everything was all right and would be from now on. I needed that from him, even if it was all a lie. No one was all right nor would be. The world was collapsing, bit by bit, one quake at a time. And I still dreamt of horrors past.

Reil had that power over me. The power of peace. He knew how to calm me, how to make me see the brightest bits of the dark and forget about everyone else. We had each other.

Until we didn't.

"Are you all right?" The voice startled me, and my eyes adjusted to the dimly lit room. Arek stood near the kitchen entrance. "Sorry, I didn't mean to scare you. You were shuffling in your sleep. It didn't look like a pleasant sleep, to be truthful."

I clutched the quilt, nestling it over my shoulders while I drew my arms around my knees. I don't know why, but him standing there left me feeling vulnerable, like a spring hare in a field of short grass, visible to hunters on the ground and raptors in the sky. I wanted to hide, but had no place to go.

Had anyone else heard me? Did I scream outside the dream? I scanned the other doorways, black holes into quiet bedrooms. Mother and Father lived through the ordeal with me, but Tulla and Wren didn't know the truth, although they'd hear versions of it from the townsfolk if they hadn't already. I didn't want to have to explain it to them. No one could ever understand why I did what I did, except me.

"I don't think anyone else noticed. I only had because I couldn't sleep."

I nodded, relieved, although having Arek the stranger see me in a sleep-induced fit wasn't comforting. "The kitchen uncomfortable? If it's not warm enough, you can rest here by the fire." I stared at the dull glow. "What's left of it." I considered adding another log. But I had already used two extra tonight which stretched our supply for tomorrow, and a third meant we most likely wouldn't have enough to get through to dinner. I didn't want to have to go on a firewood run in addition to my trip to town. It was Wren's job, but he was about as useful at felling wood as a toothless beaver.

If I put another one on, Arek would stick around longer. I wanted to get to his real story, but not in the middle of the night.

"No, it's quite fine in there. I—" Arek stopped himself. What was it he was going to say? Exhaustion had a way of weakening walls and revealing truths. Perhaps it was the opportune time for his confession. "I couldn't stop my thoughts, I suppose."

"I can't imagine what that's like." I smiled weakly, a gesture he apparently took as an invitation to sit down.

"May I?"

At least he had the courtesy to ask. I pressed my knees closer to my chest, as if there were no other room for him on the floor to occupy.

He sat with his feet facing the fire, elbows on his knees. He turned to me, staring too long for comfort, a worried pity in his eyes.

"What?" I laid my chin on my quilted knees.

"There's something else." He stared at the fire, then the room, gaze wandering everywhere but to my eyes. "I'm not sure how to say this."

My gut twisted in a knot. "What is it? Something with my family?"

"No, nothing like that." He waved my worry away but his hesitation built it back up. "I walked over here when I heard you shuffling. I admit, I watched for a moment or two. Don't take this the wrong way, I wasn't *watching you*, watching you."

Was that supposed to make me feel better?

"Rather, I couldn't keep my eyes off what you were doing."

"You mean besides moving around?"

He nodded. "You weren't the only thing moving around in here. You" —he let out a sigh— "you were moving objects."

My throat tightened and breath ceased. Why of all nights did I have to dream that terrible nightmare? I hoped the surprise and fear didn't show on my face. Father said it was easier to read The History of Tusinda written in its dead dialect than read my face.

"Perhaps you were seeing things. You said you haven't slept. You must be exhausted."

"I know what I saw." He pointed to Wren's shoes. Instead of sitting by his doorway, one lay by Mother and Father's room, the other close to the fire.

I picked up the one by the fire and tossed it toward Wren's room, the worn leather warm.

"That doesn't prove anything. Maybe Wren woke up thirsty."

"Which brings me to the water bucket." Arek pointed to the kitchen doorway. "I caught it in mid-air. I was afraid to put it back down in here, in case you sent it flying again. It could've knocked you out."

At least then I wouldn't have dreamt. I checked the bucket's corner. Of course it wasn't there because I had moved it. Without realizing it.

Arek scooted a hair closer. "You can move objects."

I turned to the fire, away from his judging stare. "It's none of your business." How much do I tell this stranger? Not talking about it may lead him to imagine things beyond the truth. Talking about it could reveal too much.

"There's nothing to worry about." I couldn't look in his brown eyes a second longer. I turned to the wood ashes. "It only happens in my sleep."

A half-truth.

It did only happen in my sleep. For the past year. Never mind what I was capable of before then.

"Worry?" A grin grew across his face. "This could only mean one thing. You have Soulmagic." He said it with giddiness, like a kid finding free sweets.

"Shh." Mother's doorway was still a black abyss. It didn't mean she wasn't listening, or anyone else. Though most everyone else would be annoyed with the noise. Mother would want to know what was being said. That woman could be sneaky.

She could also flare in anger like a tempest in the Ronth Sea. She'd be furious if I had used Soulmagic in the house. Which didn't make sense. Of all the places to use it, wasn't the house better than out in the open, amongst public eyes? It didn't matter to her. Anywhere was wrong and dangerous, and Soulmagic was downright evil.

"You can't be throwing around words like 'Soulmagic' around here. Maybe where you're from you could do that." It was an opening for him to talk about himself, rather than me—accidentally—sharing more of my secrets. That dreaded dream. Time was supposed to heal wounds, yet that nightmare haunted me more frequently the more time passed.

Admittedly, I was curious to know if other terrins viewed Soulmagic differently. Communication between terrins was limited to trade and occasional letters. Unless you had a dear loved one living elsewhere, there was no reason to write, and no one to write to.

That was assuming Soulmagic existed elsewhere. I wasn't even sure that my ability was indeed Soulmagic.

"There's no Soulmagic in Corallon," I said. "Not like there used to be before The Quake, from what I'm told."

Liar. It was rumored that an elderly lady by the name of Greet practiced Soulmagic, on the eastern outskirts of Corallon. To many in town, she offered alternative treatments that couldn't be found at the apothecary.

The apothecary. The shop with the purple glow of my nightmares. Perhaps if I had gone to Greet instead, it would've been different. I would be different.

I had to shut Arek's Soulmagic notions down. "Even if one had Soulmagic—which I probably don't—it's a risk to be out with it here. You might be accepted with open arms by some, those who could see an advantage of your ability. But I suspect you'd be shunned." I knew that all too well, without Soulmagic. "Or taken for a Raider. Isn't that the rumor these days? Raiders using Soulmagic to kidnap people?"

Arek shuffled his feet and cleared his throat, his lips turned down in a sour note. Did seeing Raiders tonight frighten him? He had seemed calm enough at the edge of Ashwan Forest, calmer than if it had been other townsfolk stumbling upon them. Perhaps after thinking about it, what could've happened, the fear seeped in.

Or was he afraid of me? How ridiculous would it have been to walk in on me sleeping, with objects taking flight?

"I need you to keep it a secret," I pleaded. "What you saw tonight. I can't have anything else tainting my family's reputation."

"But—" The sourness melted, replaced by earnestness. "Wait, what do you mean *anything else?*"

"Just forget about it. Any of it." I lowered my knees and crossed my ankles, my face fully in his view. "What you saw, it's a fluke. It's something that only happens in my sleep when I have nightmares. I'm not a danger to anyone."

"I didn't mean to say you were."

"You have to keep it quiet, then." My eyes watered. I couldn't be the cause of further hurt to my family. Our reputation had been injured almost beyond repair. Some would say it did surpass repair.

I placed my hand on his knee. "Please, not a word. I've brought you here, my family has welcomed you"—with an enormous amount of convincing, but why hound on that fact— "and is sheltering you for the night. I could've left you in the woods. My family could've said no."

"I know, and I am grateful." He had the look of argument, mouth still open, breathing heavily.

"Then what is it?"

"If you do have..." He leaned closer, whispering, "Soulmagic." He recreated the distance between us. "Then wouldn't you want to harness that power? Do something with it?"

"Absolutely not." I said it without thinking. It was the curse that came along with the ability. "*If* I were to have it, it'd be a burden to me. Not a gift."

With that, I was finished. I had no desire to carry on talking about something I knew little about these days. My sleep 'power' was a personality nuance, a flaw that meant I had to sleep in private. Nothing to harp on. In fact, I don't think Tulla had ever awakened during any of my episodes to have seen it.

"All right," he said. "I'll keep it a secret. If that's what you want."

I nodded. "Thank you." There was no reason to trust this young man. He could leave here and tell the first person he encountered. But it looked like it hurt him to make the promise.

That's what made me believe him.

CHAPTER

FOUR

As the sun threatened to rise, I cursed not having a sound sleep. A solid overnight sleep was rare these days, with the nightmares, the worsening quakes, the worry over food. Last night had all three, unfortunately.

I arose before the rest of my family. I didn't bother to check on Arek. His soft snoring from the kitchen was proof enough he was out. I slipped on my boots and my hunting cloak. While I didn't plan on actively hunting anything this morning, it didn't hurt to bring my sling and a few rocks for ammunition.

Some people believed the coldest hour of the day was in the middle of the night, when darkness was at its peak. Anyone who awakened this early, right before dawn, knew better. The night atmosphere gradually lost its heat and kept losing it until the second the sun started warming the air.

This was the coldest time.

I didn't dare leave my hands out of my cloak as I plodded through thick snow, heading south. I wanted to check on the quake damage, but I needed to get to my traps before larger predators—including humans —got to them first.

I couldn't see behind the house anyway as it sat along a shallow gradient, the snow creating a soft hump beyond.

Goodbye, family.

It was a ritual adopted every time I left the house alone. With the quakes, Raider invasions, and the unpredictable nature of people in general, any day could be the last day.

Reil didn't have the chance to say goodbye. I made sure to take that chance, even if only in my head.

I traversed the field, quite a difference from last night's journey across it. I was alone, without someone who clearly never tracked an animal in his life and talked as if to fill a void in the air with his words.

Would Arek still be there when I got back? Would he keep his promise to not tell anyone about what he witnessed last night?

As I approached Ashwan Forest, I cut right, heading for the outlook Arek and I sheltered at when the Raiders landed. Curiosity got the better of me. I may not have been able to assess the damage north of the house, but I could check here on the shoreline. The traps could wait a little longer.

I didn't have to make it to the edge to register the destruction. That was the former edge. A chunk of the shelf leading to the coastline had crumbled, etching a semi-circular ridge at the edge of the field to the forest. Piles of snow mixed with earth lay atop the sand, and to the south, several alabaster trees lay in crisscrossed shards, waves lapping on their remnants.

My heart skipped, worry washing over my skin in a cold sweat. How bad was it in the north? The last quake collapsed a short section of the northern cliff, no greater than an arm's length. The slipping dirt had created a loose slope down to the water, but didn't threaten home or town.

This looked worse.

I turned to the forest, in a hurry to complete my errands and head home. If the damage was severe, I wanted to be there to help.

Only a dusting of snow was fresh on the ground around the alabaster trees, which meant a better chance of capturing a hare overnight. When the snow fell thick it buried the trap, and the hares would completely miss it when foraging. But the quake could've jostled the traps or worse, scared off hares from foraging.

My worries alleviated as I approached the first trap. A success.

The white hare lay across the snow, a hefty fellow with long ears. I crouched to the ground, its fur and body cold. It had encountered the trap in the earliest of dark hours. Luckily it hadn't struggled much, minimizing the amount of blood. Those that do fight don't last long, but their blood and yips attract predators.

The trap was simple enough, a loop made of fishing wire designed to constrict when the hare hopped through headfirst.

The time I trapped my first hare would never leave me. Reil had taught me how to set the trap, and insisted I unsnatch it, gut, and clean it. My stomach had turned to mush, my heart aching for the poor beast.

But meat was hard to come by these days. After a while, when hunger was far beyond a grumbling in the stomach, one became desensitized to it.

I moved the trap to the base of a different nearby tree, mixing the blood droplets into the snow to dilute the scent in the old spot. Carrying the hare by its feet, I pushed on to my second trap, further into the woods.

Success again.

It was a treat to have one hare in a day. A blessing, as Mother would say, to have two. I repeated the same methods as the first, releasing the dead hare and resetting my trap. Onto the third.

As I marched to the west, there was crunching in the snow.

Other than mine.

With the hares occupying my hands, I had to make a choice. Set them down to use my sling or hope whatever it was wouldn't attack.

I slowly approached the noise, my feet quiet. The chances of an otari out and about at dawn were slim, but the quakes had a way of disrupting routines. A round lump of something hovered over my third trap, jostling in a fight with the device. The lump stood, a thin man with a wan face examining his prize.

I ran to him in a wild fit. "That's mine! Set it down!"

He startled, meeting the fury in my eyes, fright in his. He took off deeper into the forest, his footsteps nimble. I couldn't keep up with him while carrying the two hares and stopped.

If I set them down to catch up with him, others may be with him to steal my catch during my pursuit. I had to take the loss.

If two hares were a blessing, three would've been a miracle.

Although poachers angered me to no end, I tried to be content with what I did achieve. Poachers did what they did because they were either too lazy to set their own traps or didn't know how. Neither applied to me. The town could say what they wanted about me, but I provided for my family. More than what many could say for themselves.

As I walked the northern edge of the forest, I was thankful for not pursuing the poacher. While the hares were not bulky weight, they did begin to slow me down and tire my arms. The snow could do that—take all your energy in a short period. I reached the outskirts of town, appreciative of the compact snow.

With enough people and the occasional wagon to trample the white powder into a hard surface, the town of Corallon was airy and dirty. The packed snow either froze over for a slippery sheen or collected every bit of soil and animal waste people carried on their boots. The town formed an open rectangle, northern and southern sides the longer stretches of shops and homes. It took but twenty paces to go between the two. The eastern edge was partially closed off by the holy house, a long, narrow structure that had once been stables before The Quake. As horses came to be more useful as a food source rather than a consumer of food, the need for stables became non-existent. Unfortunately, the same couldn't be said for the holy house.

The west side remained open. It was the doorway to the world opposite from the holy house, out to the free wilderness, like where we lived. Although the holy would never leave Mother's heart, no matter how far from town she lived.

I trod diagonally through town. Few people were awake this early, but those that were had the same goal in mind. Trading.

It worked out best to trade early in the morning. The trade house opened its doors at the first peeks of sunrise. They had an allotted amount of goods and sometimes money, although that didn't get one far these days no matter the terrin currency. People wanted supplies for the coming day, not the leftover scraps at the end of the day. Salt fortunately was not a rarity and helped in preserving meat, but nothing beat freshly caught and cooked wild game.

I stood inside the doorway of the trade house, three men and an elderly woman waiting in line ahead of me. The line grew as I shuffled my way to the counter. As did their whispers.

The old woman eyed me, swearing incantations or prayers under her breath. Two of the men whispered to each other, staring my way until I met their gaze. They quickly turned away. The cowards. As if facing me, catching my glance, would melt them into puddles on the ground. It was amazing what a year's worth of time could do to the truth. I'd lost count of the different tales spun from gossip about me.

A woman some ten years older than me stood at the counter, accounting for the most recent trade in the logbook. "Offering?" She looked up at me and gasped. "You."

I knew better than to react with words. Instead I waited for hers.

"Not here," she shook her head. "I won't."

"I'll deal with her." The chubby woman stocking the shelves behind her turned around. She wore a dirtied apron, and had wiry hair roughly pulled into a hat that once was white.

She traded places with the younger tradeswoman. "Don't mind her. Everyone is welcome to trade. Even the likes of you, Trapper." She briefly eyed the prim woman, who huffed at the comment.

It wasn't the first establishment I walked into that treated me in such a way. It wouldn't be the last, either. I tried not to let it bother me. But sometimes I wanted to sling a rock between their eyes. Not to kill them. Just to knock them off their sanctimonious hill.

"Two hares, retrieved this morning." I pulled them from my cloak and set them on the counter.

"What's the ask?" she said, her accent a thick Corallese. Mother and Father had remnants of the accent, losing a good bit of it the past year out in our private home. Funny how we all start to sound like each other when living mostly in isolation.

"Fish." While it seemed ridiculous to give up two perfectly good animals, they didn't have enough fat to go around the whole family. Fish trumped hare any day.

"I have a tin of red sardines." She reached for a shelf under the counter and slapped the tin in front of me.

It was medium in size, comparable to my family's dinner plates. "Nothing larger?"

The largest size, a barrel—the size of a water bucket—could last us ten days. This would hold us over three, at most four days.

"All I've got." She reached for the hares.

I quickly snatched the feet in my grasp. "Since when does a tin of red sardines equal two hares?"

"Since the fish shortage."

I stared down her wrinkled, rosy face, nose and cheeks windburned from years of cold misery. Fish were hard to come by in winter, not just because of the change in the current that had once brought us an abundance, but because fewer people ventured out onto the rough seas. One mistake and you'd freeze to death in the frigid waters.

"The tin." I nodded to the shelf behind her. "And that can of lard."

"If you're not going to be reasonable, I'll move on to the next customer."

"How about we do that now?" said the man behind me, who stunk of spoiled brew.

I lifted the hares by their feet. "I've got two hares, one of them not the least bit frozen. I would've had a third were it not for poachers."

"That's not my problem."

Dong.

Dong.

The bell of the holy house stopped our negotiation. Those waiting in line placed their left hands on their right shoulders.

"Poor soul," a man two spots behind me said. "Out when the quake struck."

"Could've been any of us," a woman replied.

Another man walked into the trade house, a smile on his youthful face. It was Ludie, a friend of my brother Gareg. "Seems I walked into the wrong place. Everyone is so glum."

"Silence," the reverent woman said. "The soul needs silence to find its way."

"Then why ring the bell?" Ludie joked. I grinned, and he winked at me.

The woman scoffed and clutched the ends of her jacket at her chest. "Some people could use a reminder of the holy law." She fixed her gaze on me.

I gave her a stare down with my evil, unholy gray eyes. She shivered and looked away.

I turned back to the counter. "I'll take the sardines and the lard." The tradeswoman slid the hares off the counter, and I nodded. Perhaps it was faith that brought her to do it. Or she wanted me out of the trade house as soon as yesterday.

Or she pitied me.

I took my goods. I would've preferred to indulge in one of the hares tonight, but Mother would be content with the trade.

I slowed by Ludie, waiting to catch his attention. "You happen to see Gareg this morning?" I whispered.

His confident demeanor softened. "I was with them last night during the quake. Both Gareg and Penni are fine."

I nodded. "Thank you."

He nodded in both *you're welcome* and *goodbye*.

Gareg had been set to union with Penni before my actions had brought about shame on the family. Fortunately Penni held a prominent position in town and chose her love of Gareg over the risk her family would be frowned upon too. She held firm against naysayers, insisting he be treated separately from the rest of us Trappers. The tradeoff was that we almost never saw Gareg. He didn't dare visit our home, and most encounters were in secret with Father.

I stepped out of the trade house, the sun nearly over the horizon. It cast a yellow-gray glow over the town and snow, low-lying clouds having swooped in at the start of the day. The palpable silence made me turn to the grieving.

The holy house ritual bells rang more frequently as the quakes strengthened. It was almost expected now to lose a few souls with each quake. With the harsher winters and lack of supplies, townsfolk simply couldn't keep their homes and shops safe. And being outside during them was arguably more dangerous.

I didn't want to look over there. I didn't want to know who it was, or how overwhelmed his family was with the loss. But I saw him anyway, between the warm bodies of the standing friends and family, lying on a dark cloth on the snow. They took turns placing his belongings on his person, on the blanket. Coins, socks, a wooden carving. A folded blanket.

Reil didn't have the privilege.

No matter how much I found Spiriters' devotion preposterous, there was something about their death ritual that reached me. They believed that the deceased not only wanted but needed their personal effects to make it to The Beyond and reconnect with loved ones who have passed or will in the future.

Maybe it was the act of the ritual that was comforting, a finality of the life they had lived. Or the fact it had passed down over hundreds of generations. What else could we claim held such importance for so long?

Or maybe, a tiny part of me wanted to believe that we got a second chance with the people we loved.

A little girl, holding a woman's hand, turned around and caught my stare. I smiled softly, my heart heavy for her loss. Was it her father? An uncle or older brother?

Her face turned bitter, and she buried herself in the woman's leg.

Not even the children could stand my presence.

I sighed, feeling the items in my grip beneath my cloak, and headed back to the house. From town, our stone house was a fairly direct pathway. It was slightly uphill, but that wasn't the hard part. What made it secluded, besides my history, was that the wind held its own grudge against the land.

There was no sense in trying to keep my hood up as the wind whipped, my hair tickling the shoulders of my cloak. If I had curved to the south near the Ashwan Forest and up through the field, I wouldn't have the same problem. But that distance was nearly double, and I was anxious to get home after surviving another judgmental outing to town.

Candlelight glowed from the shut window of Wren's room. Father had said the two Displaceds were going to look for work in town, so they should be up. Hopefully the rest of the house was too.

I opened the door and took off my boots and cloak. I walked back to the kitchen, goods in hand. "I completed a trade, Mother."

She sat at the table next to Father, stirring herbs in her cup of hot water. "Ooh, let me see." Her worried face betrayed her words.

I placed the can and tin on the table. "Lard and sardines."

"You got all that with a hare?" Father said.

I shook my head. "No. That's what two hares get you these days."

"You had two?" he asked.

"Three. A poacher got away with one."

"Hm." His voice held gloom.

"What is it?" I scanned the room. "Where's Tulla? And Wren?"

"I sent them out for firewood," Father said.

Arek walked into the room, to my surprise. Had I really thought he'd run away this morning? After practically begging to stay?

"I'm sorry, Father," I said. "I used some last night, thinking there'd be enough for today—"

Father held up a hand, silencing me.

"Something has come up." He looked at Mother, then Arek, who nodded. "You are to leave for the palace with Arek. Right away."

I looked at Father as if he cursed in ancient Elsinean. "What are you talking about?" I looked for reassurance from Mother and didn't find it, her eyebrows curled down as much as her troubled mouth. "What is this?"

Arek stepped past Father, positioning himself between my parents. "I came here under King Ronin's orders."

I knew it. In honesty I didn't know what *it* was, but I knew he had been lying. I knew he guarded the truth last night better than a pickpocket guarded a newly stolen coin.

"There were rumors that a young woman with Soulmagic was living in the north, here in Corallon. After last night, I believe that to be you."

"That's nonsense. Father, tell him."

Father looked down at the table.

"How do we even know he's from the palace? He could be tricking us."

Father held up a folded paper. "Official papers."

I backed away from the table, from the vile, evil being standing in my family's kitchen. "You lied to me."

"The king needs you. People with Soulmagic."

"I'll never leave. I can't leave." I stared at Mother who gave nothing but sorrow. "How are they supposed to survive? Winter has just begun."

"Don't worry yourself over us," Father said. "We will manage."

Arek moved a step closer, and I recoiled in revulsion. "You must come with me, this morning. If you do not, I will have to inform the king of your holding of royal rations."

"You wouldn't." I wished I had shoved his lying face in the fire last night.. "You heard—you've seen—how we live here. We have no rations to give."

"I would not want to be in the position to inform the king of your violation." He nodded to my parents. "I am very grateful for the hospitality you provided when you did not have to."

"I'm sure you are." He had to have heard the vitriol in my voice. It was all I could do to keep my composure. "What does the king want with me?" I asked as if anything Arek demanded right now held true.

"I'm afraid I can only discuss that information with you. We can cover it on the way." He flashed a weak grin.

This wasn't happening.

"What about Tulla and Wren?" I implored Mother.

"They don't know about this. We will tell them you decided to help Arek find his way back to his terrin and find a new home."

"What happens when I don't ever come back?" The tears started in my eyes. I didn't want to give Arek the satisfaction that his deception hit my heart in any way.

"Don't say that, Evella." Mother placed her hand on mine. "You will come back, I'm sure of it." She looked up at Arek over her shoulder.

He smiled politely, but I wasn't convinced. Judging by how hard Mother bit her lip, she wasn't either.

"Now that it's settled, we'd best be off." Arek nodded at me. "Pack your things, say your goodbyes, and I will meet you outside."

He walked out of the kitchen. This one person, one stranger, had crossed paths with our lives to change them forever. And he walked out easier than he had entered it.

I stood in silence. In shock. How could someone be so cold and conniving? How did I ever give him the benefit of the doubt? An inkling of my trust? I knew better than to go against my gut.

"This is my fault," I said. "I let him into the house. Last night I had that nightmare. He wouldn't have seen—"

Father stood and wrapped his thick arms around me. Any composure I had left ran out the door with Arek.

I clutched my hands around Father's back and let the sobs flow freely. If Arek truly meant to tell the king about our withholding rations, that would be the end of my family. Nothing they could do would restore their place with the citizens of Corallon. I had done enough damage already. I couldn't allow there to be more.

Father released me, and Mother grabbed my hand, squeezing it.

"I'll come back." I had to say it despite not believing it. Come back and build a place of my own close by and continue to provide for the family because it was the only purpose that carried me through the days and nights. A purpose that Arek was robbing me of.

"Of course you will." She burst into tears and turned her back to me.

I gathered what few things I had— clothing, what was left of my ammunition stash, my blade, sling, and cloak. If I were to die today, there wouldn't be much to bury me with. How useful was a sling in The Beyond?

There I went again, feeding into nonsense. What did it matter? The entire world around me had turned to absurdity.

I tied my boots on securely and threw the strap of the satchel over my shoulder, beneath the cloak. Arek stood outside the front door, arms relaxed, and hands folded in front of him. How could he be so different this morning than he was last night? Or had I been blind?

"Ready?" he asked.

My lack of response was as good as any. I was outside with my belongings, wasn't I? Did he want me to be cheerful about it?

I closed the door to the house behind me, not knowing when I'd see their faces again.

Goodbye, family.

CHAPTER
FIVE

We marched beyond the field, through the Ashwan Forest. Arek's clunky footsteps had a determination to them. He was different, focused on leading the way and not having trouble in the least knowing the lay of the land.

How was I to know if he actually knew where he was going, or if it was a show?

"Is this the way you arrived here?"

He turned his head, not enough to see me sulking behind him. I kept pace but no way was I going to make it easy on him.

"Yes and no. I actually traveled town to town, inquiring about the rumors of the strange girl."

"Strange girl?"

"That's what most called her. I mean, you."

"Most? Do I want to know the other names?"

"Oh, there was Demon Girl, Witch Woman, She-Monster—"

"All right, that's enough." Never mind what they called me. How did anyone outside of the family know of my secret? Had Wren gossiped collecting firewood? Tulla when getting water? Or did this go back further—had Reil spoken about it before his death?

I thought of the young girl this morning, standing in the clutches of her mother in front of the dead man. She'd been frightened of me. And the others trading glances...Had it been they thought me a witch this entire time, invoking their stares and words under their breath? Did it have nothing to do with my actions after Reil's death? Or was it because of my actions?

We walked five paces before he continued.

"It was in town, in Corallon, that I got a real lead on you. A drunken gentleman."

So he had been to town before meeting me. He knew exactly where it was but played dumb last night to keep up the ruse. I didn't know what was worse, the lying, or that someone in town pointed him right to me.

"That doesn't really narrow it down." It could've been most any man in town at one point or another. Even Father would partake more than a man's share on occasion.

"He told me the best way to find you alone was to check Ashwan Forest. Apparently, you're a notorious hunter in these parts."

Among other things.

"I wasn't sure if I could trust him, but what else could I do? I had no other tips. Sure enough..."

"You didn't exactly find me. I remember it the other way around."

"Either way, it happened." His words came out in spurts, his breathing harder with the exertion. "I'm just glad it happened the way it did. The Raiders would've taken you if they discovered you first."

"Does it really matter?" I scoffed. "Either way, I'm being forced to leave my family to do who knows what."

He stopped, turning fully around. "You can't really mean that?"

"What? That I'm being forced—"

"No." He held up a hand. "That it doesn't matter. Do you not know of the kidnappings? Who do you think the Raiders have been snatching?"

"Young adults. Older children." I wasn't sure where he was going with this and admittedly was curious. "In their late teens, early twenties."

"Not just anyone that age. Soulmagi. Ever since The Quake, they've been targeting those with abilities."

"For what purpose?" I asked, playing into his preposterous story. The world was supposedly rid of Soulmagic. I didn't entirely believe my abilities fell under that ancient folklore.

"To convince them to fight for them or be killed. How else would they have a chance at overthrowing the king?"

I'd heard the rumors of Raiders having Soulmagic. Maybe Arek's version held true, that they kidnapped those with the ability. But how was I to believe any of this?

"How would you know that?"

"It's why the king sent me here. To take you—" He tipped his head in an aside.. "That didn't come out right. To keep you—"

"Not any better, is it?"

"To ensure you are safe, under his protection." He firmly nodded, pleased by this interpretation.

"I can ensure my own safety, thank you."

He chuckled. "I honestly don't doubt that."

We continued walking, up the slope of alabaster trees to a bald crest. Wind ripped across the smooth peak, the opening of my cloak flapping across my arm to my chest. The clouds had thickened throughout the morning, leaving a blanket of gray over our heads. Their gloominess added to the surreal feel of what I was doing, where I was going.

"Will we be on foot the entire way to Elsinea?" There was at least another days' walk to the southern border of Corallon, if not two. I could easily make it there without tiring, but what then? We'd have to traverse the waters separating the terrins. Would we simply board a ferry? Or did he expect me to swim?

"We'll follow the road south." He pointed to the thin etching in the snow down below, a pathway not often trod but enough to distinguish from the rest of the snow-covered land.

"I have transportation awaiting us, a few more hours' walk." He turned to me briefly, the wind battering his face in a gust, and he turned away.

"No royal escort to transport the precious cargo?" It was said in half-jest, but it wouldn't have been awful to travel with ease. I mean, if I had to go to Elsinea, why not in comfort?

"We can't risk the attention. The less people know about us, the better."

Was that really the reason? Or did it involve not having the money or supplies to spare for the strange Corallon girl? Or Witch Woman.

We walked downhill and stopped to dine at the small town of Chaswit. I hadn't visited any of the towns to the south in many years. Although the towns belonged to the one terrin of Corallon, these days it seemed like each town isolated itself as its own niche. There wasn't an enormous distance between Chaswit and Corallon, but even so, the conditions were an improvement. The town had three public buildings, one of which was a tavern. They, like Corallon, still went without bread. It wasn't that we didn't have the grain for it. We didn't have enough grain for both bread and ale. The latter won out.

Perhaps the starkest contrast between Chaswit and Corallon was that no one cared nor even seemed to notice me. If I had a reputation of harboring abilities, no one suspected I'd look like me, pale-faced, gray eyes as dull as the clouds. No suspicious moles, or horns, or whatever they envisioned a witch or demon to look like.

"Don't worry about payment," Arek said as we sat at a table. "I have rations."

"Rations you could've used as payment to thank my parents?" The secrets kept revealing themselves one after the other.

He coughed into his fist. "I offered, but they wouldn't accept."

Of course they wouldn't. Not from a liar like him.

I drank a cup of ale and ate a hot lard porridge. I didn't care about the taste. It was the warmth that my body craved.

As soon as we finished, Arek paid in Elsinean coin, suspicious in these parts yet accepted. We continued on our route, heading south. The darkening afternoon sky pressed Arek to pick up the pace.

For an eternity we trudged through the repeating landscape of inner Corallon. Uphill, crest, downhill, town. The further south, the softer the slopes, the shallower the crests. As I about had my last hill, Arek stopped.

He pointed to a stone cottage, a streak of smoke emanating from the chimney. It made me miss home, the warmth of the fire, Father arguing politics in the kitchen. "In there. The family let me house my animals and sled out back. They'll welcome us for a night, and we can continue on in the morning."

I still hated what he was making me do but was grateful to have somewhere to shelter tonight. The endless walking had once again grown my hunger.

We approached the cottage, a two-story house reminiscent of our first home in town. Outside, a wagon sat in the snow with a damaged wheel. Further behind the house was a low-lying stable, the occasional bark and yelp emanating from what I guessed were Arek's travel companions.

A wooden sign hung over the front door. The name Padridge was crossed out and another etched above it. I squinted to read it in the darkening night.

Gotherin.

The name caught my breath, and my hands trembled. My mouth sat agape, and Arek furled his eyebrow at me.

"What is it?"

"I can't go in there." I shook my head. "I can't set foot in that house."

"Why not?"

Gotherin. Reil's family's name. I knew they had relocated from Corallon after his death but didn't know where. I hadn't seen them in over a year, and now I stood at their threshold. I couldn't do it. They couldn't know I was here.

"You go ahead. I'll stay with the animals out back."

"Be sensible. It's warm inside, and I'll make sure you have your own room. That way no one will discover anything...floating during your sleep."

"I won't have the dream tonight." I had no power over that but wanted to believe it. I didn't mind if I did, as long as I didn't have to deal with the occupants of that house.

"Even if you don't, it'd be better inside than being out here in the open. Who knows what animals could get you, or worse, humans that would see you—"

I shook my head. "You don't understand. I can't."

"No, I don't understand. Either you explain it to me so I do understand or stop it with this silliness and go inside with me."

I didn't want to explain. I wanted to make the decision for myself without him interfering like I was some misguided child. Why couldn't he leave well enough alone?

He stood there, arms crossed, feet firmly in the ground. I don't know if he half suspected I'd push him over or my confession would knock him down just the same.

"Fine."

He unfolded his arms. "Fine?"

"Fine, I'll go in." I did want to push him now.

"All right then."

"All right," I said with contempt. Whether I agreed because of the pull of a warm fire and shelter or wanting him to stop his mouth, I reluctantly stood behind him as he knocked on the door.

It opened with a creak, a woman poking her head in the narrow opening. "Can I help you?"

"Hello again." Arek beamed a wide smile. "I've come for my animals, which you've so graciously housed. Is it possible to come inside and warm up? I can count the payment for you."

She opened the door wider. Bregga had shrunken, her muscles withered away. Her face sunk in, skin grayed, making her look much older than she was. I couldn't look away, yet I didn't want her to recognize me as we stepped inside.

The square room had a stove to the right, a small set of chairs around a wooden table and a few knickknacks alongside the walls. Wooden stairs climbed to the second story along the far wall. There were candles and books—a treat I hadn't seen in such abundance in quite some time—along with a rickety cabinet with a rusted lock, most likely their store of supplies. The wall to the left housed the fire, which burned low but steadily in front of two other chairs.

Arek took off his cloak and accepted the offered chair by the fire. Bregga looked at me, wanting me to do the same. I clutched my hood and turned my head out of the firelight.

"She's...uh...shy," Arek said in a cordial voice, then looked at me perplexed. Bregga put a thin log—closer to a branch than a log—in the fire. I made my way over to the hearth but remained facing it, my back to the rest of the house. It gradually warmed me, until I was too warm and wanted to shed my cloak. But I wouldn't dare. Instead I stepped to the corner, as if the candlestick on the cupboard was the most interesting object I'd ever seen. As I inspected the cabinet, it was surprising to see the cupboard nailed down to the floor.

"Do you get quakes out here?" I didn't turn my head but tapped the nail head with my boot.

"We do feel them sometimes," she said. "That's more to stop the thieves than anything."

As if to show her we weren't the thieving type, Arek took out Elsinean coins and counted out payment. "Here you are." He flashed his open hand, the coins shimmering in the firelight.

Reil's mother shuffled to him, collecting the coins, and recounting them before slipping them into the pocket of her floor-length robe. What was once a charming piece of clothing was now a taupe-colored tattering of threads. She wore several layers of clothes beneath it. I suspected it was her entire wardrobe.

A clanging sound came from the far wall, and both Arek and I shot glances at the doorway by the stairs.

"Just other guests. The room down here is rented out for the night."

"Which brings me to this." Arek held two more coins. "For tonight's stay."

"I only have one room."

"That's all right," Arek said. "I'm more than happy to sleep down here and let Ev—"

I coughed. Loudly. "Excuse me."

"Would you like a drink?"

"No, thank you."

Bregga took the coin. "You two decide the arrangements. As long as you keep to yourselves and don't cause trouble."

Arek raised a hand. "I assure you, we won't. Thank you."

"Now if you don't mind." She turned away and walked to the stairs. "Relina! Come fetch your dinner. Hurry it up."

A pattering of feet sounded down the stairs. Reil's younger sister, Relina, had stood at my hips the last time I had seen her. She reached past my waist now. Her round eyes and slightly upturned pinch of a nose were the same as her brother's, like I was looking at a different version of him.

"When's Papa back? Oh goodie, we have more guests?" Her face positively glowed with joy. That hadn't changed. Relina was the most hopeful child, or human for that matter. I think it rubbed off on Reil, and that was why he was able to turn my negative thoughts to happier ones.

She hurried in front of Arek and spread out her faded green frock in a curtsy. "I'm Relina. Wait, I remember you. We have your animals."

"That's right," Arek said.

"Oh, go on, leave them alone dear," Bregga said.

"I'm just being friendly." Relina glanced over at me, my face exposed from watching her in awe.

"Evella!" She ran over to me and hugged my legs.

My heart pounded my ribs. I stood in bewilderment, not knowing if I should pretend she was wrong or embrace the girl who had been family to me in a past life.

"What did you call her?" Bregga stood in shock, jaw open, the spoon in her hand dripping wetness from the pot.

"It's Evella, mama!" Poor Relina beamed with glee. I was elated to bring it to her and devastated to be the one to crush it.

Bregga rushed over, grabbing my chin, and pulled my face clear out of the hood. Her clammy hands gripped too tight. "Evella Trapper. I can't believe you have the audacity to step foot"—her words grew louder with each syllable— "in my house!" She gasped for air and released my face out of her grip. "After you—you killed—"

"I'm so sorry," I pleaded, holding Relina's delicate hands in mine. "I didn't know you lived here until I saw the sign on the door. I warned him not—"

"Get out, you murderer!" Bregga burst into tear-filled screams. "I never want to see your face again!" Her face burned red with rage, vanishing all dullness from her skin.

I gave Relina's hands a squeeze. "I'm sorry, love." I turned away from her confused face and rushed to the door. Arek stood, unsure of what to do.

"You too! You are not welcome here anymore." She took the coins from her pocket and threw them at his feet. He jumped in surprise and scurried to the door behind me.

I gasped heaping breaths of cold air, bending over from the pain. The shame. I had known better than to step inside, and I should've listened to myself. Again.

"What—" Arek's hands were open, shoulders in a shrug. "What just happened in there? What was that all about?"

"I warned you." My voice cracked with anger and remorse.

The door opened, and Bregga poked her head out. "And get your animals out now before I kill them all!"

She slammed the door, and Arek jumped at the sound.

"Has she gone mad?" Arek's confusion would've almost been amusing, were it not for the pain I had caused Bregga. "She wouldn't really kill my animals, would she?"

I shook my head, popping the hood back over it. "She's just upset." I sighed, my breath visible. "Extremely upset." I made for the rear of the house, walking around the front corner.

Arek hurried to follow, wrapping his cloak back on his shoulders. "And why would that be?"

I wanted to swat him away, to flick him off the surface of earth that he stood on. I didn't know this man well, but I did know his talking could agitate me into committing a crime.

I stopped in my tracks, pivoting around. "I remind her of her dead son."

"Why would that—"

"Because that's who I was to be unioned with."

He shrunk away, silent. Perhaps I should drop the truth on him more often.

"Your family—they said he died in a quake." He stepped back, glancing one eye at me. "Did you—she said you killed—did you—"

I shook my head. He didn't need to know the truth. He didn't deserve to know it. "If I could kill a man so easily, one that I loved and was to be unioned with, then explain how you are still standing here."

He tugged on the collar of his cloak. "Fair point. A simple 'no' would've worked too, but I understand."

"He died in a quake, just as Tulla said. Whatever notions his mother has about his death, she'll never get over the fact they couldn't go through the death ritual. He was not given his belongings for The Beyond."

"I see."

"That was a year ago, and seeing me for the first time—"

"Brought it all back." His shoulders slumped, the corners of his mouth in a frown. "I'm sorry, for making you go in there."

Be sorry for making me take this unwanted trip in the first place. But I couldn't say it. My heart was bruised, my energy gone. I didn't care where we went, where we slept. I only wanted to close my eyes and not be here anymore.

"You didn't know."

I walked to the stable and leaned my arms over the side. It was dark, with the moon covered by the clouds. All I could see were dark clumps here and there. Whatever had made the yelps before was asleep with the rest of the animals.

Arek met up with me, leaning his chest on his arms on the gate. "You still think she won't come out for us?"

I sighed in exhaustion and turned to him. His eyebrows twisted with worry, but his eyes read apologetic.

"I don't think she'll do anything if it means seeing my face again."

Arek put his hand over mine, and I recoiled.

He twisted away, resuming his position on the gate. "Then we'll sleep here tonight and be out at first light."

I didn't argue.

CHAPTER
SIX

I awakened to a wet tongue on my cheek. I opened my eyes and a furry feline mewed, as if to greet me with a good morning.

Although the cold of night cut through my cloak, the stable provided some protection for the wind, and eventually my body warmed the hay. With all the walking yesterday, I was too exhausted to lie awake fretting over the incident with Reil's mother. The day's fatigue, as far as I knew, had kept the nightmare at bay. At least for one night.

I blinked, clearing the morning cloudiness from my vision.

A cat face, the size of a dinner plate, with pin straight whiskers and sharp incisors stared me down.

I sat up with a gasp. The milky white cat shrunk back in fear.

"It's all right." Arek picked up the animal underneath its front legs. The lower half stretched in the air as he plopped it down in the adjacent pen. It had to have weighed as much as a person. "It's only a snowcat."

"Only a snowcat? As opposed to what, a sea serpent?"

His shoulders shook with silent laughter, a bemused smile across his face.

"You are aware of the reputation snowcats have?" Like being highly territorial, shredding prey to pieces, and stealing babies. That last part was probably more a product of Corallon gossip, but one could never be too sure. They did at the very least steal hares from my traps, leaving only tufts of fur. I knew when it was a snowcat because of the four-toed paw prints larger than the hare. They were one of the last large predators left.

"Perhaps their reputation is misguided." He picked up another one over the gate and squished his face up against it. It purred in satisfaction before he put it back down.

I stood, stretching my cramped legs and feeling the full force of the freezing morning air on my face. It stung my cheeks and numbed my ears.

"Here. You should drink it before we go."

He handed me a metal cup that I nearly dropped to my feet. It was hot to the touch, something I would've known if I had paid attention to the steam coming off it.

"Where'd you get this?" I stared at the stone cottage, wondering if he coaxed Bregga into helping him, despite his traveling companion.

"I left a supply bag here with the snowcats. Just a few items to have while traveling."

I sipped the hot brew, an herbal mixture with a green tint that smelled strongly of muddied grass. Thank goodness the taste was muted. Bland even.

"You have anything to eat in that supply bag?" I looked at the satchel on the ground near his feet. "How did you secure it safely—the food—while you were away?"

He grinned. "The snowcats, naturally."

"Naturally." I faked a smile. I had never met someone who frustrated me with non-answer answers as much as Arek.

"I have a square of wheatmeal, if you'd like."

I nodded, not having tasted a baked good in quite some time. He handed me the square, colored burnt brown, with hairlike fibrous strands pressed into a cracker. It was dry, crisp, and tasted like I was munching on bark. Yet nothing so delicious had touched my mouth. Hunger had a way of throwing out taste standards.

"We'd better get going. I don't want any more threats coming from that house."

I drank as much of the hot brew as I could, trying not to burn my throat as it went down, and shoved the rest of the wheatmeal in my mouth. Hay stuck to the fabric of my cloak, and I picked it off as Arek led the snowcats out of sight.

The heat of the sun did little to warm my skin as I exited the stable. I took in the peace of the morning, cherishing it, not a soul in sight for the time being. Yet how easily it crossed over into punishment. I had been away from my family for a full day, longer than ever. Did they carry on with their morning as usual? Did they talk about me over breakfast? Did they miss me?

My guts roiled as negative thoughts swarmed in. Their lives might be better without me. No cursed daughter to blacken the family name. Mom not worrying over what I've said or done in a visit to town. One less mouth to feed.

I shunned the isolation and met up with Arek, who fixed a leather harness to the last of the snowcats. The six of them stood in pairs, directly in front of the sled, a small wooden platform designed to comfortably seat one passenger.

"Are we both riding on that thing? Or did you hide another one somewhere back there?"

He sputtered a chuckle. "This is it. Don't worry, the snowcats are strong animals. They could drag twice our weight without complaining."

"Complaining? Your snowcats complain to you?" Why wouldn't they? After all, they purred and cooed with him like they didn't know how to be their wild selves.

"No complaints. I don't overweigh the sled." He grinned, satisfied with his clever retort.

I would've walked away, left him to return to the king empty-handed. The thought remained persistent in the back of my mind, a nagging I'd give in to were it not for the fact I had no money or supplies or quick transport back home. Admittedly, I was curious to see how these snowcats could pull a sled. Never mind how I was going to fit on it with Arek.

"You want front or back?" He stood by the wooden pallet, arms at his hips. "I'll have to hold the reins either way."

"Then back." I couldn't stand the thought of his arms reaching around me to steer.

"Very well." He shifted two leather loops that ran along the thin spaces between wooden planks to the front. He kneeled on the sled, sliding his feet under the loops. "Grab the supply bag and hop on."

I sat behind him, on my bottom, cradling the supply bag while my satchel slung over my shoulder. No way I'd make it far on my knees without having to switch positions. There wasn't enough room to cross my legs.

"You'll have to put your feet here, by me." He slapped the narrow strips of wood to either side of his thighs.

"I'm regretting my decision," I said under my breath.

He turned his head. "You want to switch?"

Close enough he hears my whispers. Noted.

"No. It's fine." It wasn't fine, but what was I to do?

Leave him and walk home. But then he'd tell King Ronin about our violations, and then where would we be? My family would be worse off than they already were.

I placed my booted feet by his hips and positioned the sack in the small space between us. My fingers couldn't grasp around the wood below, since two long black triangular pieces fused to the outer edges of the wood. The most unusual runners I had ever seen on a sled.

"You ready?"

How did this thing not have handles, or railing to keep me in?

My silence was as good as a yes, for Arek stretched tall on his knees and moved his hands guiding the harness. He gave no verbal command or violent crack of a whip. The snowcats broke into a run, jolting me back. Arek briefly checked on me as I gained my balance, back upright on my bottom.

As much as I didn't want to, my hands reached out to his torso. The supply sack was not only lumpy but was as unrooted as I was. I grabbed the sides of his cloak, the sack squishing between the two of us. It was still a better deal than having to constantly adjust my body to the movements of the sled.

The ride was smoother when we reached the road. There still was a considerable amount of snow to cut through, but the snowcats had no trouble. Their large paws landed on top of the snow, not through it, and despite my reservations with snowcats, they appeared content. Happy even, to be pulling us across the land.

We rode through the morning sunlight, a dim glow behind a thin layer of smeared clouds. Arek switched to riding with his bottom on his calves, crouched lower, unless there was an obstacle or guidance to give the snowcats. He carried us off the road whenever we'd see someone coming. A sled guided by snowcats would surely draw questions.

I grew to appreciate my decision of riding in the back, for Arek's body broke the force of the wind. My hair still whipped around, but if I needed to, I could lower my face behind his shoulders or onto the supply bag. Although with the bag containing not all soft things, one slight bump was liable to bruise a cheek.

At this pace, we'd reach the southern shoreline of Corallon by evening, but I still questioned how we'd travel off the island.

With a twist of his wrists, Arek slowed the sled.

"What's happening?" I had taken the last downhill with my head crouched behind his shoulders and now peeked over them. We had reached the Stohl River, the only true river running through Corallon.

"Just preparing to cross the river."

"Are we going to walk across?" The two of us juggling the supply bag, the sled and six snowcats across the frigid water was not a pleasant imagining.

"No. It's better to approach the water at a slower pace than hit it fast."

"Oh." I said it reflexively before processing his words. "What do you mean, hit it?"

He moved the reins, and the snowcats slowly crawled to the northern bank of the river.

"What are we doing?" It was official. Arek had lost all sense of reality, of what was possible in this world and what was not.

The snowcats continued at a steady pace, and the first duo splashed into the flowing water. Their heads stayed upright, paws paddling away as the others followed. The front of the sled touched water, and I clung onto Arek. I didn't care how I was seated, or if I hurt him with my grasp. We were going to topple over or sink. Either way, die. There was no getting warm from this once submerged in the icy waters.

I closed my eyes, the sled not stopping.

"See," Arek said. "No worries."

The back of the sled angled to the right, then straightened out. I opened my eyes. We bobbed on the water, the two triangular runners keeping us afloat.

"They're full of air," Arek said, reading my mind.

In front, the snowcats swam in unison to the southern shore.

"Snowcats can swim?" I said, even though obviously they could, or we would be downriver by now. I immediately regretted asking. *Please don't give a smart answer.*

"They all can," he said. "It's a question of whether they like to or not. Most don't." He turned back to me, his profile in view as he spoke. "These ones do."

"But it's so cold."

"It's cold while they're in there, but they'll warm up fast when they get out."

We drifted slightly west with the current, the snowcats pushing on to the opposite bank.

A rumble like thunder echoed across the sky. Birds squawked as they took flight from their perches. I'd been outside enough in my lifetime to know what it meant.

"No." I squeezed Arek tighter and pressed up against his ear. "Faster. Have them go faster!"

"What's—"

The rumbling grew. Branches at the banks snapped and crackled. The water swished, a bubbling cauldron of foam. A fissure formed to our left, inching closer to the sled, until the river fractured in half.

The water level dropped beneath us, sending my stomach tingling in a swooping dip. We were going to be swallowed up by the earth. Rinsed down into the abyss.

The sled shot up, the ground beneath rising, sweeping the snowcats above us.

"Hold on!" Arek grabbed me by the cloak, his other hand holding onto the reins. The snowcats continued to rise as I fell lower, a wall of freezing water rushing down over me.

The shifting of earth was drowned out by the roar of water. My cloak, clothes, boots, everything absorbed water, pulling me down.

"I can't!" Arek let out, his face twisted in agony overhead.

I slipped out of his hands and reached for whatever I could. Everything was wet, slippery, cold. I grabbed everything and nothing.

My foot hit something solid. I froze, my hands gripping an earthen wall. It grew taller by the second, the noise deafening.

As quickly as it started, the rumbling and shaking stopped.

But it wasn't quiet. The sound of rushing water nearly hurt my ears.

"Are you all right?" Arek was above me, voice weak with the noise, at the top of the cracked land. He managed to pull the sleigh over with him, and the snowcats peered down at me. Arek dangled the supply bag in the air before gaining full control of it, whipping it onto the sled.

I wanted to shout at him, but my teeth chattered and lungs struggled for air as they tightened with cold. My hands were like claws, clutching the muddy wall. Below, at least another ten, fifteen steps lower, water rushed quickly in white roils, smashing against the new southern wall of land I clung to and spreading out on the northern, flatter side until it settled down. The quake had split this section of the river in half longways, the northern bank we had been on moments ago now flooded.

"Get me up?" I used every effort to get the words out. I reached my shivering hand up as he lowered his. Our fingertips barely grazed each other.

"Hold on." Arek fell out of view and quickly returned, lowering the sled. "Grab on. The snowcats will pull you up."

The sled hung upright, and I curled my hands around the front end. I gave Arek a nod, and the snowcats pulled, a surprisingly strong effort that hauled me to the top in no time. If it had taken longer, I don't think my hands would've ever straightened out in their frozenness. Arek unharnessed the cats, and they shook their bodies, layers of fur puffing out into white clouds. They rubbed against one another, a cacophony of purrs.

"You should do the same," Arek said.

"What?" I had been entranced by the river's new landscape, momentarily ignoring my chattering teeth and body's numbness. I hadn't experienced such a violent quake like that since...since I lost Reil.

"You should let the snowcats warm you up before you start losing parts and pieces. They really are something with how warm they can get."

I wanted to ask him how to 'let' snowcats cuddle with me. Just grab one and assume it wouldn't bite my head off? But the snowcats mewed and shuffled at my ankles until I sat on the ground. They purred and surrounded me, wet but surprisingly warm.

Arek paced the edge of the raw rift, biting his cheek and mumbling to himself.

"Are you all right?" I asked. He had asked it of me seconds ago, but I hadn't bothered to ask him then, given I was clinging to a cliff and my blood was almost at a frozen standstill.

He looked back at me and despite the soft growing warmth of the snowcats, I shivered. The quake had scared him.

"I don't know," he said. "How is it that you're not shaken?"

I almost laughed. "That's the thing. With every quake, I am shaken. Yet, they're so commonplace now, what can I do? I can't prevent them. I can't stop them when they're happening. What good is it to dwell on that fear? We survived this one, and we shall hope to survive the next."

He sat down on what used to be the southern half of the riverbed and slumped his head in his hands.

"Are they not so commonplace where you're from?" Could it be that other terrins didn't suffer from quakes as much as Corallon did? Surely the counsel would hear of it.

"They are common, yes," he said. "I'm still getting used to them out in the open these past months. It's a different experience than being within sturdy walls."

These past months? Where did he live? If I asked him though, he was sure to give a non-answer. "If I'm being honest, that one was the most severe I've seen in a long time," I said. "And it did scare me."

"I don't think that helps any, oddly enough." He gave a slight smile.

"I've never known a quake to occur so far inland before. Of course I don't get away from town to really know, but they seem to stem from the coast there." I stepped toward the edge of the cliff, which now afforded a fairly expansive view to the north. "This…" I turned around. "This one was different."

Worrisome.

We turned the forced break in the journey into a meal, snacking on dried pear and the last of Arek's rations of wheatmeal. We ate in silence while my mind mulled over the strangeness of the quake. Given Raiders stayed mostly at sea, plus what I had experienced in Corallon, I had assumed the quakes were coastal. Since the river connected to the sea, did that somehow make it a conduit for a quake? Were Raiders becoming bolder in their travels?

Despite not being fully dry—and with a rekindled fear of experiencing another quake—we continued south. The landscape changed subtly, eventually rolling into a flat expanse. Although the clouds threatened snowfall, only a flurry or two hit us as the sky darkened into night. The sea permeated the air well before the coastline was visible.

"We'll camp out here tonight." Arek slowed the sled once more.

"We're not staying in town?" Dern couldn't have been far if we were near the coast. It lay further east, but it wouldn't take much longer if the snowcats were up for it.

He rose out of the sled and began releasing the snowcats. "Again, the fewer people we encounter the better. I stayed in town on the way up. Risking being recognized with a new travel companion might raise suspicion."

I unfolded my twisted bones off the sled, assessing the area. A handful of rocks speckled the land, sticking out of the melting snow. I hadn't seen animal tracks in ages, and hoped he had enough food to quell my hunger.

"I think it'd be safe enough to have a fire," he said, "as we're far enough from town."

I scanned the landscape again. The closest trees splayed on the horizon to the south, and I had no tools for felling anyway. "Any suggestions how we'd make a fire, seeing as we don't have wood?"

Arek rubbed the face of the last released snowcat, then rummaged through the supply bag. "Here we are."

He handed me a hardened clump, shaped like a brick. "Forever flame."

A dark powder, like soot, laced my fingers. The block looked like compressed ashes, something that had already been burned twice over. "I thought these were fake. Just a story people told."

"I think you'll find a lot of what you learned in Corallon to be true isn't. And what isn't true, is."

I stood in disbelief at the brick. One snowcat pounced playfully at another, a reminder of my ridiculous preconceptions of how the world worked.

Arek used his hands to clear a circular pit in the snow. He took out the two cups used this morning and filled them with snow, then took back the forever flame. "I need a stone. Something smooth but hard."

I searched the ground, then thought of my sling sack. I pulled out one of my ammunition rocks and handed it over.

"Perfect." He struck the corner of the brick. It sparked, the black substance burning, flames spreading out to the rest of the brick. "Here you go." He handed back the stone. "I'll warm up some water and boil the dried pears. Makes for a sweet porridge."

I looked at him, shocked. Sure, Arek cheated fire with his savvy royal goods, but he had a confidence about him out here. Even as he guided the sled, he looked comfortable in keeping directions, and had a sense of his surroundings.

"Could you take out the two blankets from the sack? I know they're not much, but if we stick together by the fire and with the snowcats, we should stay warm enough."

I reached in the bag and pulled out two thin blankets, nowhere near the newness and condition of Arek's cloak or boots. I had no intention of snuggling up to him like a snowcat to stay warm.

"I'll sleep on the sled, if you don't mind." It'd be drier, although the distance off the ground would make for a colder surface than if I stayed in the insulating snow.

Arek was ready to argue his side, but he closed his mouth, sending out calculated words. "If you wish. Take three of the snowcats."

Three of the animals walked over to me and laid at my side. My mind was going to explode. "How'd that happen? Do they understand our conversation?" I stared at their cute yet frightening faces and had a crazy thought. "Can they talk?"

Arek laughed, a hearty chuckle in which he had to support his belly and prevent himself from falling over. The big smile revealed dimples in his cheeks. The fire's light darkened the arches beneath his strong brows and cast a glow over his face, the stubble heavier along his jawline. He looked older and mature, the most relaxed since I met him. His joy was almost contagious, if I had not felt so stupid.

"I'm sorry," he said, wiping his eyes. "No, they can't talk."

I scoffed, throwing my hands in the air. "Well, I don't know! You told me I'd find things that I thought aren't true are, so maybe that's one of them."

He nodded. "Fair enough."

He calmed down for the most part, letting out a chuckle here and there whenever recalling my question, as he made his bed for the night. He dug out another section of snow near the fire and used part of his cloak as a pillow, while the rest of it and the blanket wrapped over his body with the three snowcats.

I was more than ready for sleep, but annoyed he hadn't answered my question. How did the snowcats know to come by me? And why did they feel comfortable around me, a stranger?

As I looked at Arek already asleep by the fire, stomach full of porridge, I thought back on the first night we met. He wore the wrong clothes, had no weapons, and lacked an overall sense of survival skills.

Yet today he exuded confidence with his knowledge of wildlife, directions, flow of the river. Despite all that, the quake had given him a fright.

As much as I didn't know this stranger lying across from me, he had revealed part of his true self today.

And all he left me with were more questions.

CHAPTER

SEVEN

"Evella." My name echoed through a haze. "Evella!"

I shook awake, my eyes taking a moment in their grogginess to register Arek's face above mine. His hands held my shoulders.

I snapped back to reality and sat up, shying away from his grasp.

"You were having a nightmare again."

I looked around at our camp. The snowcats moved sleepily, licking each other in greeting. The fire still held strong, the brick not having changed size or color, no noticeable change in any aspect. It really was a wonder. How easy was it to get a forever flame? If they were abundant in another terrin, was it possible to trade for them? How easier life would be with the task of fire simplified. No more felling trees, sawing trunks into smaller pieces, drying out wood. It would save trees, not to mention effort. At least one member in my family would be free to do other things—help hunt and trap, make repairs or improvements on the house. Perhaps give time to read, to train in another trade, or learn more about other terrins.

Arek offered another cup of the herbal brew, and I gladly accepted. It was only the second time drinking it but the taste had grown on me. It immediately provided warmth and alertness.

He tidied up the supply bag, then sat amongst the snowcats. One rubbed its face on his leg, then the others followed, vying for his affection.

It was hard not to smile, but he helped it fade when he reminded me of the nightmare. "What is it that you dreamt about?" He looked at me forlorn, like a parent tending to a child after a tumble. "Was it the same as last time?"

It was always the same. The purple light. The bottle in my pocket. The pain. Sometimes the pain was worse in the dream than it had been in reality.

"Was I—moving things again?" I skirted the question but did want to know. There wasn't much I could've moved nearby. I couldn't imagine heaving a snowcat into the air, its weight more than mine. But what if I had moved a rock? It could've fallen on top of either one of us.

"There were a few things spilled out of the supply bag, but I have a feeling it was one of the snowcats rummaging in the middle of the night." He pointed to the collection of pawprints going every which way in the snow. "You know, it might help to talk about it. Then it won't seem so frightening anymore."

"We'd better get going." I poured out the little that remained in my cup, the snow sizzling from the hot liquid. I didn't talk about that night to anyone. What was the point? Mother and Father had been there, and Mother especially would not want a word mentioned of it to anyone. It was something to erase from memory. If only my memory worked that way, picking which events to remember and which to easily wipe out.

Arek nodded and rounded up the snowcats. Why should I tell Arek, of all people? I don't know the first thing about him. What, in the little that he's told me, holds true and what has been a lie? It's not that I don't know him entirely. Obviously, he has a way with these snowcats and knows his way on a sled through the terrain. If he indeed wanted to keep a low profile, then he was right to have camped where we did. He was smarter than he first seemed.

Which begged the question, why the act in the Ashwan Forest the first night we met? Did he think that was the only way to get what he wanted? He could've knocked on our door and asked for shelter.

But then he wouldn't have had the leverage of alerting me to the Raiders at the shore. Guilting me into feeling like I owed him something. I took in a deep breath, the air freezing yet refreshing, were it not for the terrifying thought forming.

What if Arek was working with Raiders? What if he had landed with them? Of course, how did I not think of it before? He'd built my trust, convinced me to accompany him, and at any moment he was going to hand me over. Was this how the others went missing?

"All ready," he said. "It shouldn't take long to get to the coast from here."

I nodded. If he was with the enemy, then I needed to come up with a plan. To do that, I needed time. He needed to think nothing had changed and that I fully believed we were going to see King Ronin in Elsinea.

He locked his feet on the sled and stayed upright on his knees until I boarded behind him. How I would've loved to bathe and change out of my clothes. Despite the cold, I had built up a grime on my skin from sweating in my sleep. My cloak still smelled of burning wood and stale ale from the tavern yesterday, and my feet begged to be slipped out of my boots to breathe.

This wasn't the time or place. Even if I could bathe, I couldn't wash and dry out my cloak. As for my feet, once they got cold from exposure, it would be near impossible to warm them back up.

I reluctantly took my place, and Arek moved the reins, the snowcats trotting their way south.

He was right, it didn't take long to reach the rocky coast. Before the sun reached a quarter way up the sky, we stood on the bluff overlooking the sea a fair distance west of Dern. Large boulders and stones stacked along the southern end, where Corallon split from Iogaton, as if a dense egg of rocks cracked in half, spilling out the hardest bits of earth on the border.

Even with the clouds clearing, Iogaton wasn't visible to the southwest or Tusinda to the southeast, much to my disappointment. Supposedly, Corallon branched away from the surrounding terrins the furthest, creating the widest expanse of sea between terrins, while the southern terrins remained closer to each other. I had no idea how long it would take to traverse the sea to either of the nearest terrins. I didn't even know if we'd head to either one.

"I'm guessing taking a ferry is not an option."

Arek gave a curt shake of the head. "We'd have to go into town, purchase fare and wait around for the next ferry. Too conspicuous."

"Do you have a plan?" I kept my eyes on the water, little waves of white caps sprinkling the surface in the wind.

He grinned slyly. Of course he had a plan. The young man without a sense of survival wasn't him. The real him carefully plotted.

"It'll be best to go by water the rest of the way, the same way I came up. It's quicker than having to cut across Midmarea. We'll stay close to the terrin's shore when we're near in case we need to land for any reason."

"How long will it take?"

"A good part of daylight. One positive of heading this way is that we'll be moving with the current." He pointed to the water ahead, as if the boundaries of the current he spoke of showed themselves. "It'll save us time and the snowcats energy."

"The way you said that, sounds like there's a negative too?" I asked, hesitant to find out.

"Unfortunately we'll have to unharness the snowcats here and carry our ride down."

That didn't seem so bad until we ventured down the bluff to the water. The rocks were slippery with saltwater, and it took the both of us to carry the sled. Arek took the brunt of the weight, staying steps below me, but that meant I had to fight the weight pulling me down, and with no grip on the rocks it made my legs shake. The descent took longer than I had estimated from the top.

Somehow we made it to the lapping water at the bottom without scrapes or twisted ankles. Arek placed the sled in the water and let it float while he harnessed the cats on the rocks. He sat on top the sled, then reached out a hand to help me. I didn't want to soak my boots in the water, knowing it would take most of the day to thaw out my feet. I accepted his hand and stretched one leg out, my boot end finding grip on the sled. He pulled me over, and I nearly overshot the sled. Arek quickly moved his hand to catch me, and I crouched low, my face near his. His breath puffed white in the cold, his eyes locked on me. It was for a mere second, but my body froze, his gaze sending a flurry within me I didn't welcome.

"Are you all right?" he asked.

"Mmhmm." I gained my balance and took my position, embarrassed over my slipup. And my reaction to his closeness.

The snowcats swam away from shore. It was the first time I stepped off Corallon, my home. My heart ached with sadness. I did miss my family, but more so, I wanted them to experience this. I wanted them here, to see what I have seen and will see. There were sketches and maps of other terrins, Corallon the furthest north, an arrowhead pointing west. That was most of what I knew of the other lands—their shapes and placement on a map. How they all looked like they'd fit into one land if squished back together. But who on Corallon really knew what they looked like? What they smelled like, felt like? Despite conniving Arek and the situation he put me in, there was a piece of me excited to see the rest of the world.

"This is the longest bit." Arek's words blew in front of him instead of back to me, and I strained to hear. "We could head a little west to skim the shore of Iogaton, but it wouldn't be for long. Best to go straight down to Midmarea."

Now I was drifting off my world, into the unknown. I had to trust Arek even though it was the last thing I wanted to do. He had successfully navigated to Corallon, so why not trust him to get back to Elsinea?

Unless he hadn't come from Elsinea at all.

My thoughts of Arek strayed further to the sinister. I hadn't come up with a plan yet. Was I supposed to escape? The further we traveled from Corallon the dumber that idea seemed. If he was working with the Raiders, was there a way to trick him into admitting it before he handed me over to them?

Unfortunately, the sea gave me more time to think, to sink lower in conspiracy theories. It was like the openness, the sheer vastness of water around us and below us, released the borders of my rational thinking. My mind twisted and warped everything that had happened, questioning what was true, what was planned, what was coincidence. I never felt so clueless and helpless. For as much as I longed to journey across the sea, I wanted to see land. Somehow that would get my mind to stop roaming.

In the eternity of time, the sun had risen over our heads, a dull bulb of heat doing little to warm me from the salty wind at my back.

"There." Arek pointed ahead. I squinted, the water reflecting the sunlight too brightly. The horizon was a blue straight line meeting faded blue sky. I popped up, peering over Arek's shoulder. There, far ahead, lay a tiny brown dot. Then, as my eyes adjusted, the rest of the land spread out from it.

"Midmarea," he said.

As we approached, it was evident Midmarea was much larger than Corallon. We skimmed close enough to see the sandy beaches running along the coastline. The sled was a speck next to a behemoth, and for some time there was no end to the northern border.

How different it was from the uninviting rocky shores of home. How I longed to land ashore, feel the golden sand in my toes and explore the green hills beyond. And no snow, in winter! How could this place, far away yet not so far away, look so different from Corallon?

"We'll stop once we wind around to the west. There's a small harbor with enough business that we wouldn't look suspicious. Give the snowcats a rest and grab a bite to eat."

I was guiltily giddy with excitement. Even if I couldn't wander inland, at least I could say I had touched Midmarea. Would Tulla even believe me?

Soon we made the turn heading due south. The western shore loosely resembled the northern cliffs of Corallon. A few houses dotted the skyline above. One's roof slanted crookedly, like it would slide off with the slightest gust. Another house was broken in half, its two stories of rooms open to the sea air.

The quakes.

Part of me had wished it on them, wished others suffered as much as we did with quakes. But seeing the wreckage, the familiar signs of fissured land, shattered homes torn to rubble, the linear veins of collapsed ruins, was dreadful. It was wrong to wish it on anyone. No one deserved to be ruined.

My desire to explore vanished. The reports Corallon received were true.

The world was dying.

We approached the harbor, a small inset of coastline. The horizon between water and sky vanished, were it not for dark blue seabirds swooping and cawing at the surface, breaking up the illusion. There were no buildings or wooden-planked docks. A handful of vessels anchored out in the water. A man in a rowboat oared in the direction of a two-sailed lugger, three men aboard waving to him.

"A ferryman?" I asked.

Arek nodded. "It's how they get to shore. Unless they want to get wet, or risk beaching their vessel. Outgoing tide gets really low."

I dipped my fingers in the saltwater, warmer than the river and sea by Corallon, but not warm enough to want to bathe in or swim. Especially since the air still had enough chill to cool my exposed hands.

"Oh no." Arek contorted his hands, and the snowcats sped up. He looked off to the right.

I scanned the water west. "What is it?"

He stretched his arm out. "You see the thin strip of land out there? That's Hefris. Aim for the middle then trace the water slowly back our way."

I did as he said and made out a thin pole jutting out of the water.

"Raiders," he said.

Spit caught in my throat. "How do you know?" I managed.

He urged the snowcats to move faster, a heavying wake growing behind the sled.

He didn't have to answer. The stick wasn't a stick at all, but a mast. A second one appeared to its right. The vessel surfaced, a growing metal tube across the water. Two triangular sheets hung off the masts, seawater glistening off the billowing material. The vessel was close—almost in sling range.

This was it. Was Arek playing this up? Was this the moment I was to be handed over?

A rusty creak carried over the water. A man appeared on the deck, followed by another, until four figures stood, balancing on the vessel bobbing in the water. One of them, with long dark hair, pointed something at us.

A weapon.

"I won't go!" I wiggled away from Arek and turned toward the shore. If I had to swim, so be it.

"What are you doing?" Arek grabbed me by the cloak and pulled me back. "Are you crazy?!"

I swung onto my back, boots in the air as a dart whizzed above me. "Are you trying to get me killed?" I yelled. "Was all this just to surrender to them?"

"I'm trying to keep the both of us alive!" Another dart struck the sled, sticking to the top of the triangular runner.

Arek turned around briefly. "Here, hold the reins."

I stayed low and grabbed the reins, not knowing what exactly I could do with them.

Arek flicked his hands in the air. His face was focused and assured as he turned to the Raiders. His eyes closed before opening them the same moment his hands flung out in the air.

The blue seabirds swarmed overhead and headed straight for the Raider vessel. They circled the figures, and one of them bent to his knees, threatening to descend back into the vessel. Another grabbed his arm and kept him above deck, pulling him to his feet.

The birds formed a thick swarm and charged the Raiders. They pecked with their beaks and flapped their wings in the men's faces. The shortest man, swatting violently to no avail, lost his grip and slipped, falling into the water.

"Now." Arek turned back to me and ripped the reins out of my hands. He guided the snowcats with urgency, and the sled caught speed, the distance from the Raiders swiftly growing. I looked back at the vessel, the three men still battling to get the fourth out of the water.

"I don't think we'll make that stop after all," Arek said.

"I second that."

He yanked on the arrow sticking out of the runner, breaking the shaft close to the point. He examined it before throwing it out into the water. "Those were sleeping darts, by the way."

"What?"

"What they were shooting. The point would hurt and injure, but they wanted to knock you out."

"I don't understand."

"The shaft had a resin inside. It would've entered your body through the tip."

"No, I mean, you said they wanted to knock *me* out."

"What did I say about Raiders? They just attempted to take you on their vessel. They want to use your abilities for their purposes."

I shook my head, digesting the words. "How would they know about me?"

"Because they know about me," Arek said. "Not to mention *I* knew about you. They either found out through somebody or guessed what I was doing traveling north."

"Was that why they landed in Corallon? They were following you?"

Arek's shrug registered through his thick black cloak. "Seems the likely explanation."

I stared at the water, the Raider vessel behind us a mere blip on the horizon.

"So you're not secretly a Raider trying to abduct me?" A tinge of embarrassment washed over me.

"What? Are you serious?" Arek slowed the snowcats, who eagerly took the break by treading water. He turned around, facing me as much as he could with the space on the sled. His oval face looked more angular, stronger, the longer he let the stubble go. His eyebrows bunched together and his lips flushed a deeper pink, either from the sun or narrowly escaping or both.

"All I've ever wanted to do was protect you."

My heart skipped a beat. I felt foolish and confused at the same time. He said the words as if he fully meant them.

The worried crinkle above his narrow nose softened, and he stared at me long enough to notice just how close we were to one another.

He sighed and leaned back. "I was assigned this mission. No matter how I felt about it, I promised King Ronin I'd bring you back safely."

I nodded. Of course. This was his job, and if he didn't perform it accordingly the king would see to it he may not get another one.

I bit my bottom lip, staring at the rippled water.

"What is it? Don't believe me? Look, I know I wasn't truthful when we first met. And I don't know if you'll ever realize how sorry I am, how terrible it made me feel. But I had to—"

I held my hand up to stop him.

His mouth remained open for a second until he relented.

"If that's the case, then be truthful with me now." I sat taller, feeling in control for the first time in the last several days. We were on a sled after all, and he had nowhere to go.

"Very well," he said. His eyes were softer, his mouth serious.

Now that I could be fairly positive he wasn't out to toss me off to the Raiders, there were other pressing questions. "How did you do that? With the birds?"

"It was bound to come out eventually. I had hoped you would figure it out on your own."

"Figure out what?" I most certainly had not lived up to his hopes.

He let out an amused sigh. "You're not the only one with Soulmagic."

"What?" Had I heard him correctly?

"How do you think I control them? How do you think I've tamed these snowcats and guided them to run and swim and not attack you?"

"I—" I shook my head. "I figured you were a good trainer." I shrugged, not knowing how to explain how I justified the occurrences of the past two days of travel.

His grin broke into a laugh, the same hearty laugh that produced those dimples that were annoying and handsome.

He calmed down, waving a hand in the air. "Sorry. I shouldn't laugh.

You didn't know, and I didn't tell you. But I'm telling you now. And there's something else you should know."

I braced myself for whatever would come out of his mouth. My world was upside down, sideways, completely shaken up.

"There are more where we're going."

CHAPTER

EIGHT

As we cleared the western shores of Midmarea, my mind was reeling. If only Arek had been up front with me, had told me that first night catching me in my sleep, that he had abilities too...

Maybe I would've gone with him. Without his coercion.

But deep down I knew that wasn't true. I wouldn't have willingly left my family to fend for themselves, to survive the winter in Corallon, without being threatened.

Arek hadn't known me for more than a moment, but that was long enough to know what he had to do to pull me away from my home.

He was clever and capable, and even though he wasn't in concert with Raiders, a part of me held doubts to his motives.

"I think it's best if we continue onward." Arek sat on his knees with an air of confidence, a strength in his voice that hadn't been there before. Maybe there was some relief revealing the truth to me about his powers or outrunning the Raiders. "The snowcats are tiring, but I think we can make it the rest of the way. That'll put us there earlier than expected."

Even though the Raiders were nowhere in sight, as my habitual checking behind us indicated, I welcomed his plan. "If you feel they're up for it."

Did he feel what the snowcats felt? If he had a way to communicate with them, command them, did that mean he could also receive information from them?

There were too many questions to ask about his powers, and Soulmagic in general. It was hard to hold a conversation without him turning around so I could hear, which distracted him from the snowcats and me from checking on the Raiders' status every two blinks.

But there was one that nagged me. "Are you telling me you could've controlled the otari that you scared off? Allowed my shot to hit him?"

"Still upset about that? Of all the things we've been through these past days, *that* is what bothers you?"

"If you wanted to discuss what bothers me, then the snowcats had better be prepared to guide us past Ulopra and back around the planet until we hit Corallon again."

He laughed it off in a huff, seemingly not taking my comment too seriously.

We rode in silence until we reached the next shoreline, a rounded scalloped land ahead.

"Elsinea?" I asked.

"Indeed." The snowcats tugged harder, as if seeing the destination motivated them more. The poor things had to be exhausted, yet their speed defied my assumption.

From this distance, Elsinea looked wide, a bit of earth splayed out over the water. It wasn't until we got closer, seeing the palace off in the distance above the rest of the land, that I remembered it came to a point in the south where the palace sat.

I don't know how my preconceptions of Elsinea had formed. I pictured lush trees and bushes with broad leaves swaying in the sun, fruitful farmland producing grains and vegetables, too much for the farmers to know what to do with. There'd be shops upon shops, selling the most basic fare to the exotic, with fabrics I had never seen and spices I had never tasted.

The clear picture in my head was wiped away as we skirted around the west side. Farmlands checkered the north with straw-colored fields. A far cry from plentiful bounties, but conceivably that was attributed to it being winter, even if the climate was more temperate.

The waterway was the narrowest one we traversed yet, with the terrin of Devrenim to the west, the coast clearly seen across the water. Trade would be much easier between these two terrins from the distance alone.

We approached a harbor further south on the coastline, not unlike the one in Midmarea in shape and size. But this one bustled with ships and vessels of all forms. And people. There were people everywhere.

Arek slowed the snowcats until we glided into shore, onto a strip of mud formed from small hulls sliding in and out of the water. I got off the sled and helped push it further up, out of the way of others wanting to use the slip. Arek worked on unlatching the animals out of their harnesses. Their paws and fur quickly browned with the thick mud but they didn't seem to mind.

"Arek! You are back!" A burly man with a round belly and even rounder face held out his arms before resting his hands back on his belly.

Arek tossed a coin to the man. "Good day, Samish. See to it they fill their bellies and rest."

"Certainly."

Arek swished his hands in the air and the snowcats rushed to Samish, who held his hands out. "Slow down, one at a time." They followed him in single file to a wooden building with a crooked roof, set back from the water enough to not be hit by the changing tide, yet too close to not get wet during a storm.

"He'll get the sled, too," Arek said as if I had wondered. "We'll walk from here. The palace is on the top of the hill so we'll cut through town."

I nodded in excitement and apprehension. The sheer numbers of people gave the island its own feeling—a hurried, rushed sensation that quickened my pulse and step. As we passed folks going on about their day, I couldn't help but notice their pallor, faces no cleaner than ours from Corallon. Most wore clothes as dull and tattered as my people, their bones skinny behind the draping fabrics. There was more variety in people though—hair styles in short chops to thick curls, heads wrapped in thin fabrics, braids and plaits on both the men and women. Citizens of northern Corallon had a texture about them, a weathering of the skin that only the cold air and wind could do to a person. Here, skin looked younger, plumper, fresher, even in those who looked as starved as those in the northernmost terrin. They came in all shades of skin, from the darkest of brown to the creamiest white. As more Displaced came up from southern Corallon and surrounding terrins, the town of Corallon became more of a mix of peoples, yet not as diverse as this.

I was one of the palest in the crowd, a ghost eyeing the wonders before me. And I received side-glances and curious scans as if that's how everyone else saw me, too.

Only a few shopkeepers wore brighter and newer clothing on their fuller bodies—felt hats and ruffled shirts, colorful scarves and stiff boots like Arek. The air rang with an underlying aroma of pig manure, with the occasional whiff of warm wheatmeal crackers and root vegetables seasoned with spices. A wan customer haggled with a vendor over a sorry wilted head of cabbage.

"It's not how I pictured it." I practically yelled it to Arek, the noise of the streets a constant high volume.

"No?" Arek weaved through the people on the street, turning this way and that through a maze of stone and wooden buildings. They were built so close to each other they relied on each other for support. If one wall were destroyed, the whole city would collapse.

"I guess I figured if you lived by the king, you lived like the king."

Arek pulled my elbow, moving me out of the way of a cart moving too fast through the crowd.

"It may have been like that, before."

"Before The Quake?"

He nodded. "But we're not getting our rations." He eyed me like it was my fault. People like me didn't contribute surpluses to Elsinea. That was because we never had a surplus of anything these days. Except snow.

I followed him through the rest of the town, moving further south.

The land narrowed enough that the sea was visible on either side of us. We reached a series of wooden posts, a gate taller than four men.

"I thought you were going to walk me off the island."

"Over here." He led me to a turret with a rounded doorway, a man standing guard. Another turret sat at the other end of the gate, again with a manned guard.

Arek nodded to the guard, and he gestured for us to walk through the doorway. Two women in finer dress gossiped and giggled past us on their way out.

"The palace is on the very edge of Elsinea," Arek said. "You would fall off the edge if you went out a back window." We walked through a narrow walkway then turned left into a courtyard. He pointed to the large circular tower in the back of the triangle that formed the palace walls, a tower partially concealed due to a bridge that ran parallel to the front gate. It seemed reasonable for the bridge to be manned, adding another layer of protection for the king from the common folk, but no one stood by the rounded archway into the smaller courtyard.

"The Quake completely tore the palace from the surrounding land. Major repairs had to be made in the back and both side walls."

"Is that what the wooden sections are? Repaired damage from The Quake?" The two side walls were a mixture of metal near the foundation, and wood on the second story. Some patches were of older stonework. The palace looked to have been built piecemeal, at different times with different materials in a rush to make it whole again.

Arek nodded. "They couldn't replace it with metal like the rest of the palace, because the Raiders got to the metal stores first."

That, I knew. Raiders had hoarded metal from all of the terrins, not that there was much from Corallon to be had. But they used it for their ships like the one we encountered off Midmarea, or saw on the shore of Corallon. If ships were their only use of metal, how many ships did they have? Or did they use metal for something we didn't know about?

The palace courtyard was much quieter with fewer people, a tranquil place compared to town. The crashing of waves could be slightly heard over the murmurs of the finer-dressed folks, assumed to be in King

Ronin's court based on their flowing dresses and stately pants and coats. Their attire and overall cleanliness made me feel like a heathen.

"Arek?" I asked, Arek looking at ease and in his element. "Should I clean up, I mean, before we meet the king? Is that not advisable?"

He stopped in his tracks and stared at me, head to foot. "Maybe a little. I don't think I can pull off a change of wardrobe."

"Perhaps some water to splash on my face, at the very least?"

His stare went off to some part of the east wall, which wasn't just a wall, but a two-story building with windows and archways. Bedrooms for the royal court?

"I can manage that. I doubt the king can see us right now anyway, with how early we are. How about a bite to eat, too?"

Nothing sounded better. "Yes, please."

"Then we need to go down here."

I followed him to the archway etched into the bridge cutting across the courtyard. An open door stood in the side of the archway, with stairs leading down. Wall torches guided our way to a basement.

It was the sort of walkway that I wouldn't have gone down had I been following a total stranger. But when we reached the bottom, the noise alerted me that it was indeed frequented by others. A woman with a dirtied apron passed us, either oblivious to us with her concentration or she simply didn't care.

"Servants' quarters," Arek said. "The basement runs beneath the whole structure, with tunnels across the courtyard. It's where the string leads to, on the bells in the rooms."

I raised my eyebrows. Was he speaking Elsin or gibberish?

"When someone in the court needs something, they ring a bell in their room. The string attached tugs a bell on the other end, down here. So the servants can fetch the hot drink, or clean clothes."

"I can't even imagine living like that."

He sighed, again staring off into space. "Me neither."

"You mean you don't have a bell in your room?"

He cleared his throat, cheeks reddening. "I'm more on the other end of the string."

I nodded, not knowing whether to believe him. That was nothing new, though.

"The most important room in the palace is down here." He hurried ahead until we turned into a larger room with a higher ceiling than the hallway. "The kitchen." He breathed in the scents of the room.

A fire burned aglow near the center of the back wall, and a tiny window lay open high into the stonework, letting in cooler air while letting out smoke. Four servants milled about, one crushing grain, another bent over the stove with something boiling in a pot.

"Arek! You're back!" A skinny yet sturdy woman in her forties greeted him with a hug. "It's been too long."

How many people knew Arek, and knew he had gone away? Did they know why I was around him? I still didn't really know why I was around him, but here I was.

"Oh, how is it you're more handsome than last I saw you?"

Arek hastily accepted the hug and quickly pulled out of the woman's grasp.

She mumbled something else to him, the noise of pouring broth overpowering it.

"I can't stay for long, I'm afraid." Arek stepped back from her. "Nera, I was hoping we could get a bite to eat before reporting back to the king." He looked at me. "And maybe some hot water to freshen up?"

"Of course." The woman swatted her hand. "You two sit down. Miss...?"

"Oh, I'm Evella." I gave a slight wave and nod. How was I supposed to address her? Was a cook in the king's court different from a cook anywhere else?

"I am Nera. Miss Evella, please. Make yourself comfortable." She pointed to a wooden table with thick chairs.

Arek led the way, and I followed him, sitting at the table. The chairs were heavy and made annoying scrapes dragging across the floor of large flat stones.

She returned with a tray of cut squash, a cut of meat, two large heads of broccoflower, two glasses of ale and a wet cloth.

"For your face and hands," she said.

"Thank you."

"This looks wonderful." Arek grinned.

"I snuck a little taste of the lamb for you. You know how the king hates the fatty cuts." She rolled her eyes. "And don't give me that attitude about the animals."

Did Arek know that about the king? What else did he know, and how? I must've been looking at him funny because he stiffened in his seat.

"What?"

"Nothing." I took a bite of the squash.

"It's not nothing. You had a look on your face."

"What look?"

"Like you were trying to solve me, as if I were a puzzle. I'll just let it out now, I don't eat meat, if I don't have to. It doesn't sit well with me, having a connection with animals. Doesn't seem right to command them *and* eat them."

That wasn't the reason for the look, but what he said made sense. Who knew how deep his connection was with animals. Would they think he betrayed them by eating their kin?

I dismissed the talk of food and chose my words carefully. "I don't really know much about you, besides the Soulmagic bit." I said the last half in a whisper. "How did you end up in service to the king?"

He took a bite of the broccoflower. "I grew up here, within the palace walls." He glanced at Nera ever briefly. "And once the king found out I had Soulmagic, he's had me helping him with a mission."

I took a bite of the lamb. "This is wonderful." I wanted to ask a follow-up, or several, but I savored the bite. "I haven't had lamb in years." I closed my eyes, half guilty for enjoying this while my family was back in Corallon surviving, half in utter pleasure. As I let it escape down my throat, I looked up. Arek's mouth snarled up in disgust over my feasting.

"What? Animals aren't a part of my Soulmagic. Do you know how valuable meat is these days?"

He relaxed in defeat. "I get it, I do. But I can't help how I feel."

"I'll try to be more discreet." I took the last bite and chewed slowly. "What's the mission you're helping with? Finding me?"

"That's part of it. A small part." He dabbed the corner of his mouth with his sleeve. I handed him the wet towel, and he waved it off. "You use it to wash up."

I wanted to lick the juices off my plate, it had been so delicious. But I wiped my hands in the cloth and used the reverse side to clean up my face as best I could.

"And the other part of the mission?"

Arek stood, taking one last gulp of the ale. "That, I'll save for the king."

CHAPTER
NINE

Arek led me out of the kitchen through a basement corridor. It was narrow with rooms shooting off from it to the left and right. We passed one room with children around Tulla's age or younger, seated on long benches and facing one wall. A woman stood at the front of the room, pointing to her mouth as she spoke. "The pernicious pupil picked on the petulant peasant for a pear."

I would've asked Arek twenty questions about the classroom, but he hurried on by, as if we were on a tight schedule.

Corallon hadn't offered classes in any subject since the last schoolteacher died in a quake over two years ago. Either no one had the knowledge, or confidence in their knowledge, or time to devote to teaching others. They were too busy trying to survive. At least I had a chance to glance over maps and absorb the general idea of Elsinor's history. Tulla had only been exposed to the basics of writing and reading when the classroom closed. Any other information she learned was passed to her from the rest of us.

And what did I know, in all honesty? My perceptions of Elsinor had been dramatically off this entire journey, and I hadn't even set foot on or seen the majority of terrins. We were kept in the dark, and these children gave me a sliver of hope they might grow up knowing more than me.

We passed a few more rooms, some storage for crates of supplies, others empty. It was evident when we arrived in the grand turret at the back of the palace because the walls curved and guards stood at the doorways, keeping an eye on who entered and exited.

"What's behind there?" Two guards stood by a thick wooden door, metal slats nailed into the boards for reinforcement. Torches on either side on the wall burned low, providing only enough light to make out faces.

"The dungeon." Arek's mouth curled down. "You don't want to find yourself in there."

One guard had rings hanging off his nose, the other with a long beard parted into braids. Just what kind of criminals were housed here? Thieves? Poachers? I swallowed hard. Murderers?

In Corallon, it was nearly impossible to arrest anyone for a crime, let alone keep them indoors and feed them. It was considered punishment enough to leave them free to survive, if they weren't killed first. I hadn't thought about what I would've done with that poacher snatching the hare from my trap if I had caught up with him. I merely wanted my hare back. There was nowhere I could take him for punishment, and would I have had enough reason to kill him?

We took the stairs along the outer wall, spiraling up and around until we reached ground level. A woman and man entered the front door looking clean and stately, the courtyard and bridge off in the distance behind them.

For as much as I had envisioned the palace being a bright, open building with tall ceilings and adorned with tapestries and candles, it was the opposite. The atmosphere was damp and dark, especially in the basement. But even on the ground floor, few windows let in natural light, and the views afforded a sliver of a glimpse of sky. It felt like a prison on the edge of the world.

"Do they not keep fires going to warm up the place?" I rubbed my arms underneath my cloak.

"The king is very particular about where and when fires can be lit. You'll find a few torches here and there, but he's a bit paranoid about the wooden structures, especially on that side of the palace." Arek pointed south, supposedly where the palace lost part of its structure during The Quake. "He keeps one in The Great Hall, though, where we're going."

Apparently, that was supposed to provide consolation, but I was too nervous over what I was walking into. It would help if Arek would fill me in, but he insisted I hear it from the king himself.

It was difficult to get a sense of the layout. At first the corridors were much like home, radiating out from the center. But then we made cuts to the left or right, and I lost my direction. We passed a doorway leading to a large room with two fair-sized windows to the outside. The stone floor and pieces of furniture—a rocking chair, a made-up bed, a cracked mirror—held a layer of dust. The room was so void of life it nearly sucked the air out of mine.

I stopped at the doorway. "What is this place?"

Arek sighed but gave in to my questioning. "That room belonged to Alora. King Ronin's sister."

Vaguely the lineage came back, the king having a brother and sister. They did not survive The Quake while their father, King Crohl, died just days before, leaving then Prince Ronin as the only survivor in his bloodline.

"They haven't used the room since...?"

"Not since her death, no." Arek spoke of it matter-of-factly. We were both too young to have a connection with her, or the royal history around us. "Supposedly that would be given to the queen, if the king were to ever union."

"Separate rooms, after being unioned?" Reil popped into my head, his smile, his playfulness under the blankets as we lay together in the abandoned icehouse, keeping each other warm.

Arek shrugged. "I don't make the rules around here." He turned to me and leaned closer. "Mind, there *are* rules here, Evella. Things are different than Corallon, so I need you to keep an open mind and follow my lead."

"Should I be worried?" He certainly didn't help with worry. "Will he kill me if I bow to the wrong person, or say the wrong words?"

Arek's face softened with a smile. "He's not like that. It's more important that he feels you're listening. Just hear what he has to say, all right?"

I nodded. It wasn't all right, but it didn't matter what I thought.

We crossed a wider hallway formed around a rectangular building within the circular walls. The straight sides reached the ceiling as if it had grown like a weed through the turret. Breaking the monotony of stonework were narrow arched windows of stained glass. Arek stopped as we rounded the corner and guards greeted him.

"The Great Hall." Arek let out a hand, and I walked in before him. For the size and lack of splendor of the place, it could've simply been called The Hall. The stained-glass windows along the longer walls did not show their vibrancy due to the low light, and two enormous tables set aside took up most of the length of the room. The middle was empty, a wide corridor leading to the enormous yet simple throne. As Arek promised, a fire burned bright behind the throne in a massive ornately carved opening in the back wall. Chairs sat lower on either side of the throne, two men seated in them, both dressed in faded black tunics and pants.

A line of people waited ahead, facing the throne. Arek and I stood at the back of the line.

The woman in front of me held a brown sack and dropped it to her feet, impatient from waiting, and arms tired.

"Pardon me for the wait." A man with a white beard and thick white eyebrows waved a hand at the head of the crowd. "Let us continue." He sat in the middle chair, carefully adjusting his tunic, a darker black than the others beside him. I looked at Arek, adorning his black cloak. It must've been a chosen royal fabric to distinguish those working for the king. If that were true, why hadn't anyone questioned Arek's cloak in Corallon, or elsewhere? Then again, the king's Rationers came to town once or twice wearing dark clothing, and I thought nothing of it.

A man holding the hand of a young boy approached the king. "Pella has reached the age of eight, Your Greatness. I would ask you to allow him to begin classes here at the palace, under your protection." The man took off his hat and gave a shallow bow.

"Come here, Pella." King Ronin waved his fingers until the boy approached, then held up a hand to halt his ascent. "Do you want to attend classes?"

Pella nodded. "I've been practicing my reading, sir. I struggle with the bigger words, but I promise I can learn." The boy was quite impressive in his confidence, showing more than me at the moment.

His father nudged him. "It's Your Greatness," he whispered.

"Oh, sorry, Your Greatness."

King Ronin smiled and dismissed the error. "Very well. I'll draw up the contract but do me a favor."

"What is it?" Pella asked.

"I want you to read it, not your father, and you to sign it. It is your decision to make the commitment. Do you understand what I am asking?"

Pella smiled and nodded with excitement.

"Go on."

The father and boy stepped out of line, and we moved up a pace.

The king stood up from his throne and leaned over, scanning the crowd. "Arek! Please come up here."

Arek nodded at me, and I followed him past the people who either gave curious looks or hateful ones. It wasn't a good start to my time in Elsinea. I didn't want to be known for receiving special favors from the king.

King Ronin smiled. "Is this her?" He scanned me, eyes passing judgment whether he intended to or not.

"Yes, King Ronin. This is Evella Trapper, of Corallon."

I tucked one foot behind the other and quickly bowed my head in a nod. It looked more like my forehead had tried to crush a pea on the wall. It was awkward, the silliness flushing over my cheeks with heat. Nobody taught me any of this in Corallon. There wasn't a need to.

"The pleasure is mine to have," the king said. "Let me introduce you to Haro and Icad."

"We've met," Haro said, his face thin, nose hooked and chin triangular.

"I'm sorry?" I hadn't set eyes on this man ever before.

"You were merely a child. A baby. Your father is Hemil."

"How do you know that?"

"I told you we've met."

The king held up a hand. "Haro has flawless memory. Anything he sees or does, anyone he meets, he can recall as if it just happened."

I stood with my mouth slightly ajar. I didn't need to ask Arek. He mouthed the word. "Soulmagic."

"That's extraordinary." It truly was, but I wanted to know more about his encounter with Father. Had they known each other years ago? What was their connection? Or had it been in passing? With flawless memory he could be capable of remembering strangers on the street.

Haro grinned at the compliment, a diagonal slit of lips across his face. If the king hadn't been so jovial and cordial, I would've been taken aback.

"And Icad?" The man on the other side of the king was just as skinny as Haro. He had long black hair and bangs across his forehead, with a small round face and dimpled chin. "May I ask if he has—"

The king grazed my elbow with his fingers. "Come, walk with me."

I turned to Arek.

"If you'll excuse us, that I may borrow her company for a moment?" King Ronin asked Arek, more as a friendly gesture than for actual permission.

Arek closed his eyes in a brief nod. "I shall wait in the corridor just outside here."

"Very well," the king said.

I walked beside him, daring to glance at his clean boots, his simple clothing. His face, despite the white hair, looked young, younger than Father but older than Arek. I wondered if he had white hair since birth.

"Was your journey all right?" He seemed genuine, yet oblivious to how he disrupted my life, my family's lives in summoning me here.

"It was fine enough." The contempt cut through my voice, and I bit my cheek.

He played with a thick silver ring on his right hand, rotating it around his finger. "I want you to see something."

We wound around steps until we reached the top level of the turret. The wind blew strong as King Ronin led me along the upper walkway down the western side of the palace walls. The sun hung low, the air slowly cooling with the vanishing light. We reached the top of the western turret, the one Arek and I had entered.

"What do you see down there?" He leant out his hand, palm open to the terrin below. A terrin that had been the heart of the kingdom, the center of Elsinor.

"I see more people in one place than I have ever seen before." It may not have been the answer he was looking for, but it was what came to mind first.

He chuckled. "I imagine for someone hailing from your terrin, that holds true." He sighed, placing his hands on the stone wall that reached my chest. "Yet there are far fewer people than Elsinea has ever had before."

It was near impossible not to stare at the large jewel on his finger, a kicking two-headed stallion etched on the front, with ornate gilded leaves around the band. It blaringly contradicted the rest of his attire. Then again, I had expected everything in the palace to be as ornate as the ring before arriving, not the opposite.

He squinted, his thoughts far off. "Perhaps you are too young—you are how old?"

"Nineteen."

"Ah, yes. You're too young to have been around, let alone remember, but I came to this position after The Quake."

I nodded, knowing that much.

"Nothing has been easy for me, or the people, in that time. If anything, conditions are worsening. There's starvation, people do not trust one another, and there seems to be a fight to the death over simple belongings these days."

"I'm afraid it is the same in Corallon." If he had known that already, it didn't hurt to remind him of the plight of my people. "It doesn't help the quakes are getting worse."

He turned to me, his pale eyes cloudy with tears under white bushy eyebrows. "That is why I have called you here. We need people like you. People with Soulmagic."

I shook my head. "Arek said as much, but I'm not sure I understand what purpose I'd serve. You need me how?"

King Ronin stepped back and gestured for me to follow him. He trod slowly, deliberately along the walkway. "My father, unfortunately for those like you, feared those with abilities. Some escaped his proactive intolerance by going into hiding, but most…"

I nearly gasped. I'd heard the rumors of The Great Culling, of rounding up those with Soulmagic before my time. It was one of the reasons Mother didn't want me using my powers. How was I to know what was true? But here the king was, confessing the sins of his father, King Crohl.

"It was a very dark time indeed. When I came to take the throne, I forbade the banishment of Soulmagi. I had to wait nearly two decades for the next generation of young adults to show their faces—show their Soulmagic. Of course, I was aware that those with abilities could show them earlier, but I didn't want them too young."

"Too young for what?"

He turned, grabbing my hands in his. They were surprisingly warm in the cool gusty air. "There is a great power controlling the quakes. One you cannot comprehend, and it will only get worse. The Raiders are growing in number and have sought those like you—any Soulmagi old enough to fight—to be in their army. They will use such power to defeat me, to defeat us in trying to unite the terrins."

"Is that what you want? Unification?"

He laughed nervously, letting go of my hands. "My dear, that is the only way we can stop The Raiders, stop the quakes. It's the only way to help those who are starving and homeless. We must unite as one again, one land of Elsinor." He continued walking. "It is the reason why I push having classes in Elsin. To have a unified land we need to understand one another. We need to all speak the same language to learn from each other, to improve trade."

"You think Elsin is the language that should be universal?" The split hadn't been enough to tease out the languages that had swept across large areas when all lands were one in Elsinor. In fact, families made it a point to pass on their language to their offspring, even if it wasn't the main language of their terrin. As for Corallon, most spoke Elsin, but Father and Mother did teach me words from old Cora—otari being one of them. And many traders found pride in keeping the old language.

"Elsin is the most broad and common language." He waved a hand. "But never mind that for now. What's important is that you are here."

I braced to hear just why.

"I have gathered my own group of people with Soulmagic. Much like yourself. We cannot defeat The Raiders, this overwhelming power manifesting the quakes, with our basic weapons. We need to have our own special…"

I am not a weapon. Do not call me a weapon.

The king caught himself. "Skills."

"You want me to fight in your own Soulmagic army?"

He closed his eyes, a practice in patience. "I would like for you to train with Arek and the others to help defend our people, your people, against the evil that is rising. I know it must've taken a lot for Arek to convince you to come here."

I suppressed the urge to roll my eyes keeping in mind my audience.

He tipped his head, staring at me with curious eyes. "You're angry, over how you came to be here."

I straightened, surprised. "I didn't mean—"

"No, it's all right. I can sense you're trying to hide it. Call it a gift. When you have to interact with as many people as I do, you get a sense of who they are. Sometimes, feeling something intensely is better than feeling nothing at all. Emotion can be a powerful tool."

I let the words stew. The longer I stayed silent, the more I suspected he read my mind.

He turned to me, exhaling some of the awkwardness out of the conversation. "So what shall we do with you? To put it bluntly, as King, I can order you to train. But I know even I cannot force you to put the real work in. That is up to you, and only you. I can only hope you'd want to do it, for the people." He stretched his hand out again to the north. "For your family."

He admittedly tugged on my heart, but at the same time released a hint of disdain. He was no ordinary person. He was king, and he knew how to manage his people to get what he wanted.

"The decision is entirely yours," he said. "I'd hope you'd want to find your strength, hone your Soulmagic, for yourself. To get to know who you really are."

I glanced behind me, at the town of Elsinea below, the all but barren farmland beyond that. At Corallon well beyond sight past the sea. If I said no to his offer, what would that mean? Going back to Corallon, to my family. Watching chunks of our land crumble to the sea. Seeing more people die from the quakes, from the cold. From starvation.

Nothing would change.

No, it would change. It would get worse, as it has been doing for years.

What was my other option? I could take action.

I could try.

What better could I do for my family than to defeat The Raiders? Stop the quakes? I was tired of bandaging the damage. Tired of scraping by, having no power over what was happening to us. What if this was the way out? What if my strange ability had the power to help abolish the evil decaying the terrins?

I couldn't help but imagine the black cloud over my family's head being lifted. The cloud I created with one decision on one night, that tarnished the family since. I could change the way people felt about the name Trapper. They could move back to town, or out of Corallon altogether. The world would be at their feet.

I sighed, the cold not deep enough to see my breath. The wind would've carried it away anyway.

I turned back around and looked at King Ronin, at his pale weary eyes beneath his white slugs of eyebrows.

"I'll train."

CHAPTER
TEN

We rejoined Arek within the large turret.

"I will summon you to report back to me, in time," King Ronin said. "I'll be curious to know of your progress."

He looked at Arek, who nodded in reply. "See to it she begins training immediately. I'm anxious to see what she's capable of."

King Ronin glanced at me with a smirk. "I think she may surprise herself."

As quickly as he had taken me aside, the king nodded goodbye and rushed off to the main hall or wherever his sidekicks were taking him. The one with the long hair, Icad, glanced at me, a little too long for comfort.

Arek nudged my elbow, pulling me out of my trance.

"What's his power?" I asked. "The creepy one."

"It's best not to be around that one." Arek's eyes narrowed.

"What is it? Is his power fending off people with evil stares?"

Arek chuckled. "That's just his normal human power. Come on." He led me through the turret out into the courtyard. "I admit, I don't like him. I don't feel safe talking around him or breathing around him for that matter."

I quickened my pace, Arek rushing across the courtyard as if we were now unwelcome.

"You know how I've been saying that your powers could be used for good, to the benefit of the people?"

"Yes. King Ronin had said as much."

"Oh, I see. If it comes from the king, then you're able to accept the call?"

I looked away, my lips pressed together holding back a rude retort.

Arek held up his hands in surrender. "Whatever gets you to help out." He continued his brisk pace. "Anyway, I can't speak for everyone, but I think there are some abilities, some Soulmagic, that shouldn't be practiced. It crosses a moral boundary for me."

I stopped him with the touch of his shoulder. "Now you have to tell me."

Arek sighed, looking back at the turret. No Icad in sight. "He can see through other people's eyes."

I tucked my chin back. "Like, an empathy power?"

"No, literally." We stepped into the stairwell under the bridge, heading for the basement again. "He can get inside your head and see what you are seeing. The worst part is that you don't know he's doing it, until after he has. Sometimes not even then."

Invading someone's head? The implications in terms of weaponry during warfare were far-reaching. He could spy on the enemy completely undetected.

"Can he hear as well?"

Arek nodded. "It's as if he takes over your consciousness. I don't think he has control of your thoughts, or your body's movements, as far as I can tell. It's like being a fly on one's shoulder, hearing and seeing everything."

I hadn't allowed myself to imagine other people with Soulmagic, let alone the types of powers they could have. I wrapped my hands on my arms, chilled at the thought of someone invading my head. If that existed, what else were Soulmagi capable of?

"I wanted to get out of there because the more distance you put between yourself and him, the less able he is to use his powers. It's a strength in proximity kind of situation."

"Good to know." I bit my bottom lip. "And thank you."

He stopped me in front of one of the rooms off the basement hallway. "We'll stay here for the night and head out tomorrow. You're welcome to this room. Nera prepared the bed and brought your belongings."

The bed was thin, but Nera had covered it with two blankets. A basin and wooden chair with my satchel on top rounded out the sparse accommodations. Between the journey on the sled, attack from Raiders, crossing town, and conversing with the king, I could've slept standing.

"I'll be down the hall." Arek paused in the doorway for a second, giving a brief smile before heading down the hall.

I closed my eyes, taking in the silence and solitude. A night in the palace—another story to tell Tulla. I opened my eyes quickly and rushed to the doorway. "What do you mean head out tom—"

But Arek was gone.

"Where are we going, by the way?" Normally a thought like that would've kept me up all night, but I was too exhausted and slept through sunrise. A servant had awakened me, my presence surprising her when she came to retrieve the bedding. "Why isn't training at the palace?" It seemed like the safest place to use Soulmagic. It was fully guarded, enclosed, and people nearby dared not question the goings on of the palace.

"Some of us need resources not readily available at the palace to train. But most importantly, we need space to move around. Really flex our skills."

I raised my eyebrows. For my nonsensical ability, I needed objects, preferably small and lightweight. What did others need?

After lunch, we replenished our supplies with what the kitchen could spare and walked the southwest corner of Elsinea. Part of me wanted to stay in the relative luxury of the palace, while another part felt unease amongst the palace walls. Knowing Icad and Haro roamed nearby didn't help.

As we approached the dockside building where we'd left the snowcats, it dawned on me that the palace wouldn't be a great place for Arek to practice his skills. Who wanted to walk around the corner and be greeted by a known predatory animal?

"How are they?" Arek asked the keeper Samish, who rubbed his belly bowling over the waist of his pants. He may have been a good animal caretaker, but his waistline suggested he took advantage of customers and visitors. No person was that hefty without partaking in shady business.

"Full bellies and a rest was all they needed. I don't know how you've trained them for this kind of work, but I swear they're ready to take you to Corallon and back."

My throat caught at the sound of home. Had this man figured out where I was from?

Arek looked at me with a side-eye, wondering the same thing. "We won't be traveling that far, but good to know." He tossed Samish an extra coin. "Thank you for your help."

"Not a problem. Do you want me—"

"I'll fetch them," Arek said.

"They're out back."

Arek gave one nod of the head, and I followed him out a back door. The snowcats slumped lazily in a pen, while two horses in an adjacent pen stayed on the far side of theirs. One whinnied as a snowcat stood up. Even the horses knew what snowcats were capable of.

Arek scratched the neck of a snowcat that purred at his boots. "You've rested a good bit, but I don't want to overwork you another day."

He turned back to me. "We'll walk with them and the sled across town, and leave from the eastern shore." He brought the snowcats to alert, then wound up the harnesses, handing over the wad of leather and buckles to me. "Can you manage that? We'll have to carry the sled together, but I'll need a hand to keep the snowcats in line."

I nodded and shoved the harness in my satchel. Some of the loops poked out, but if it stayed put, I didn't mind the awkward bundle beneath my cloak.

He moved quickly, guiding the snowcats in front of us. I grabbed underneath the right side of the sled, and he the left.

"I want to get there before it gets dark."

"And where is there?"

Arek looked in my eyes, studying them, like I was the one hiding something. "I commissioned the king to let us train off Elsinea, on another terrin. At first he refused, but my proposal made a lot of sense. I mean, there are no people—that we know of, and it's never visited."

"You don't mean—" There was only one terrin that fit such a description. The Unnamed Island. The Quake had left it uninhabited, or if there were people there, they did not bother to claim a name. No one dared to travel there, for it came with a reputation all its own.

"Spokizar." Arek's voice cracked, and he cleared his throat.

It was the only word I knew in Old Reni. *Ghost Island*. Not an official name, but a nickname derived after the ghosts that lived in the mist.

"Don't worry," he said. "Whatever you've heard about it, they're nothing but tall tales and wild theories. We've been there for some time now and haven't encountered many ghosts." At this he grinned, a wide smile showing his white teeth against his tan skin.

"You're enjoying this, aren't you?"

"A little." His grin vanished. "In all seriousness, we can train there in secret. We have the space and resources. Plus, no one ever crosses Mariner's Gauntlet if they don't have to, due to the rough seas."

"That's wonderful. Sounds like quite a treat." It was a sarcastic remark covering up the regret building up over my decision. Had I made it in haste, wanting to please the king? Or did I believe I was doing it for the right reasons? My increased worry pointed to the former.

"Hey, have you ever considered that the king has Soulmagic? Like, he has the power to convince people to do his bidding?" It wouldn't be that far-fetched if creepy guy Icad could invade minds. I'd agreed to all of this after one conversation with King Ronin. But, Arek did plant the seed along our journey, giving me time to mull over whether I had a responsibility with my powers that I had no control over.

"While he's a big supporter of our kind and has placed his hope in us, I would think if the king had Soulmagic he'd hone his craft too—and be using it to defeat the Raiders himself."

"Maybe he knows he can't do it by himself and wants our support."

Arek shrugged. "Maybe. But, even if he had your power, or mine, wouldn't he have used it for his people any number of times?"

Arek could be right. He did seem to be closer to the king than most of the people I encountered at the palace.

We walked to the opposite coast of Elsinea, swooping around to the north to avoid the heaviest crowding in town. By the time we reached the coastline, we had switched sides on the sled four times over. My arms and calves ached, my hands sore from their tight grip.

Waves crashed upon the shore, white caps foaming on the ripples. Spokizar was across the way, across the treacherous chop that stirred like a hot brew on a bumpy carriage ride.

"Don't worry. As long as you hold on tight, we should be fine."

I handed Arek the harnesses, and he worked on the snowcats. My mind wandered across the water, Spokizar a sliver of land with deep green trees juxtaposed to the blue sky.

"We should go." Arek led the first pair of snowcats in the water. "We're losing daylight."

I pushed sluggishly to the sled, holding it still enough in the water for Arek to board. If I stopped to think about it too much, I would turn around.

I clenched my hands along Arek's cloak as usual. He grabbed my wrists, wrapping my arms clear around his torso. "It's for the both of us," he said. "Trust me, they don't call it Mariner's Gauntlet for fun."

I wasn't sure if I had trust in him. Had he given me enough reason to trust him after he revealed the truth of his appearance in Corallon?

It didn't matter, because the snowcats swam in a wild fury through the breaking waves, and we were off. Water splashed in smacks along the sled, spraying us with seafoam. I quickly got over the fact that I held on to Arek to stay afloat and pressed against him even tighter to avoid getting wetter. Not only was the water frigid, but the wind worked against us, tearing my eyes and freezing my nose.

His body rose over the wooden slats as we crested the swells, his knees hitting back down as we swooped through the water valleys. He was right in saying it was for the both of us. I held him down on the sled as much as he anchored me to it.

I was glad the last food I consumed had been a while ago in the palace's basement, for it would have surely flung back up had it been sooner. The snowcats pedaled their paws with fury. It was a mystery how they could even see or keep their heads above water long enough to breathe. I hoped with everything they were heading us in the right direction, because I surely couldn't make out Spokizar from this vantage point.

"Hold on!" Arek yelled, seeing the wave before I did. It rushed us from the left side as we crested another.

I closed my eyes as tightly as my arms around Arek. If I broke ribs, we'd deal with that later. I braced for the impact, but the sled lifted instead, the left side toppling us over, my bottom slipping off toward the surface of the sea.

Water filled my ears, my nose. The cold stunned my body, my arms and limbs pedaling, grasping for anything to grip onto. I felt the metal of the runner and slipped my hand over it, pulling up with all my strength. I gasped for air as my head came out of the water.

I solidified my grip but couldn't pull my body on the upside-down sled. I frantically looked to my left, to the right. Behind me. "Arek!"

He was nowhere. The snowcats miraculously kept afloat treading water but didn't pull the sled in any direction.

A swell of water pushed up next to me, and Arek's idiotic gorgeous face appeared, hair slicked down with seawater. He gasped for air, and I used one hand to pull him closer to the sled.

"Are you hurt?" he asked, as if I were the one who took eternity to surface.

"I'm fine," I said, teeth chattering uncontrollably. "You?"

"I lost my boot there." He reached up and threw the wet boot on the undersurface of the sled, along with the supply bag. "Found it, though."

I shook my head.

He looked ahead at the snowcats, and their forward swimming commenced. "I'm not sure if we can flip this back upright, so we'll have to wait it out."

"We're going to freeze to death."

"Not if I can help it."

The sled moved steadily, floating quickly over the waves. When no feeling remained in my fingers, and my grip on the sled all but vanished, the waves died down. Seabirds flew overhead, and eventually my feet scraped bottom.

We plodded onto the stony shore, gray and brown pebbles smooth and slippery in the water. As soon as the sled was far enough on land to not drift away, I collapsed. My body was frozen inside and out, and my muscles refused to move, but I had never been so happy to touch land.

"Come on, we really will freeze to death if we don't get out of these wet clothes."

I let him take my hand, and he heaved me up, first onto my knees, then onto my feet. The weight of the water in my cloak, in my boots and clothes, pulled me to the ground. I decloaked and slapped the garment on the ground. It had to have weighed as much as Tulla.

Arek took off his cloak and stripped down to his bare chest. So much had changed when I first met him, thinking him naive and immature. He was anything but naive, and in front of me, he stood strong, his muscles taut and sculpted, a level of confidence that only came through experience. Something on his shoulder caught my eye, a patch of roughness breaking through the rounded muscle—

He caught me staring, and I blushed. Merely a survival mechanism to keep my body warm, despite not feeling a bit of warmth at all. It had nothing to do with the young man showing me a side of him I hadn't seen before.

He wrung out his lightest layer and hastily put it back on. He scanned the coastline, tall evergreen coniferous trees along the short stone shore. Hadn't the sky been a clear blue overhead when I had seen it from Elsinea? Standing here, it was nearly as gray and drab as the rocks we stood upon.

"I'm wondering where the—"

A sharp arrow whizzed by, and Arek ducked as I hit the ground.

"Raiders again?" I asked.

"It came from ahead."

I scanned the tree line, and two more arrows zipped our way.

"Stop—" It was all Arek got out before rushing behind a rock.

I grabbed my sling out of my soggy satchel and lifted a stone from the ground. Although the sling was wet, it didn't mean I couldn't fight back.

I raced to the nearest tree, hiding behind the trunk, an arrow nearly skimming my shoulder. I waited a beat, right when the archer would be grabbing another arrow. I stepped to the side and whipped the sling, sending the rock in the air.

My right foot slipped out from under me, and my back hit the ground with a thud, knocking the wind out of me.

"Evella!" Arek shouted my name, but my eyes saw stars.

I heard the snowcats before seeing them, their paws pouncing on the stones. They reached me and worked on whatever held tight to my right ankle. I looked up, eyes clearing. It was a branch, a snarly vine the animals broke through with their sharp teeth.

Arek stood in full sight on the shore, waving his hands. "Stop! It's—"

The ground shook. The snowcats whimpered and backed away from my ankle. Cones fell out of the sky, hitting me below, green needles raining down. I rolled onto my stomach, looking ahead to find a place to grip, a place to crawl to. But I couldn't focus on anything. Everything shook.

"Evella!"

Reil reached out his hand, too far for me to grasp. I closed my eyes tight, using all the strength I could within me. He fell down, down, so far down...

The cracking of the earth pierced my ears, and I curled up into a ball, protecting my head with my hands. *This is not the same. Reil is gone. This will pass. You're fine. You're fine.*

I longed to be in my house, under the kitchen table. Arek was right about the difference. Being outside for a quake was unbearable. *You're fine.*

Something heavy lay on top of me, breathing and warm as the earth shook.

Arek's arms were over me, his chest on my back, taking the brunt of the falling tree debris.

The grumbling fainted into silence. All I heard was his breath near my ear.

"It's over," he whispered.

I opened my eyes, the snowcats returning to lick Arek's face. He slowly stood and gave me a hand to my feet again.

"Are you all right?"

I nodded. "You didn't have to do that." I pulled the pine needles off my clothes and out of my hair.

"I didn't think," he said. "I just…did."

I licked my cold lips. There was something else I wanted to say about it, but I couldn't quite pinpoint it.

"Everyone unharmed?" A girl's voice rang out from the trees, in the direction of the arrows.

"We're all right," Arek shouted back. "No thanks to you." He grabbed my hand in his, his fingers much warmer than mine. I craved the warmth. Or did I crave the touch? Could he sense my body still shaking?

"We thought we'd get some practice, that's all," she said.

"We weren't going to really hurt you," a male voice called out.

As I followed him out of the cover of the trees back onto the stony shore, the brush ahead rustled. A large man. A young woman.

People appeared from the darkness of the forest.

Arek let go of my hand, cold numbness returning to it. He looked at the forest people, then back to me and sighed with a grin.

"Evella, meet the others."

ELEVEN

"It was Merja who spotted you two." The soft-spoken girl looked remorseful. I had never seen such long hair, her gray-blond tresses reaching to her knees. Her skin was only slightly less blond, a gray-cream. "She said we should test out the new girl, see what she could do." She shot a glance over her shoulder.

"Such a tattletale." A lean, muscular woman half a foot taller than the timid girl crossed her arms. Her jet-black hair was shaved around her head, except for longer strands that swooped across her forehead, not long enough to tuck behind her ear.

"I'm guessing you're Merja," I said.

The woman turned one side of her mouth into a grin. Her black as night skin highlighted the contours of her muscles, and her sleek black clothes hugged her body like a second skin. "The only thing I am right now is unimpressed."

"Give her a chance." The man's deep voice had come out of the near-giant standing behind Merja. Two pairs of Merjas stacked atop each other would not have equaled the size of him. He was bald with a big bulbous nose, sturdy and strong yet not without extra weight around the waistband and under his chin.

"Such a softee," Merja said.

"That's Darvo and Merja," Arek said, rejoining the conversation after checking up on the snowcats. "They're both from Tusinda."

I nodded. Although the terrin of Tusinda was directly southeast from Corallon, I had yet to set foot on it. There were two things I knew to be true about Tusinda, based on what Father had said—it was close enough to experience a taste of Corallon's weather, and there had been a great fire there. Something to do with the cindite they mined. Seeing as Corallon hadn't received any shipments of cindite in quite some time, Tusinda was not quick to recover.

"And I'm Ulda." The long-haired girl waved her fingers nimbly. "From Ulopra. Sorry about your ankle."

I looked down, my ankle free of the tightening vine. "That was you?"

"Mmhmm." She blushed, whether embarrassed to have swept me off my feet, or with pride in her skill.

"What about the arrows?" I glanced at Merja.

"What if it was?" Merja said.

One of the two figures behind her spoke up. "Definitely Merja." His clothes matched those of the young man next to him, an old brown leather jacket and dark brown pants. It was obvious they were twins, same square faces, dark messy hair cut short along the sides, their ears sticking out only slightly. But what distinguished them from each other were the scars. The one who spoke up had black mottled spots around his eyes over his otherwise pale skin, like a permanent blindfold. The other had the same mottledness, but stretching from his right cheek across his face to his forehead.

"That's Jahel and Joris," Arek said, "from—"

"Iogaton." It came out before thinking. But the scar was a telltale sign of Flesh Plight, well-known to have plagued Iogans after The Quake. Physical isolation and a temporary ban on trade had saved the other nine terrins from encountering it, but there'd been no escaping it on Iogaton. Assuming the twins were a year, two at most, older than me, they must've been babies when it happened.

"How dare you assume." Joris' pale face turned redder, somehow making the diagonal scar more prominent.

"Just because we look like we do?" Jahel frowned.

"I didn't mean—"

The brothers looked at each other and burst into laughter.

I stood, confused. Was I botching up meeting these people I was supposed to train with? How was I the fool when Arek and I were the ones attacked upon landing?

"Of course we're from Iogaton." Jahel's eyes sparkled within his black mask of scars.

"This is going to be fun," Joris said.

I looked to Arek, who didn't give much consolation.

"Let's go easy on the new girl, all right?"

My teeth chattered from standing on the unprotected shore, and, admittedly, from fear of being here. With all my hunting and trapping experience in the wild, I hadn't been more unnerved than around these people. What other powers did they possess? What if one of them turned on me? Would my self-defense skills be enough?

Arek read my face. Either Father was wrong in saying I was hard to read or Arek had a special ability. "Don't worry. I know this is all very new and a lot to take in. Let's get warmed up by the fire and take it one day at a time."

I heard *fire* and that was good enough for me to give the evening a chance. I followed the group through the forest of pines and firs, Arek telling me about the tallest and darkest of the trees, the brunsam fir. Their needles stacked one another into a thick mat, weighing down the rough brown branches and blocking out the sky.

We trekked a few hundred paces, taking half that to completely submerge into the forest. The sky darkened while a constant cover of gray mist loomed overhead. The walking helped to warm up my blood, but not enough to stop the shivering. Or abate the underlying gloom. Maybe it was the newness of the place and people, but something clung to me since I touched ground, like cold fingers hanging onto my ribs.

We reached a small opening, an area of forest floor with a handful of trees cleared out. A fire pit sat near the middle of the circle. Judging by the scattering of pots and pans, utensils and satchels, this was their home base.

The twins worked on stoking the fire, bringing the sorry whiffs of cinders back into a steady crackle of flames. Why didn't they use a forever flame? Or were some things kept secret, even from the rest of the Soulmagi?

"Let me show you your new home." Ulda grinned, baring perfectly aligned white teeth. Of all the inhabitants of this island, she expressed the most excitement about my presence. She pulled me off to the side, where a mound of branches and sticks supported a four-corner structure, brunsam fir branches covering the outside.

I lowered my head through the doorway and peeked inside. There was a raised flat area to the left that made for a bed, a heavy rock as a nightstand, and a set of leashes hanging on the opposite side.

"Oh, sorry, forgot to take those out." Ulda grabbed the leashes and walked to Arek, who had started a chat with the twins by the fire.

"Wait." I hurried after her to the fire. "Arek, is that your shelter?"

His hand swatted the air. "Don't worry about it. I can fix another. I didn't think you'd want to have to make your own shelter after the journey we've had."

What made him think I couldn't make one? Or that he was more capable of doing so than I was? His journey had been longer, in fact.

I grabbed the shared satchel of our things and plopped it down on the ground next to Arek's shelter. I walked the perimeter of the clearing, checking out the rest of the sleeping quarters. A similar shelter to Arek's sat across the way, with two beds. I assumed it belonged to Jahel and Joris. Continuing around, a sturdier structure sat between two trees. This one had a tarp over the supports, with branches covering the tarp.

Darvo startled me from behind. For as large as he was, he had traveled quite quietly. Obviously versed in hunting with such skills. "That's my place," he said.

"How do you get inside?" I studied the structure, no noticeable door in front. Only a covering of branches with slivers of tarp between.

Darvo placed his fingers beneath the front wall and pulled. A door swung open to the side. The tarp had been cut on one side and across the top for a doorway, the other side serving as the hinge. Darvo had a sizable smile, proud of his work. "I don't care much for rodents." He sealed the door closed. "If you don't like them either, you'd best use more than just branches."

I nodded. While Corallon was too cold to be roughing it overnight—let alone the lack of big game to necessitate a longer hunt—it still had its share of rodents. They liked to chew through the binding between stones and beneath the dirt floor to get inside homes, invade storage pantries, even make holes in clothing.

While I wouldn't want to find any nibbling on my feet, rodents were the least of concerns in this place.

"My place is back there." Ulda pointed to a mound set back from the rest, a soft hill that formed east of the clearing.

"I should've guessed." The outside of her structure was laced with vines and white and yellow flowers. Her Soulmagic came in handy when it came to decorating.

I gave her a brief smile and surveyed the shelters again. Something was missing.

"What about Merja? Where does she stay?"

"Up here." Merja said, annoyed. At least she dignified my question with an answer. High above Darvo was another tarp, tied between two trees like a hammock. Merja stood on a platform, a wooden triangular pallet wedged between three trees. She shuffled with some supplies I couldn't see from below, done with giving me the full tour.

"She's our little magpie," Ulda said.

"Don't call me that."

I looked up at the hammock. "Does her Soulmagic have to do with supersonic hearing?"

Ulda giggled. "No. She uses PN."

I blinked heavily and shook my head. *Piercing negativity?*

"Psychic navigation," Arek chimed in, tearing himself away from the fire. His clothes were drier than mine, although I hadn't paid much attention to my goosebumps lately. "It's like she has a compass inside her head. She has the ability to make a mental map of an area."

"That's why I call her our little magpie. That, and she made a nest for herself." Ulda giggled.

"Go ahead and say it one more time," Merja threatened from above.

Ulda leaned to me in a whisper. "What's more, if you give her an object off of someone or an animal, she can track them, like a target."

The powers Merja possessed seemed infinitely more useful than what I was born with. I stared up once more and met Merja's eyes before she backed away again on the platform.

"I'd better get to making that shelter," Arek said.

I shook my head and stopped his movement. "I'll make it. You all have made your own homes here. I'm perfectly capable of doing the same for myself." I grabbed the leashes where Arek had set them down by the fire. One of the curled-up snowcats beside Jahel snarled at me. I let go, and the snowcat returned to its warm utopia.

"At least let me help," Arek pleaded.

If I was to be taken seriously here, I'd have to command to be taken seriously. That meant not cutting corners. It meant doing things for myself whenever I could. "Thank you, but you should tend to the snowcats. The journey had to have been harder on them than us."

He reluctantly nodded as I made for the trees. I collected what branches I could. One of the felled trees left in the clearing had a good portion of wood unhewn. Darvo leant me an ax, and I hacked and chopped and cleared twigs off branches.

Not wanting the others to see, I tried to move the smallest of twigs with Soulmagic as I worked. I had to prove to myself that I could do it without having to be asleep, dreaming of past horrors. It took all my might to shake a stick, and even then, I wasn't sure if it had been me or Darvo as he smashed a beetle with a heavy footstep.

My structure differed from the others in that the roof leaned from the ground to halfway up a tree. It was large enough for me to sit up on a low bed in the tallest part, my feet in the lowest. I'd managed to fill in the backside of the shelter with upright sticks. Tomorrow I'd find or make some mud to fill in the gaps.

Arek's satchel had surprisingly kept most of our items dry. He procured stiff solid boots for me much like his own, insisting they'd serve me better on the island terrain than my usual boots. I changed into the other set of clothes I packed—a heavy tunic and fur lined pants, although the fur had nearly flattened to nothing, and holes had formed around my knees. I hung my wet clothes to dry by the fire. Not as close as I wanted though, because the others began to cook up supper.

Even though my stomach growled as the aroma of vegetable stew hit me, my muscles, bones, willpower, had been sapped. I needed rest, and to get my head straight. I was camping on Ghost Island after all, with six other young adults that had more powerful—and useful—Soulmagic than me.

The others hung around the fire, speaking loud enough to hear they told stories and poked fun at one another, but not loud enough to make out the stories. It reminded me of my family, whom I ached to correspond with. I had wrongfully assumed I'd end up in the palace and could write to them. Having seen this place and the route to get here, it was doubtful anything would be sent off the island.

As I tried to relax, a foggy mist rolled in, carrying with it a foreboding chill penetrating my skin. A slight breeze blew in my shelter. I pulled my cloak over my body, keeping me warm, and providing a sense of security—whether false or not—from the eerie fog. The more it thickened, the more melancholy washed over me, an unwelcome wet blanket of sorrows.

The breeze echoed in my ears, a movement of air that turned from a whooshing to whispers. I held my breath, scanning the shelter. Hairs raised on my arms as something moved over me then lowered, the whispers echoing within my shelter. The floor beneath me had two swishes, like someone had taken a stick and carved parallel lines in the moist dirt. A symbol?

I sat up, the cloak draping off me.

A twirl of mist in my shelter and another line appeared, wider, spaced further away from the other two.

"Show yourself." My shaky voice echoed my hesitancy. Did I really want to know what lurked beneath the thick vapor?

A knock at my roof, and the fog disappeared, along with its haunting murmurs.

I straightened at the sight of Arek. "Did you see that?"

"See what?" Arek asked. "I thought I heard you talking."

I had an overwhelming sense that the fog was meant for me. That, or the others would think me crazy for the connection I felt to it. "Nothing. I must've nodded off and dreamt." I covered the slashes in the ground with my feet.

"You need to eat something. Keep your strength." He set down a wooden bowl of cooked vegetables. He squatted low to be level with me sitting up on my lumpy makeshift bed. His hands were folded together, back crouched uncomfortably.

"Thank you. Sit down." It came out more assertive than intended. "I mean, if you want."

He sat on the ground, wrapping his arms around his legs. Like the first night we were together, in my house by the fire.

"Not too bad in such a short time." He lightly jiggled a stick in the wall, and it released from its hold.

"It'll do for tonight." I grabbed the stick from his hand and shimmied it back in its place.

Arek grinned. "Well, if you don't have controllable magic skills, you do know how to function out in the wild. At the very least, you'd provide us with a good supply of kindling."

I didn't like that he made me smile for a second. Behind him, the others had dispersed, their conversation dying down. Darvo and Joris remained, exchanging tall tales.

"I'm still angry with you, you know."

"Really?" Arek opened his mouth in fake shock. "I couldn't tell."

Damn him for making me smile again. "You tricked me, getting me to come with you, using my family against me."

He chewed on his bottom lip, remorse oozing from his face.

"But, I guess it's easier coming from someone who doesn't have a family." It wasn't meant to be a jab, merely an honest remark. If I hadn't felt the love and connection with my family, could I have used the same tactic on someone else? Especially if the king demanded I bring that person back?

"I need to confess something," Arek said. "The woman you met in the kitchen."

"Nera."

"Yes, Nera. She's...my mother."

"What?" I sat up taller.

"Not my *real* mother. She died in The Quake. Nera was my mother's best friend and took me in as a baby. I don't remember my real mother at all, but I never thought of Nera as anything else but my mother."

My underlying anger gave room to pity. It wasn't fair. It wasn't fair he did what he did, then to come out here and make *me* feel sorry for *him*.

But I did feel sorry for him. He *had* been a Displaced, just a whole lot earlier than when I met him. Life in the palace was the only life he knew, so why wouldn't he carry out what the king asked of him?

I was more than confused. Too much happened today, in the past few days, to really face and understand. It was too soon to let out the mixed emotions, especially to him. "She seemed very kind."

He perked up. "Oh, she is. Who knows where I'd be if it wasn't for her."

"Certainly. For all you know, you could be sleeping in the wild on Ghost Island with a bunch of magical outcasts." I chuckled.

"There are worse things, I suppose."

A howl echoed through the night. I looked at Arek, and behind him Joris and Darvo's conversation halted.

"If there are worse things, I don't want to know them." I meant it as a joke but it wounded Arek. It wasn't entirely his fault I was here. It was part of King Ronin's plan. And yes, there were worse things. I could be in the hands of Raiders, or at the bottom of Mariner's Gauntlet.

But I was here in this strange place to make a difference. To stop the Raiders. Stop the quakes and all their destruction. For my family, and all the families left in Elsinor's terrins.

"So what's the plan for tomorrow?" I hoped the change of subject showed him how I really felt about being here. That it wasn't the worst thing.

"We will see what the island has planned for us." He stood, brushing the dirt off his hands.

"What does that mean?"

He stepped outside of my roof, bending slightly to meet my eyes. "You'll see."

TWELVE

The sheer exhaustion from traveling had hit me as soon as my head hit the pillow last night. Technically it was a loose sack of shoots and dirt, but it didn't matter. My muscles relaxed, and I had no desire to use them until the morning.

Luckily, I did not have a nightmare, at least not that I remembered or realized. Although it was morning, there was little sunshine to be had. The doorway to my makeshift lean-to was covered in gray mist. It was too dense to make out the center of camp, the fire all but a pile of ash.

I was struck with that same feeling I had since my arrival. That someone else occupied the air I breathed, the space I took up. I had investigated the three slashes in the ground last night after Arek left, making sure nothing lay buried in the dirt. I erased them with my feet from view, though they lingered in memory.

Outside, Jahel wiped his nose in his sleeve, collecting twigs and branches for the morning fire. I wiped my eyes, attached my satchel to one hip, blade on the other and slipped my cloak over my shoulders before venturing into the open.

"Did I wake you?" Jahel broke a branch in half and tossed it on the baby flame.

I shook my head. "No, I was up." The cool fog sat low to the ground, thick enough to hide Merja's tarp hammock above and Ulda's carved out hollow ahead.

Jahel's stoking the fire drew me back to Corallon. Beyond making my own place during the short season, I had planned on training Tulla and Wren to better help out. If only I hadn't taken so long to teach them, taking sole responsibility. They had no choice now but to rely on themselves. Either they could get along without me, or they couldn't. If they couldn't, would I have any family to go back to?

I shook it off. *Don't think that way, Evella.*

I pointed to the fire. "I could help with that."

"I got it covered."

I hid my disappointment. Everyone needed to know that I was useful, that there was a purpose for me being here despite not knowing myself precisely what that purpose was. For now, I had to rely on what I did know how to do, and that was to survive. Fire building, hunting, trapping. The family name wasn't Trapper for nothing.

Merja climbed down from her treetop platform, wearing the same black outfit from last night. The back of her top had a special quiver sewn in, housing her cindite arrows. The sight of her bare arms gave mine goosebumps. It made no sense—I was the one from the coldest terrin, yet everyone else appeared fine with the persistent damp chill.

Merja moved nimbly, the little stubs of branches somehow supporting her weight. Add tree climbing to her list of abilities, whether related to Soulmagic or not.

Merja bent down in front of Darvo's shelter, grasped the end of the tarp peeking out at the bottom, and shook. "Wake up, little fella."

"Go away." Darvo's voice rang in the air, muffled.

"Jahel is making breakfast." She stood at the door, leaning one arm on the structure. She looked at me and raised her eyebrows before turning back to the door and knocking. "Come on, we have a fresh batch of birds' eggs."

The door swung open, and Darvo came moping out, shuffling his feet forward and ducking to miss the top of the door frame.

Merja patted him on the chest. "Big day today."

"Why is that?" Darvo's voice was raspy, and he grabbed the ladle out of a bucket, sipping on water.

"She always says that." Ulda walked barefoot to the fire wearing a blue bodice over a fluffy cream shirt and pants that ended at her knees. Baby's breath and tiny blue heather flowers were weaved into her braided hair. She looked like a flower in human form. No one would've guessed how sinister she could turn the forest.

"Aren't you cold?" She was standing there in bare feet, bare ankles and calves, and there I was, looking like I had spent the night in Corallon. "I mean, your feet?"

"It's a perk of my ability," she said, her smile warmer than my cloak. "I can make plants flower and grow, roots shoot and dig deep. But I can also command the ground to be warm beneath my feet." She winked.

Did that mean she was telling the truth? Or wasn't?

Arek stepped out of his shelter, the shelter that was almost mine had I not been so stubborn. He stretched his arms and wiped his face, the pulling and tugging on his skin somehow helping him become alert.

Joris joined Jahel by the fire, and the rest of the crew followed suit. They fried eggs in a pan over the flame, and warmed up the same brew Arek had given me the other morning outside Reil's mother's house.

The faint thought of Reil reminded me of yesterday's quake. Their frequency was alarming, as if they'd snowballed out of control of Raiders' hands. If indeed they were responsible. Was it possible, whoever was at their command, had been overpowered by them somehow? I grew nauseous at the thought. "Was there any damage from the quake yesterday?"

Joris took a big bite of crushed wheatmeal with berries before answering. "If there was, it'd be on the southeast side."

I almost didn't make out what he said.

Jahel jabbed him with an elbow. "Have some manners, brother." He pressed his lips and met my stare in apology. "Since we've been on the island, every quake has sliced off some of the southeast corner of the island. After the first ten, we stopped checking."

"And stopped counting," Joris said.

First ten? That meant at least a month or two, perhaps longer depending on how frequent they were in these parts.

"Just how long have you been here?" I eyed the group and swallowed hard. "If I may ask."

"If I may ask." Jahel chuckled with his brother. "Now you're the one who sounds like she grew up in the palace, not him." He pointed at Arek.

"Come on, you two." Arek glared, seemingly not amused.

"Four months, give or take, for me and the big guy," Merja said. "Closer to eight for the earliest of us." She glanced at Arek and Ulda.

"You've been out here for that long?" Too many things ran through my head. Being away from family that long. Surviving on this island. How much time they've gotten to know each other, hone their powers. How was I to ever catch up? And when was I to ever leave?

"Don't make a fuss over them," Merja said. "The quakes. If anything, being on this island makes us the safest lot in Elsinor."

"That's why we're here." Arek chimed. "To train, beat the Raiders, and stop the quakes."

The others either cheered aloud with a whistle or hoot, or lifted their mugs. Darvo did both.

"What's it like? The training?" Maybe if they'd brief me on it I'd be less queasy.

"It's best to show you," Merja said.

"Agreed." Arek grabbed the pan and ladled water on it, the sizzle boiling off bits of burnt egg. The others emptied their mugs, Darvo wiping his on the shirt tail hanging out his vest. He wore a black jacket over it, the same material as Merja's outfit. I guessed it was the infamous Tusindan severn, a fabric that could handle both the heat of the mines and the cold above ground. Cold of course was relative, coming from Corallon, but Tusinda had a handful of deep cold spells during their winter, according to Father.

They headed northeast from camp, an unspoken trodden route they must've traversed a hundred times before. I followed, my nerves jumbling more as we hit hillier terrain, the trees sporadically interspersed among large silver rocks.

Ahead stood a tree with chiseled bark, an arrow carved in it pointing to the right. The longer I looked in front of me, the more I made out a path. It not only wound between trees, but beneath and above. One tree had strange wooden blocks hanging over a limb, another had pegs scattered up the bark. Objects strewn about along the ground and within the branches—a pottery wheel, a wooden barrel, a square metallic sheet, a bit of rope. Nonsensical items in a nonsensical labyrinth.

"What is all this?" I asked.

"You wanted to know what training was like," Merja said calmly, leaning up against a tree.

"*This* is training? What are you supposed to do? What are all these things for?"

Jahel and Joris looked at each other, then at me. Merja kept an eye on a scar on her hand, and Darvo rebuttoned his vest realizing the misalignment after his first go-around. Even jovial Ulda stayed quiet.

Arek took a breath and stepped closer. "We think you're supposed to start here." He pointed at the nearest tree with the right arrow etched into the bark. "And continue down the line to the end, without falling."

"Or being trapped," Ulda said. "Don't forget that part."

None of this made sense. "What do you mean you think?"

"Huh?" Arek acted as if it were a preposterous question.

"One of you had to set this up." I scanned their faces one by one. No one read guilty, yet they were hiding something. "Right? Someone had to. Was it the king? Did he send people to set it up for us?"

The crowd remained silent, and I resisted the impulse to scream. As soon as I would get one question answered, three new questions popped up.

"No one knows," Ulda said.

"What do you mean no one knows?"

"That's what I meant by what I said last night," Arek said. "What the island has planned for us."

"I don't understand." They were saying words, but the words they chose weren't supposed to go together.

"It's the magic of the island," Ulda said.

I looked at Jahel and Joris, pity on their scarred faces.

"This was set up shortly after we arrived," Jahel said.

"We tried to catch anyone in the act, changing the course, coming to and from the island," Joris said. "We even took turns staking it out overnight for several nights. Nothing."

"There's no one. It's here, and it's for us," Merja said. "That's all you need to know. That's all that matters." She tapped Darvo before starting on the first marked tree. She nimbly climbed up and made her way across a branch, stretching out to the next marked tree.

It couldn't be all that matters. How were we supposed to know that this was for us? To help us hone our skills? What did any of this course have to do with our abilities? With my ability?

I stepped next to Arek, staring at Merja's progress as he did. "Are you telling me you're fine with this showing up out of nowhere?"

He sighed, then turned to me. "I've seen a lot of craziness in seeking out people with Soulmagic." He pointed to the twins. "Take Jahel, for instance. He can make any room dim until you can't see your hand in front of your face. I've seen him dim the sun in this forest."

"Really?" Not that there was much sun to work with here. But how did he make that happen?

"And his brother Joris, can see in the dark. He has natural dark vision."

I nibbled on my bottom lip.

"Can you tell me how that happened, those twins getting complementary Soulmagic abilities?"

I stared at the brothers, who critiqued Merja's progress. "I didn't even know such skills were possible."

Arek placed his hand on my shoulder, not patronizingly, but in support. "Not much of any of this makes sense. Someday we may figure it all out. But Merja is right. For now, we need to work on improving control of our abilities so we can complete the king's mission."

I didn't want to be content with that answer, but Arek was right. Nothing made sense, and there were too many questions to have answers for right now.

A grunt came out from the top of a tree in the distance. A light fog had built up over the course, a smoky canopy enveloping the treetops. It took a second to find Merja curled up in thick netting, hanging from a branch.

I gasped. "Is that what you meant by traps?"

Ulda nodded. "No one has gotten further than Merja. She keeps getting caught in that same spot."

Merja used a knife from her boot to cut herself down and landed with an oomph.

"You're going to have to reset that," Joris yelled out.

"Don't even." Merja stuck out her hand, not bothering to look Joris' way. She fought with the netting, mumbling what I assumed were words not meant for human ears by the look of her face.

"How far have you gotten?" I asked.

Ulda smiled softly and nodded to a spot somewhere ahead. "I keep tripping up on crossing the mud pit." She turned to me. "In order for me to command the plants, I have to see them. I need to see the stem to make a flower, or part of a tree's root to get it to burrow the way I want it to. With that mud pit, I can't see anything. Not a root, a seed, a stem. It's something I'm working on—not having to see what I know is already there below."

I nodded. I wanted to tell her I needed to work on manifesting my ability while awake, but it sounded outrageously silly.

"How about you give it a try?" Darvo leaned in closer, patting my back hard enough that I stepped forward. "The twins asked me to ask you."

That didn't say much about the twins' bravery.

Merja returned, arms folded, her tight pants and boots dirtied and face scraped. "Make it to where I was, and Darvo will throw Jahel and Joris in the mud pit."

"We didn't agree to that," Joris said.

"But I did." She sneered.

I looked at Arek for support, or relief, or some excuse to get out of this. He simply nodded.

"The fog looks to be thickening." I grabbed what I could to stall, but I wasn't wrong. It did thicken, a dense quilt of cloud hovering over us.

"Shouldn't we wait until it clears? It would make everything slippery, not to mention hard to see."

"Not sure we've ever had a clear day here." Merja stared me down.

In no way was I ready for this. But would I ever be? I had to start somewhere, but in front of everyone?

I had to earn their respect. The only way to do that was to try.

I set my cloak down and approached the first tree, my breathing fast and heart racing. My hands were cold and hot, sticky to the touch. I pulled myself up, my boots grasping for grip on the bark. Blasted new boots may have been great for the forest floor, but had no give. I managed to heave over a limb and righted myself. The next two limbs were easier to reach, and I climbed them fairly easily, feeling a little more confident.

I walked out on the long thick limb pointing to the next checkpoint, a tree across the boulders. Merja had walked along this limb with agility, but I hadn't paid a whole lot of attention to how she made it across to the next tree. I shimmied down the limb, it bending lower the further I stepped away from the trunk. The next tree was too far to reach without leaping for it.

What if I didn't make it? I'd flop on the rocks below. Or reach it and break the limb, or lose my grip and…

I closed my eyes. All options pointed to the rocks below.

Why didn't I watch Merja more carefully? I'd been caught up in why this existed instead of listening to Merja's advice.

My clammy hands grew colder, a chill rising from my feet, up my ankles, to my torso. I opened my eyes to a wall of fog. Whispers echoed through the air, words unintelligible. The same voice whispered over itself five times over.

Gethhhhhh…

Toooo…

"Are you hearing this?"

"Hearing what?" Arek shouted up.

Gethhh… The whispers grew louder, and the wind picked up, overshadowing the voice.

There it was. Ahead of me, swaying slightly in the wind.

The rope.

The next tree had a rope strewn around a taller branch. If I could summon the rope's end out this way and reach it, I could swing over. Is that what the whispers were? Telling me I had to get to the rope?

All eyes were on me. I felt them more than saw them from above. They so much as didn't blink in case they'd miss what spectacle I'd give them. I didn't even know where to start with my power.

I reached out my right hand, my left clutching the shorter branch above me. The fog dissipated as I aimed for the bottom of the rope, my hand open, arm stretched out. I felt incredibly stupid.

"What's she doing?" One of the twins whispered to the other.

"Shh," Ulda said. "I think we're going to see her Soulmagic."

I let out a big breath and tried again, aiming my hand at the object. I closed my eyes, shut them as tight as they would go, focusing on willing that rope end to my hand. My arm shook, and stars appeared beneath my tight closed eyes.

Come on. Come on!

I dared to peek, opening one eye slightly. The rope was nowhere closer to my hand.

I'm a fool.

If Soulmagic wasn't going to work, maybe I could use what would work.

I retrieved my sling out of my satchel and unraveled it.

"Uh, uh." Merja stepped closer to the tree, wagging her finger. "No weapons. This course is for Soulmagic training. We all agreed."

Once again, I looked at Arek for support to find none.

"She's right," Ulda said.

Merja whipped around. "You don't even use weapons."

Ulda shrugged. "Makes it easy to follow the rules then, doesn't it?"

I warily put away the sling. Trying Soulmagic again meant acting the part and failing. There was no point.

I slowly worked my way back to the trunk and lowered myself down, each step thickening the water in my eyes. I wanted to run away, to hide from the others. I didn't belong here. Not with them. Not with powerful people who were in control of their Soulmagic.

I reached the ground and reluctantly faced them.

"Impressive," Merja said, chuckling, then walked away.

I couldn't hold the tears back any longer. They flowed down my cheeks.

"Don't worry about her," Ulda said. "It takes prac—"

I ran, in between Ulda and the twins, past Darvo and Merja, catching Arek staring at me with concern. More like regret in wasting his time bringing me here.

Regret was the right word. It fit the both of us.

CHAPTER

THIRTEEN

I retreated to camp, not knowing where else to go without getting lost in this place.

My bed coverings weren't enough to comfort me. It had been foolish to play along, to think I could make a difference along with these Soulmagi. They clearly had more experience and control over Soulmagic.

It wasn't like me to give up. To run off like that. After all, it took me years to excel at trapping and hunting, but those skills could be taught and learned. One was either blessed with Soulmagic or not, or in my case, cursed with losing it.

I'd nearly convinced myself to return to the training course, swallow what little pride I had left, when the fog encroached. Faint whispers danced in the air around my head. They multiplied, repeating nonsense, and I couldn't make out a thing in the thick of it, my tear-filled eyes unable to focus.

Gethhhhhh...

Toooo...

I moved to cover my ears, but another sound stopped me. A snap on the ground outside.

I sat at attention. Perhaps it was one of those rats Darvo hated so much. But it had a weight to it. Something substantial.

Footsteps.

I tiptoed out of the shelter. A snowcat or two poked their ears up in the air. "You heard it too?"

Then, behind my shelter, through the fog. Panting. Running.

I raced behind my shelter, the snowcats seeming not to care about my stupidity chasing after something unseen, without weapons. It wasn't going to get away, this presence that had loomed over me since arriving. Not if I could help it.

"Wait! What is it you want?" I shouted into the retreating mist, the trees and plants slowly revealing themselves through the vanishing cover.

My breathing quickened and pulse pounded in my ears. "Do you want us gone? Do you want *me* gone? Are you trying to help? I don't understand."

No whispers or swoops of mist answered. If some being set up the training on the island, why would it want us gone? Also, why stay hidden? If it wanted to help, there were more direct, easier ways.

I hadn't realized how far away from camp I had trotted into the woods until I turned around. I could barely make out the two trees supporting my shelter.

Something crunched to my left, and I stiffened.

"It's only me." Arek held up a hand and smiled faintly.

I let out the tension in my lungs. "What are you doing here?"

"I came to see if you were all right, and then I heard shouting." He looked behind me, at the empty forest. "Who were you shouting at?"

I mimicked his stare behind me, as if whatever it was would magically show up now. Of course it didn't. "Nothing. It's—no one."

Arek tipped his eyebrows down, his lips a line of concern. "Are you all right?"

"I'm fine."

"Don't be so hard on yourself. We all—"

"I'm not!" It certainly didn't sound true coming out. "I'm fine. Just let me be."

Arek nodded weakly and turned to go. But something seemed to compel him, as he stiffened his shoulders and turned back around. "Do you absolutely loathe me?"

Loathe was a strong word. I loathed the quakes, and those who caused them, those who killed Reil. I couldn't put Arek in that group. As much as I wanted him to be inconsequential in my life, he had already changed it. All I could muster was, "What?"

"If it takes you that long to respond, I have my answer."

"No." I shook my head. I didn't loathe him. There was some other feeling there, I just didn't know how to define it. What to name it.

But his questioning of it irritated me. "How am I supposed to feel about you?" I crossed my arms. "My family and I take you in, trust you, and you betrayed us."

"I'm trying to help them. Help us. Help whoever we can. And honestly, I don't think you'll ever be able to harness your abilities if you keep holding this against me. It's like a poison."

How dare he assume anything about me. "I didn't ask for this, Arek."

"None of us asked for this. None of us want to be away from loved ones, but you know what? We don't want to lose any more loved ones either. I don't have a whole lot left to lose, if you haven't realized."

He brushed his hand through his hair in frustration. "Don't you want it to end? Aren't you tired of the destruction?"

I was tired of the destruction. It took the love of my life away from me. It took the possibility of new life away from me.

"Let me be as clear and honest as I can be. I'm so sorry. I know they trusted me, and I'll never forget their hospitality. I had to do what I had to do to get your help. Because you are special, Evella. You have capabilities no one else has, that may help end this. You said so yourself, the quakes are more frequent. The Raider sightings are increasing. We're running out of time." He placed his hands on his hips, his eyes pleading. "Haven't you ever done something not so good, for the overall good?"

My hand curled into a fist, the urge to punch him strong. I wanted to push him to the ground. To silence him. I wanted this situation to go away, vanish forever. I wanted to be back at home, pretending things weren't getting worse. Pretending that Arek was wrong.

I had done something not so good. Something terrible that I had to do, for the good of both of us. My stomach knotted, and a sourness grew in my mouth. My eyes clouded with tears, and I couldn't bear to say anything to him, focusing on not falling apart.

"Evella."

"Leave me alone!"

A woman's voice echoed through my fuzzy ears. "There!"

Something took hold of me, wrapped itself around my torso.

I opened my eyes and rocks, twigs, even the ends of my hair, floated in the air. I didn't think about keeping them afloat or worry about dropping them. I stared at them, my body completely still.

Ulda commanded the sticks to drop.

Merja glared wide-eyed, and I took a few breaths. The rocks fell with a crash.

"You can let go now," Merja said.

Darvo's thick arms loosened around me.

"What…happened?" I asked.

"Whatever it is you were thinking, it got your soul twisted up," Arek said. "It broke out into your surroundings."

I knew what had done it but didn't want to admit it. It wasn't going over the events of the nightmare that activated my power. It was the feeling, of what I had lost that night that did it.

"Evella, what is it? What were you thinking?" Arek's face screamed concern. "I only want to help you."

His pleading tugged at my chest.

"Is that what you can do?" Merja asked.

"What do you want, Merja?" Arek's irritation bled through his pores.

"We all felt bad about what happened at training. Right?" Ulda sneered at Merja, who conceded with a shrug. "She tracked you down so we could tell you."

"So no secret rendezvous," Merja said.

"We weren't having a rendezvous." Arek's cheeks shone pink.

"I heard something," I said. "When I went to check it out, Arek followed me." I pleaded with my stare not to tell her anything else, although I did wonder if Merja could track down the mist.

"Now we know it wasn't anything, so everybody back at the course," Arek said. "Including you, Evella."

I sulked, despite Darvo patting my back for encouragement. What was the point? How was the course supposed to get the powers out of me? It seemed a waste of time, yet if I didn't participate, it would only increase the animosity between me and the others. Especially Merja.

And now that she saw at some level what I could do, I wouldn't hear the end of it. But how was I to get it out of me? How did I make it happen just then? Were my powers so out of control that it took three of them to subdue me?

I halted, the others stopping ahead of me. *To. Geth.* It wasn't an old language. It was a word. Could it have been? The slashes in the ground, burned in my brain. They weren't markers for treasure, or ancient symbols. They were two individuals, becoming one. A team. "Together. We need to work together."

"Huh?" Darvo held his mouth agape.

"You've been training by yourselves on the course, right?"

"I've gone the farthest," Merja boasted.

"But why individually? Maybe you're not supposed to do it that way. Look at what you did for me back there. Merja tracked me down, Ulda guided the sticks and leaves. Darvo, your strength calmed me down."

"Sorry," Darvo said. "I hope it wasn't too tight."

"It was perfect."

Heat crept over his cheeks in a flush of red.

"That's my point," I said. "Everyone has their strengths. Why aren't you defeating the course together? Isn't that what we'll have to do in order to beat the Raiders?"

"I don't know," Arek said. "I assumed we each had to be able to conquer it to—"

"To what?" Merja retorted. "Attack Raiders by ourselves? She's right." She glowered at me, eyes narrow. "Been here a day and you've erased months of work."

"Don't say that," Ulda said. "We have all improved."

Merja marched ahead, and Darvo and Arek followed.

Ulda stayed behind, walking slowly by my side. "Don't worry about her. She's upset she hadn't thought of it."

"I don't mean to upset anyone. Even if she wants me to fail."

"She doesn't want you to fail. None of us were at this level of controlling our abilities before we arrived. After my father passed away, there was a period of time where I couldn't seem to do anything."

We traveled through the empty camp, the others getting further ahead of us. "I'm sorry. Was it during a quake?"

Her eyes turned downward to her feet. "He fell ill three winters ago, shortly before I had turned fourteen. There wasn't much anyone could do for him. I made him herbal drinks and gave him what I could from nature to heal, but..."

I simply nodded.

"Mother didn't care if I honed my powers or not. But Father, he knew about magic. Sometimes I wonder if he had abilities and escaped being hunted down during The Great Culling. If he did, he never told me." She faintly smiled. "He taught me that my power comes from the soul. It's the core of Soulmagic, hence the name. For whatever reason, or maybe no reason at all, our souls connect with something. And we have the power to use that connection."

"Did he train you?"

"Not in this sense." She pointed ahead, the fork in the trampled trail coming up. "More like he nurtured my soul. He also taught me that when the soul is bruised, so are your powers. A lesson I truly learned after his death."

My attention piqued, stopping my feet. "You think mourning his death suppressed your powers?"

Her lips pressed in a thin line. "I think that when he died, a piece of me died with him. And that affected what I could do."

It had been over a year since I had some control over my ability. It stopped when the nightmares started. And those started after...

"What you did back there was amazing." Ulda perked up. "How strong was your ability before?"

I continued onward. "Before what?"

"Before your soul was bruised." Her hand wrapped around my elbow. "I am right, aren't I?"

I bit my lip, her intuition a bit scary. Reil had been the only one who'd seen what I could do, yet no amount of my power could pull him up from his fall, as the earth crumbled beneath his feet into the sea.

"For one, I had more control over moving things. It was like what you said with your powers—I had to see the object to be able to move it. I couldn't summon something that wasn't already there."

"Like fetch the water bucket at night when you don't want to get out of bed?"

"Exactly. Unless I could see it through the doorway. But you saw me back there. It's chaos."

"We just have to figure out how to tap into it."

"The only other times I can move objects nowadays is in my sleep, when I'm dreaming about—"

I had just met Ulda, and no matter the level of kindness she had shown me, certain topics were off limits.

"When I'm having nightmares. That's when Arek caught me using my powers. But if before, I could only move objects visible to me, then how is it that now I move objects in my sleep, with my eyes closed?"

Ulda's smile grew into a large grin. I half-expected her to clap or squeal in excitement. "Very interesting. I think that's going to be a key factor in getting your ability back under control."

"You think so? How?"

"Maybe there's something in this nightmare that makes you feel a certain way. Whatever happened to you, to bruise your soul, it's causing you to feel a certain way. Your emotions have a greater impact on your ability than simply sight that you relied on before. Think about it. What if experiencing whatever you went through, then healing your damaged soul, made you stronger? Made your powers flourish? Made some new connection to your abilities?"

Her enthusiasm was contagious, but my personal reality fought back. "It seems the opposite has happened, though, suppressing my powers. Do you think yours improved?"

"Certainly. Of course, it took time to heal. But as I did so, it became easier to command plants. It's not really commanding, either. It's connecting, like I said. When your soul is whole, the connections made can be very powerful."

There either was something to what she said, or it was all a load of snowcat droppings. Nonsensical talk.

"If you ever want to talk about it—what happened to you…"

I didn't want to talk about it, with anyone. It was my story and mine alone. But Ulda was being kind, her default nature, as I was coming to learn, and she put me at ease. Her demeanor was more mature, like talking to someone much older and wiser than me, trapped in a young body. Death had a way of doing that, dimming the light of youth too quickly in its wake.

We caught up to the others at the course. Arek glanced quickly at us before returning to his conversation with Joris.

Ulda turned to me, devilish grin on her face. "He's very…attentive to you."

"I think he's worried I'll flee. That all of this will scare me off."

"Well, are you? Scared off?" Her eyes turned big.

"Surprisingly, no." I didn't have a home to go back to. Sure, it was there. But I was on a mission now, to stop the death and destruction across Elsinor. How could I face my family if I quit on the first day?

"I don't think that's it—fear you'll leave us."

"No?"

"You know, I was smitten by him some time ago."

Not what I had expected. "Arek?"

She nodded. "We were the first two to arrive here for training. At one point, I thought we were the only two people in the world who had Soulmagic. I started to believe we were destined to be together." She giggled and shook her head. "Silly thoughts, I know."

I shrugged. "It's not silly, if that's how you felt." I couldn't blame her for feeling that way. It had felt the same with Reil when I was her age.

"I put that behind me some time ago, though. It's not wise to fall for an Oather."

"An Oather?" I had heard the term once or twice on the lips of townsfolk in Corallon. From what I could gather, Oathers were severely loyal to the king. "I wasn't sure they really existed."

"I thought you knew, that he carried the mark. That's why I've been worried about him, since your arrival."

I wasn't making whatever connection Ulda had.

"Imagine how hard it must be to fall for someone you can never be with." She read my growing confusion I didn't bother trying to hide, and she patted my hand. "Oathers can't be unioned. And with the way he looks at you—"

"What?" He didn't look at me any differently than he looked at others. Did he? "I'm not sure what you're talking about." Arek was the first person I'd ever met with Soulmagic—that I knew of. Having taken our journey together did provide me a connection with him I didn't feel with any of these strangers. But that was the thing, they were still strangers to me. Just because I felt a connection with Arek didn't mean I wouldn't develop that same relationship with the others. Already Ulda was trying to become friends.

"Sometimes it happens when we least want it to. Or in his case, when he's not allowed to." Ulda raised her eyebrows. "You can't deny he isn't handsome, at least."

I stole a glimpse of him, his brown eyes as dark as the bark in the forest, dimples that appeared as he chuckled. He was handsome, but that didn't mean our relationship would amount to anything beyond what we already had. Which was... I didn't know how to define what we had. Just that it was something.

How could I even think about the possibility of more right now, with anyone? After what happened with Reil. The confrontation with Reil's family on this journey.

I had the training course to tackle, and the only relationships I needed to focus on were those that would turn us into a team.

FOURTEEN

"We all saw it," Darvo said.

"Really?" Jahel rubbed his chin.

"Didn't happen if we didn't see it," Joris said.

Merja elbowed him. "The question is whether or not she can do it again. On purpose."

All eyes planted on me.

"Let's try to tackle this as a team." Arek employed his usual deflection.

"No," I said. "I'd like to try again, if that's all right." I needed a victory behind me. How could they trust me as a member of the team if I didn't display a reason to trust me?

"Are you sure?" Arek asked.

"I need to show them, and myself, what I can do."

He let slip a soft grin.

Ulda spoke softly at my side. "Think about channeling your emotions. Whatever it is you feel during that nightmare. Do you think you could conjure up those feelings now?"

I thought of the black cold, the purple light. The blood on the table. The pain. It worked my body into a sweat, my breathing into panting. I swallowed hard, pushing the memories down. Obviously, I could channel those emotions. Almost too easily. That's why I constantly buried them down, trying to make them vanish forever. It was the only way to move on from it all. Wasn't it?

I hadn't really questioned it before. As far down as I tried to bury everything, it lingered there, at the surface, ready to invade my thoughts.

Maybe Ulda was right. Maybe the reason why I couldn't use my powers was because they were tethered to those emotions, to the memories I avoided every day.

I climbed the branches of the first tree. When I shimmied along the long branch, I stopped, staring at the rope's end. This time I didn't close my eyes or try to fling magic out of my hand. I felt the emptiness in me, like a black hole hungry to be filled. The branches on the other tree shook, and a handful of needles broke off, some reaching my face, others falling between the two trees.

"Great," Merja said. "Maybe we can fill the lungs of Raiders with pine needles."

Jahel slapped her arm, and she replied with a vicious stare. Jahel stepped back, and Joris chuckled at his brother's momentary cowardice.

There were many objects in front of me. The tree branches, needles, rope, tree trunk. I had to balance the amount of strength I was summoning with focus. I didn't want the entire tree to collapse on me— not that I believed I was strong enough for that to happen. But, as Merja joked, I wanted more than mere pine needles in my hand.

At last the rope wiggled, and its end bent upward and out, gliding to my palm. I became so excited that it fell off track, heading for my shoulder and nearly whacking me in the face. I caught it though, and Ulda clapped for me while Arek threw a fist in the air.

I'm not sure if the others knew what to think. It didn't matter.

I swung to the second tree. From there I had vertical tree trunks to jump across, a farther distance between them the closer I got to the third station. There wasn't a whole lot I could think of to help me, except at the last step. It was too far to jump across, and I raised a large stone from below to serve as a floating step. It worked.

Somewhat.

I moved the flat rock past my current high stump and leapt. My foot didn't miss, but the rock slowly fell beneath me. I lost control of it, fighting between my balance and lifting the rock to support me. I dropped to the ground slower than a freefall. When I stood in front of the others, I didn't care if I looked like a failure. I didn't care if I hadn't gone as far as they had. I made it further than ever before. Using my power. It was a miracle.

Ulda met me halfway to the start and gave me a hug. "That was brilliant. Oh Evella, you're going to be great at this."

"You really think so?"

Joris nodded. "It took Jahel fifteen days to get that far."

"What?" Jahel threw his hands on his hips. "No, it didn't. You were worse than me."

Joris leaned closer and whispered. "If darkness is his power, memory is his weakness."

I chuckled, elated to have rediscovered a piece of me I thought was gone forever. And I began to feel like I belonged here, with the others. That I'd be one of them soon.

Ulda stood on the long branch of the first tree, pulling my attention from the others. "What are you doing, Ulda?"

"If we have to work together, we'd better get started. Evella or I can manage this first one if any of you had difficulty." She winked at me.

The twins shrugged at each other and followed up the tree. As Ulda crossed using an outstretched branch from the second tree, Merja and Darvo worked their way up the trunk. Arek and I took up the flank.

"You belong here, you know." Arek's smile killed me, weakened my knees without warning. "Not only for your Soulmagic, but for your instincts."

"Better watch it," I said. "I'm starting to believe you."

Despite a handful of squabbles on how best to complete each station, and a few show-offs on who had the better solution, the training course began to look defeatable. Darvo's height and strength helped in forming a bridge with his body. Merja's navigation skills came in handy with the spinning platform, guiding us when to leap off, the dizziness affecting us too much to judge for ourselves.

Jahel and Joris worked together in the copse of trees. Jahel darkened the area, which chilled my bones despite its wonderment. It grew so dark in our area of forest that the night bugs began to buzz and screech. That made it possible for Joris to look for something we might've missed in the daylight with his special vision, and sure enough, he spotted a heft thread. The ultrastrong thread strung up as a shortcut between trees had been about as fictitious as forever flame back in Corallon, but little surprised me nowadays. Ulda helped Merja in the spot she had gotten stuck a number of times, actually purposely setting off the net trap then raising it to use as a way to climb to the next station.

After supposed months of individual attempts across the group, we made it together in less than half a day. It put smiles on everyone's faces, including Merja, although I got the feeling she still would like to beat it by herself.

"I can't believe we never thought of that before," Jahel said as we walked back to camp to break for the day.

"It's so obvious now." Jorel's mouth hung slightly open, dumbfounded.

I walked slower, letting the rest of the pack pass me up. Merja tapped me on the elbow with hers, hands in her tight pockets. "Good going, kid." She flashed me as much of a satisfied smile I'd ever get from her. It didn't rival most other smiles, but it meant more than anyone else's.

Arek slowed his pace, and I eventually caught up with him.

"Looks like we make a good team," he said.

"The question is, for what? What is the plan? Keep training?"

He shrugged. "Merja has already suggested we try using different powers at each station."

That could be a good exercise in teamwork and pinpointing who could do what. "But what's the point?" I stopped as the others nearly pulled out of sight. "How are we translating this to defeating the Raiders? Are we supposed to confront them? Wait until they attack us? What is the plan?"

Arek scratched his forehead. "I promised you I'd be honest, right?"

I nodded. Whatever he had to say, I'd take it.

"I don't know what the king has planned. But you and I are to report back our progress when he summons. I'm sure he'll give us more information then."

"And in the meantime?"

"Keep doing amazing things." He gave a lopsided grin.

Dinner was served shortly after returning, a meal that I partook with the others this time around after filling mud in the crevices of my shelter. Despite the joviality of the company, which Ulda reassured me was quite rare these days and therefore appreciated, I couldn't get my mind off the mist. It had helped me solve a problem, but why? What was this entity that loomed over the camp? And should I tell the others about it?

Arek must've sensed my mood, for he tapped on my shelter as darkness blanketed the forest. "Just wanted to see if you're all settled now. Need anything more for your shelter?"

"Is that really why you're here?" Snark laced my voice, unintended.

He arched an eyebrow in surprise.

"I'm sorry," I said. "You didn't deserve that."

He shrugged. "Maybe, on some level."

I sighed, letting out the guilt that I'd let sink deep earlier today. "No. I took my anger and frustration out on you, back in the woods today."

"If you hadn't, you may not have rediscovered your abilities." He pointed to the foot of the bed, and I made room for him to sit. "I know you owe me no explanation, but..." He raked his fingers through his hair. "If you ever wanted to talk about it, where that stems from, I'm here."

"I'm guessing Ulda said something to you?"

The worry softened around his eyes. "She's a good friend. Maybe not the most quiet one, though. But I mean it. I only want you to work out what it is that needs working out, so your soul can be at peace. If I can help you with that, I will."

I bit my bottom lip. If I was to let it go, I needed to let it out. Ulda would've listened, but it didn't feel right telling her. And now I know secrets are not her strength. "You had asked me a question. One that struck something in me."

He looked at me quizzically, forming wrinkles at the bridge of his nose.

"Whether I had done something not so good for the common good." My lip quivered, my eyes welling up with tears again. "You know how I was to be unioned, with Reil?"

He nodded softly.

"I didn't tell you everything when we visited his family's house. I—I couldn't tell you. I didn't know you, and well—"

"I understand. We were strangers."

I took a deep breath. "Before Reil died, we were happy. In all the terribleness around us, we had each other. With our union quickly approaching, I found out I was pregnant."

Arek's eyes turned solemn, and his demeanor quieted.

"I was eighteen, and was I ready to be a mother? I mean, Ulda is nearly seventeen. And seems more mature than I was. Maybe more than I am now. I was terrified. But Reil comforted me. He knew what to say, how to act. He assured me we would be fine. I believed him, every time I doubted myself.

"Then one day, we were out hunting near the north cliffs, and a quake struck. The earth split, right between us. I reached my hand out for him as he slipped away. He fell so fast with the earth, into the sea. I tried using my powers. I tried pulling him up with my mind, raising him in the air onto sturdy land. I had never tried to move a human before, but I had to try. I didn't have time to think about it, I just did it. But I failed him."

"You can't blame yourself for what happened that day," he said softly. "It was the quake, not you."

"Please." I held up my hand. "If I stop now, I may never get it out."

"Alright." He shuffled on the bed, turning toward me but giving me space.

"When he died, it felt like my soul was ripped out. I thought for a while that I didn't want to live. I had my parents, my sister and brothers. But I didn't have him. I didn't want to raise a baby without him. I didn't want to see pieces of him in our child. In her eyes or his nose, how he or she would walk and talk. And the world was only getting worse. No child deserved to live the life I, and the world, would give it."

"Oh, Evella." He placed his hand on mine. I welcomed the warmth and the connection to another human. But I didn't want to be touched. I didn't deserve it. I pulled my hand slowly away.

"I went to the apothecary in town. I'd heard the rumors, about what some of his potions could do. I stole one of them— cloverbain. But he caught me as I was leaving and came after me. I had never run faster in my life. He stopped at the doorway of his shop and yelled at me. He warned me that what I had stolen wasn't enough. I took it anyway. I had to try."

I started sobbing, not caring anymore how it looked to cry, to be this open in front of Arek. I had kept it inside for so long, the words spewed out of my mouth.

"He was right, it wasn't enough. I fell terribly ill, and my parents rushed me to a healer on the outskirts of town. He figured out what I had done, as my parents showed him the empty bottle. I nearly died as he cut me open and sewed me back up. I don't remember much of those moments. But what I do remember was the pain. It's what I relive in my nightmare, over and over again."

"I—I don't know what to say." Arek looked down again at his knees.

"I wish others felt the same way—not knowing what to say." I wiped my eyes with my sleeve. "Whether the healer spoke of it, or the apothecary, I don't know. Word spread quickly about what happened with the Trapper girl. Eventually it reached Reil's parents."

"That was it, wasn't it? Why Reil's mother treated you so horribly when she saw you?"

I nodded. "She will never forgive me for losing the last bit of her son she could've had. And no one in town who knew ever looked at me the same way again. My parents decided to move us out of town, because of the looks, the whispers, sometimes the face-to-face insults people felt they had to share."

"Evella, listen to me." He sat up straighter and looked right into my teary eyes. "You don't deserve to be treated that way. No one does."

My lips quivered again. "The answer is yes, I have done something not so good for the overall good." I nodded. "I did what I thought I had to. I did what was best for that child. No one deserves to enter this world as it is, let alone with a broken mother. I had to think of my family, with another mouth to feed. About me not being able to provide for them in taking care of a new life. One that would constantly remind me of the life lost in their father. So if people wanted to treat me terribly, I didn't care. No punishment they inflicted on me could be worse than the one I had already suffered."

"That doesn't make them right, Evella." He reached again for my hand but stopped short, resting it on the bed between us.

"I fear that, no matter the progress I made today, I will never be able to control my ability as I had done in the past." I wiped the wetness on the back of my hand. "Ulda had said that when her father passed away, her soul was bruised. That she lost some of her power and had to heal herself before it came back. I immediately thought of losing Reil, that maybe his death had permanently bruised my soul. But that wasn't it. That wasn't what I thought of back there on the course. Now I know."

"What do you mean?"

"The baby, that child, had a piece of soul. No matter how young, how small it was, it took some of me. I feel like I never recovered from it. I never healed. I don't think my powers will ever be strong again, because my soul will never be whole again." I lost what little composure I had managed.

I wept with heaving sobs, my stomach muscles contracting, my lungs spewing air and sucking for more between cries.

Before I knew it, Arek's arms were wrapped around me, holding me tight.

I rested my head on his shoulder and let the weight of my grief, the grief that had accumulated the past year, release.

FIFTEEN

Everything felt different the next morning, like old remnants of myself had returned. I wasn't sure how to act, especially around Arek, with this new level of connection.

We stood in silence at the training course a little too long, and I had to break it. "Thank you, for last night. For listening." And consoling, and not thinking I'm a monster for what I had done. I only cared what others thought on Corallon because of my family, because of how they treated them knowing my not-so-secret secret. It didn't bother me what they thought of my actions. They didn't know me, know what I had gone through or would be through. Most of them would never be in the same situation to have to make the decision for themselves and everyone they loved.

But, with all my bravado, with the walls I gladly placed between me and the citizens of Corallon, the hard as stone exterior...I found myself caring what Arek thought of me. I didn't want him to think less of me, for it to come between us in any way. Why I felt that way, I didn't know.

"Of course," he said. "I think last night was a breakthrough for you. If you can channel what you were feeling, that connection..." He leaned even closer. "Terratics believe that once you die, you are returned to the earth. You live on in all the pieces of it."

"That goes against what you believe though, doesn't it?" I asked.

He backed away. "How do you know what I believe?"

"I saw you, after the quake at my house. Clutching your guardian. That means you're a Spiriter, that you believe you go to The Beyond, with what you accumulated in this life."

Merja swung along a rope ahead of us, Darvo catching her whether she wanted him to or not.

"It's how Nera raised me, yes. And what most in the palace practice. I go through the rituals when I'm around her. Maybe deep down I do believe in it." He shrugged. "Perhaps Spiriters and Terratics are both right. Perhaps our bodies return to the earth while our souls continue to the beyond."

"Or vice versa," I said. "Or none of it." I wasn't in the mood for taboo talk, but I had Soulmagic, as well as everyone else here. We were taboo. As if on cue, Ulda formed a nest of branches and leaves to land in.

"I can't say what's true in our death or not," Arek said. "But that part of your soul you feel is missing—what if it's back in this earth? In everything around you. You just have to communicate with it. Feel it."

"Is that how it is with the snowcats?"

He paused, glancing behind him as if the snowcats at camp had followed us here. "Ever since I was little I had a connection to animals. I came upon a trapped dwarf fox once when I was four. Its leg was stuck, sliced open and bleeding. I swear I felt its pain in my leg. I felt its hopelessness. Had it been left there, unseen, it would've died a slow agonizing death. I wanted it to die quickly, in peace. And when I wished that internally, the animal died in my hands. Right then." He shrugged. "Somehow my soul connected with it. That's what you have to do, Evella. That's why it's Soulmagic."

Whether it was a deeper understanding, or my confession last night, or a renewed enthusiasm to regain control over my powers, I had an endless energy. Every attempt we made at the course that afternoon led to a quicker time to completion. There was less arguing and more doing, holding out a hand to help each other and making sure no one strayed behind.

By dinner my legs ached from being on my feet all day. My

shoulders and chest were sore from pulling myself up and climbing. Merja discovered a shortcut that utilized veering off the course and scaling the base of one of the mountains in the northeast corner of the training area. Jahel and Joris argued it was cheating, while Arek and I agreed that when in combat, there were few rules to follow. I likened it to hunting, in that anything and everything was a resource. You weren't confined to a closed-off area. You made your own, and used what you had. If the mountain was available to climb and skip over an entire section, so be it.

But there was another type of exhaustion. The kind Ulda told me was due to using Soulmagic. It was an overall lethargy, like the lively energy in me had been sapped. It was more than muscle aches or joint pains. Everything felt sluggish.

The fire crackled, the little sunlight left lying low in the thick clouds. I welcomed the fire's warmth, since my sweaty clothes began to overcool my body. I asked Ulda for some womanly advice on a more substantial bath than using the buckets of water we refilled for the camp. The narrow creek provided enough fresh water, but wasn't wide or deep enough for a full body bath. The sea was an option, although its mood changed by the blink, and I didn't care to have a film of salt on my skin and hair.

"There's a pond, south and east of the training course. You can't see it from the clearing but it sits in a sort of valley at the foot of the mountains. I can walk you there if you'd like."

"That's not necessary, as long as it's not hard to get there."

"At least let me give you a lantern."

I walked across camp with her to her shelter. Especially in the night sky, the fern-covered door blended in with the rest of the unit, built into the side of the hill. If I had been a stranger walking through the woods, I wouldn't have noticed the place if I wasn't looking for it.

I bent low and entered the shelter. Couldn't say why, but I had pictured it round, like my family's house, with completed walls and ceiling. But it was nothing of the sort. It was hard to tell the shape, with edges that looked like corners in odd places. The roof and walls were carved from the dirt, and roots made an intricate network holding the dirt in place above our heads. Vines and branches covered the walls, sprouting colorful flowers. It smelled like humid dirt and fresh leaves, hyacinth and moss adding an earthy perfume to the air.

Ulda retrieved a glass lantern, a narrow cylinder with a metal handle, the whole thing barely large enough to encase a candle. It wasn't a candle, but a wick with oil in a reservoir beneath it. She refilled the reservoir with a pink fluid.

"Most people know that cherrymums produce a lovely fragrance. What they don't know is that cherrymum water isn't water at all. It's an oil that can be burned."

I watched in fascination as she lit the wick and handed me the lantern.

"Mind you it burns fast, but that should be enough to get you there, have a quick dip, and head on back."

"Thank you." I was tempted to stay to pick her brain on the rest of her flora knowledge. What else could plants provide us that we didn't know about? But since the lantern was lit and the night ageing, I needed to get going.

"You're welcome. You can return it in the morning."

I nodded in thanks again, and she walked me out of the shelter.

"It's lovely, by the way," I said, knowing how much she wanted me to see her place. "Your shelter."

"Oh thank you. I do what I can." Her shoulders nearly reached her ears, cheeks pink. "Remember, head to the course, but then make a right. You'll see a side trail heading southeast we've made from going back and forth to the pond."

I hurried along the trail to the training course, worried about the quick-burning cherrymum oil. I practiced levitating the light in front of me, which provided comfort and eeriness, casting shadows that distorted branches and needles, creating sharp objects and shadow beasts in the night. My focus had been on longer stretches of airtime for the lantern that I nearly missed the side trail. I turned right, the pathway narrower and less traversed than the main trail.

There were a few trip-ups on rocks, but I made it to the edge of the pond. The blackened-out stars indicated the presence of the mountains.

Were it not for the clear night sky I wouldn't have known they were there in the pitch black. Now that I thought about it, I hadn't seen a clear sky since arriving. It was beautiful and spooky. People didn't call the island Spokizar for nothing.

I set down the lantern in an admittedly shaky landing on a boulder near the shore, discovering not much of a shore of rocks or sand. It was as if the forest decided to end right there, dirt, leaves, needles and branches along the ground like any other part of the forest.

The water had to be frigid, despite the steam coming off the surface. Was it really steam? The water had to be warmer than the outside air, which did hold a chill at this hour, but my gut doubted the water held any warmth. For one, the sun didn't shine anywhere on this island. For two, if it were warm, the others would frequent this place more often.

Undressing away from the warmth of camp was bad enough. I placed my folded clothing in a pile atop my boots. My dipped foot in the water confirmed my prediction. The water was not only cold, it baffled the mind it wasn't frozen over.

There was no taking my time, wading further out, getting used to the temperature. Best to dive in and do it. "All or nothing, Evella." The words didn't give me the strength I wanted them to. I cursed there not being a rocky outcropping to jump from.

I closed my eyes and ran out in the water, my mouth open in shock. I made it as far as my waist. "Sweet Spirits!" Holding my breath, I ducked below the surface, running my numb fingers through my hair before rising back up. It was hard to tell what was colder, the portion of my body in the water, or the newly wet portion out.

"Yoww!"

I ducked low enough for the water to reach my shoulders and stared in the direction of the yell. A head popped up out of the water, crisp white breath escaping into the moonlight.

"Arek?" I wrapped my arms across my chest, as if he could see underwater. I couldn't help instinct.

"It doesn't get any easier," he said between gulps of air.

"What are you doing here?" I half shouted, half shivered it out.

"Figured I could use a bath."

I bit my cheek. "At precisely the same time I'm taking one?"

"Why not?"

I let out my breath in a tisk. "Because."

"You know, you're right. That's a valid reason." He splashed water my way, too far away for it to reach me.

"Maybe I wanted some privacy." I stepped toward him, splashing him back. Mine just nipped his face.

"It's night. No one can see what's going on." As he looked at me, I was sure I wasn't completely veiled by the night.

He stood, the water reaching up to his waist, rolling off his chest and arms. The night definitely didn't hide everything.

He dipped back down in the water, then stood up again. He repeated the up and down three times.

"What are you doing?"

"I thought maybe the exposure to the air would make the water seem warmer." He dipped down again. "But nope. There's no getting warmer."

I chuckled, lips surely blue by now. A silence passed over us as we looked at one another. I couldn't see how brown his eyes were, or even the dimples in his cheeks. But there was a recognition. A pull to him. A rawness about being bare underneath the water in front of each other. It felt like we stripped away all the facades, the haunts of the past, the bruises and scars acquired on our journey.

Ulda's comment about the way Arek looked at me buzzed in my head. "That mark, on your shoulder." I reached for him, but he quickly held his shoulder as if he'd just realized how unclothed he was.

"You saw that?"

I nodded. "That first day here, on the shore." I'd forgotten about it until now. "Is it true? That you're an Oather?"

"It was why I couldn't come back from Corallon without you." He looked back up at me. "Sometime after seven, eight years of Nera raising me in secret in the palace, King Ronin found out. He wanted me and Nera thrown out for our betrayal. She pleaded with him to let me stay, and I couldn't see her like that. I couldn't stomach that her life would be ruined because of me. I swore I'd do anything for her to stay. He agreed to let us both stay, if I were to take The Oath." He moved closer, so close I nearly backed away, but then he turned, baring his shoulder.

I gasped and ran my fingers over the two-headed stallion etched into his cool skin. I didn't need to make out the details. I knew the design. "It's the same as his ring."

"He uses it, to brand his Oathers. We swear loyalty to him for life, he makes sure we have his mark for life."

"Does it really mean you can't union?"

He winced for an instant before looking away, as if he didn't mean for me to see it. "There is to be no other we give our lives for. To give someone our hearts is to sentence them to death."

King Ronin had seemed almost affectionate with Arek at the palace, almost as a father would. But now I questioned if it was all a performance, reveling in his power knowing this man had been coerced into loyalty since a boy.

I wanted to comfort him as he did me, heal his wound and free him from his decision made long before I knew him.

"Don't do that," he said.

"What?"

"Pity me. I saved myself and Nera. Always had enough food, decent clothing, shelter in the palace. It's a choice I made."

"When you were just a boy." I wasn't helping him feel better, pointing out the wrong in it all. But I couldn't stop. "It makes me hate that I've agreed to this, being a part of his plan. I had grown up thinking either he's clueless what life is like in other terrins, or he doesn't care, as long as it benefits him. Your story makes me believe the latter even more."

"You didn't agree to do this because of the king. You agreed to do this to stop the destruction. Just like I agreed to The Oath to give Nera a better life. Always remember that."

No matter how true the words, they didn't make me feel better.

"Evella?"

I waved my arms through the water as if treading, even though my toes played with the rocks in the dirt at the bottom. "Yes?"

"I don't think I can last much longer in this cold."

I chuckled. "Me neither."

"You first." He nodded toward shore.

My jaw dropped. "You would like that, wouldn't you?" I splashed him again. But I looked at my pile of clothes on shore and got an idea.

"All right." I grinned. "Me first." I waded through the water up until the point it became too shallow to be hidden. It was hard to distinguish the clothing items from one another in the pale light, but luckily my cloak sat on top. I raised my hand, and the cloak floated over the water, my hand catching it just as I lost control over it. I turned my back to Arek and put on my cloak while standing, wrapping the fabric around my torso, concealing what need be concealed.

"Hey, that's not fair."

I turned back around and shrugged. "Your turn." I walked up to the shore and worked on the rest of my clothes, the cloak not bad at drying me off.

Arek remained frozen in the water, biding his time.

"You don't think I'm going to leave you all by yourself, do you?" I couldn't keep back the glee as I folded my arms, enjoying the warmth of the dry clothes.

"All right then." Arek stood, his chest out of the water.

For a second, I thought he was going to go for it—make a run naked to the shore. But he twisted his hands in the air.

He wasn't going to get off this easily. I darted for his clothes down the shoreline.

The forest behind me rustled, twigs shaking and small paws patting.

A swarm of tiny forest creatures appeared, too fast for me to beat. Squirrels separated his garments and two birds swooped down for his shirt. They clutched it in their beaks and flew to Arek, who clasped it in his fist with a grin.

The squirrels stared me down, squeaking as if snarling at the enemy.

"Fine." I put my hands up. "You win."

Arek approached the shore, shirt on. "You know I'm going to have to get you for that, right?"

"What? I—" I ran to the protection of the forest before he could catch me.

CHAPTER

SIXTEEN

"Hey!" Arek's shouts grew fainter as I weaved through the forest. As I slowed down to catch my breath and give him a little time to catch up, I realized I had been giggling.

I was having fun. I couldn't remember the last time I allowed myself to have fun. Free time in Corallon was short, and with the constant worrying about food and warmth and not dying from quakes, it was hard to let go of it all.

I scanned the forest behind me. Arek should appear any moment now.

But I couldn't see far. A thick blanket of dense mist slowly drifted through the trees.

"Arek?" My labored breathing turned to panic breaths. "Arek!"

The mist quickened its approach, enveloping me in its soft snare. The whispers began, nonsensical words overlapping and growing in volume.

Along with them, a footstep.

Whatever it was, it was in front of me. I felt it. I held back a scream, ashe thing breathed. It was alive and it stood before me.

"Arek is that you? You got me back, now stop it."

There, as the mist cleared between me and it, a figure appeared.

It was a man, dressed in dark brown that blended with the night forest. He was slightly taller than me, with a small but muscular build and a short thick beard. His eyes caught the moonlight, as if the mist and moon worked together to present him to me.

Instead of scaring him off or throwing the lantern at his face—which I couldn't because I'd foolishly left it at the shore—or running like mad, I spoke to him.

"Are you real?" Both Arek and Ulda thought I had imagined noises, imagined the sense of someone watching me. Maybe I had, and my mind was so far gone and confused in this place that I conjured up a person before me.

The mist swooshed around him before settling back down near the ground.

He stayed still, except for a dark raised eyebrow. "As real as you."

"What do you want? Who are you?"

"You first. It's the least you could do considering you set foot on my island."

"Your island?" I studied his face, which remained dead serious. No one knew for sure if anyone lived on Spokizar. If you asked around, most would comment the only thing living on that island was indeed dead, in the form of ghosts. There were other theories as well—like it was a safe haven for outcasts or thieves. Was I looking at such a thief now?

He placed a hand on the hilt of a blade at his waist.

I was out here in the woods, weaponless. He had the upper hand, and what did I have? The ability to move a cloak in the air. I didn't even know my way around the island. If he did live here, he'd be better at that, too.

"I'm no one," I said.

"I highly doubt that." He stepped with one foot out, leaning on his other, relaxing his posture. Like he could stand there all night waiting to get information out of me.

I didn't know how much to tell him. It wouldn't hurt to give him basic information, would it? At best he would leave me be, and at worst he'd kill me. Those were the options regardless of me opening my mouth.

"I'm Evella Trapper, from the terrin of Corallon."

"Corallon? That's a bit of a ways, isn't it?"

It was hard to gauge whether he was surprised or knew that about me already with his nonchalant way of speaking. "Not unmanageable entirely by sea. Much longer if you traverse the terrins on foot." Not that I would know just how long.

"What is a young woman from Corallon doing here?"

"Ever been to Corallon in winter?"

"Can't say that I have."

"If you had, it wouldn't seem so out of place for one to leave it."

He tilted his head to one shoulder. His reading of me made me question talking to him at all.

"That may be true." He wagged a finger and paced. "If we were talking about any other terrin. But Spokizar?" He stopped, turning in the dirt to face me. "That doesn't seem like a getaway destination for anyone."

"Yet here you are." The annoyance bled through my voice. "Between the two of us, only one has stated a reason for being here."

He closed his eyes, chest bouncing with a chuckle. "Right you are. Also, only one of us has lied to the other."

I took a step away from him, the sense of an impending battle too strong for comfort. If I had to resort to Soulmagic, so be it. Hopefully I could wield it when it counted most.

He held up a hand. "I didn't show myself to cause trouble. More to confirm what I suspect about you and the others."

Speaking of others, where had Arek wandered off to? "You're the one who has been spying on me, aren't you?" I bit my bottom lip. "Just what is it you suspect?"

He cleared his throat. "All right. I guess it's my turn to give a little." He folded his arms across his chest. "You and your friends are Soulmagi. You've come here to practice your abilities in secret. I must admit it's the perfect place for it. What I don't know for sure is why you're doing it. I have my guess, of course."

"And what would that be?" He was correct so far but admitting that would put the others in jeopardy. There was still no telling who this man was, or what were his intentions.

He did the head tipping maneuver again, setting me with unease. Could he invade my mind, like that vile man Icad at the palace?

"I think you are forming an army of sorts. Training to fight who I could only guess is King Ronin."

I scoffed, unintentionally.

He raised both eyebrows. "I missed the mark? Why else would you train to fight? Who could you possibly—" His face turned pale and serious. "I got it backwards, haven't I? The king put you up to this."

The mist around the man swirled off, spinning around me in a vortex, my hair billowing in its circle. "Calm down," the man said. "I'll explain it to her."

The mist returned to the ground, halting at a standstill.

"What is going on?" I asked. Maybe he did have Soulmagic, and the mist was his manifestation. "Do you control the mist?"

"I think we'd better move this along. It's worse than I thought."

I eyed the forest around us. Was there something coming for us?

"My name is Fulric. And you've already met Alora." The mist raised in a wave that rippled back into the forest where it was too dark to see. "I don't think she'd appreciate you thinking I controlled her." He glanced down at his feet, acknowledging the mist.

"She's—" How weird to refer to a vapor as an entity, as a female one at that. "She's been watching me, hasn't she?"

"She sensed something in you on your arrival. A greatness the others do not possess."

"So you have been watching the others, even before my arrival?"

"Of course. Who do you think set up the courses they've been toying with?"

"It was you? But why? Why have you hidden yourself from them yet help them train?" There were too many answers he needed to provide. "Why reveal yourself now?"

He held up a hand to stop my questioning. "We have hope that once you hear the truth, you'll use your powers for good."

My chin tucked closer to my chest in surprise. "That's what I plan to do. That's why we train. We want to stop the quakes. For good."

It sounded valiant and noble to say it out loud. I was a part of this, a part of a group set out to change Elsinor for the better.

"Yet you haven't heard the truth yet." He stretched out an arm, offering his hand. "Come with me. I'll tell you all about it." He must've registered my shivers. "I can at least offer you a warm fire."

Should I wait for Arek to find me? Or retreat back to camp? I could find my way back in the dark. Eventually. "Why should I trust you?"

"What do you have to lose?" He looked directly in my eyes. "The way I see it, I'm armed, you're not. Although I see your Soulmagic has finally made an appearance, so I guess I'd better watch my tongue." His cheekiness needed knocked down a notch. "Listen, you need not fear me. If I wanted to kill you, I would've done so already. But that is not my intention."

His words didn't help much, but—he probably could've killed me in that mist, and he hadn't. How could I return to camp and tell the others I met a man, yet have nothing else to say about him? That I left him in the woods? What did this man know that I, nor anyone else here, didn't know?

I didn't offer my hand, but took two steps toward him. He took that as sign enough, and turned into the forest, waiting for me to follow.

We hiked close to the pond, heading east, toward the foothills of the mountains. The mist—Alora—didn't follow us directly, but drifted over the lake into the trees, meeting up with us. We didn't speak, only walked. I wondered if the others started to worry about me, especially Arek. He'd have returned to camp by now, realizing I never made it back.

We walked long enough my body warmed from it, then circled over a slanted hill. Tucked away on the other side, etched up the base of a mountain, was a round entrance.

A cave.

No wonder the others hadn't found him when they searched the island. They would've had to be in this very spot to have seen it.

I scrambled up the stony rock face leading up to the cave's mouth, mimicking Fulric's foot placement ahead of me. My calves and thighs burned, the climb stinging my muscles and tendons. It wasn't a tall climb in the least, but after today's training, I had little left in me.

A fire burned low in the center of the floor, near the entrance where the smoke could exit. Fulric revived it with a fresh block of wood. The cave was not much bigger than Ulda's shelter, but with no plants and more furniture. What I could make out in the firelight was a pile of belongings, remnants of the last few meals, and balled up fabric that looked to be dirty clothes. A small ladder leaned on a shelf, a wooden platform that I guessed was his bed. He also had a rudimentary desk and chair, and a pile of books—beaten, worn books that looked like they were pulled up from the sea bottom and dried out over too hot of a fire.

"Sorry, I didn't have a chance to tidy up." He flashed a smile. The fire's light made his features clearer. He had black hair, cut short and matted down, which blended in with the thick beard reflecting a streak or two of silver.

I sat by the fire, warming my hands.

"So what is this truth you wish to tell me?" It was getting late, I was further than I had ever traveled from camp, and my body begged for sleep.

"Right. Get to the point, shall we?" He smiled again and poked the fire. "You didn't contradict me when I said the king put you up to this— coming here and practicing Soulmagic."

"I didn't contradict it, as much as I didn't contradict or agree to anything else you said."

"But you did. In your own way." He stopped messing with the fire and looked across the flames at me. "I didn't bring you here to argue with you."

"Why did you bring me here, then?"

"What you don't know is that King Ronin is the root of it all. The destruction, the starvation."

My face crinkled in cynicism.

He scooted a step closer around the fire, his face clearer without having to see through the flames. "Why do you think the people who manage to kill Raiders end up having the fewest quakes?"

"That's not true." Something in the recesses of my memory emerged. A Corallon man had claimed to kill a Raider, years ago. The time afterward was the longest stretch without quakes in Corallon I could remember having. "Maybe it's because that's one less Raider to cause a quake."

"Clever. That would fit the narrative," he said. "But that's not why. I know the truth, because of her." He pointed out the cave of the mouth, the mist hovering in the trees below.

"This is ridiculous." I shook my head. "I'm listening to a man who talks to mist." I stood up. "If anything, you've been isolated in this place far too long, and it's showing." I moved to exit the mouth of the cave.

"I didn't tell you her full name," he said. "It's Alora Aspernath."

My feet stopped before my thoughts caught up, and I spun around. "As in, the king's dead sister?"

"Dead. Nondead. It's a bit tricky to categorize her." He took in a deep breath and let it out slowly in a sigh. "Please, sit down and listen to what I have to say. If you don't believe me, you can carry on with your fool's errand."

I considered the options, but resigned to my curiosity. "Fine." I returned to my bit of cave floor by the fire.

"In order for any of this to make sense, we must go back, before you were born, I assume. Back when the world was one place. Elsinor."

I blinked hard but held my tongue.

"Back when King Ronin was prince, he convinced his father, King Crohl, that people with Soulmagic threatened the throne. He told stories of secret meetings amongst the commoners, tales of Soulmagi practicing in basements and backrooms. He planted the seed in King Crohl's head that he had an enemy, and his enemy was Soulmagic."

"Is that why King Crohl persecuted those with Soulmagic? Hunted them down?"

Fulric took a long blink, seemingly frustrated. "That's what they want you to believe."

I closed my mouth tight, awaiting the explanation.

"No, King Crohl placed a ban on all use of Soulmagic. Of course, it was only as good as it could be enforced. Still, it was tough on those who relied on Soulmagic for their livelihood. Neighbors started snitching on each other. Traders suspected and reported other traders. If caught, there were heavy penalties."

"But not death?"

"Never death. King Crohl was adamant about that," he continued. "Soulmagi were still people, after all. But Prince Ronin thought otherwise. He wanted more to be done to stop Soulmagic. Specifically, he wanted the elimination of it, and only one way guaranteed that result. One King Crohl would never agree to. So, he went behind his father's back and ordered The Great Culling."

"King Ronin told me that was his father's doing."

"He would say that. Most people thought the same, since it was during his father's reign. As for King Crohl, in the end, he had been misled. He was wrong about who his enemy was, for he'd been living with the enemy in the palace the entire time. His own son."

"What are you saying?" I mulled over the implications. *In the end.* "Did Ronin do something to his father?"

"Ronin wanted the throne more than anything, and wasn't willing to wait through his father's reign to get it. He devised a plan to kill his father."

I shook my head. "That can't be. Someone had to have seen it or known about it. They couldn't tell King Crohl was murdered?"

"Ahh." Fulric wagged a finger. "You are right, in that someone did find out. His sister Alora got word from one of the servants, who had accidentally walked in on Prince Ronin, wielding Soulmagic himself."

I squirmed on my square of cave floor. The thought of King Ronin having Soulmagic had briefly crossed my mind when I had met him. It wasn't that far-fetched to think it true.

"Prince Ronin knew his secret had been jeopardized and stormed in on Alora's meeting with their father. According to Alora, it was a horrible but swift death for King Crohl. Prince Ronin flicked his hand, and something in King Crohl snapped, as if his heart burst at that very moment. His eyes turned bloody, his nose and ears streaking red.

"Ronin then turned on Alora. What he didn't know was that his sister was a Soulmage, too. It was suspected to have come down the line from their mother. Even so, there was nothing Alora could do in time to stop his attack, so she did what she could in defending herself."

"Which was?" I clung to every word. Somehow this was becoming believable, even if it was unbelievable.

"She expelled her soul from her body before it perished, and fled here. This land was the furthest she could get her soul away from the palace. Away from her murderous brother. And since then, she's been forever tied to it."

"That mist is Alora's soul?"

"It is the form her soul has taken."

"And you can communicate with her?" With the scratches in the dirt in my shelter, surely Alora communicated with him in ways I couldn't even imagine.

"Yes."

We sat in silence, the fire crackling. Finally I organized my thoughts enough to pull up an obvious question. "Who are you, then? Why are you here?"

He sighed, his face turning grim. Yet there was a sparkle in his eyes, a longing. "She was my friend. My lover." He kept his gaze on the fire. "We are soulmates, and as long as a part of her lives on, I cannot leave her."

"You are tied to this island, forever?" It was a somber prospect. I didn't know how long I could go on and not see the sun, even if it was the low winter sun in Corallon.

"I can go as I please, but I do not like leaving her." He nodded to the cave entrance. "She has the ability to travel, but it takes much out of her, and it can't be for long, else she could dissipate. Evaporate until there's nothing left of her."

Reil's face popped into my head. His arm outstretched, reaching for his last hope. Me, on sure-footed land, trying to raise him back up. What was worse, losing a soulmate completely? Or having a lingering piece of them, that wasn't all of them, bound to you?

I wrapped my arms around my raised knees. My head added to the hurt of the rest of my body, and the fire began to warm me too much, speckles of sweat forming on my neck and brow. I wanted more than anything to go back to camp, to forget this evening. If I did go back, would I ever see Fulric again? Would I have the chance to ask him all my questions?

"Why the training?" I asked. "Why help us?"

"When the first of your group arrived, Alora and I assumed there was only one reason for people with Soulmagic to seek out a private island. To do exactly what Prince Ronin lied about to his father—to form an alliance to go against the king. It comes as a shock to find out it's the opposite."

"I think the shock is all mine."

He tipped his head and glared into the fire again. "I suppose it is."

My stomach lurched, and I stood, fanning my clothes for cooler air. "How do I know to trust you? That any of this is true? And don't say because there's no reason not to trust you, or some play on words like that." I stared him down, wanting the hard evidence. As if Alora the Mist wasn't enough to convince me.

"There is a way—to prove to you I'm telling the truth. King Crohl, he wore the Royal Ring. It's a ring passed down from king to queen to king, and so on, down the inherited bloodline. The only way to pass it down is for the owner to willingly give it to the next of kin."

"Was it a thick band with gilded leaves and a two-headed stallion?"

"You've seen it?"

I nodded. "King Ronin wears it now." *And uses it to brand his Oathers.* I set aside the repulsion the thought brought me. If the ring had an enchantment or some property like Fulric described, King Ronin wouldn't have obtained it. "If anything, that proves your story isn't true."

"Ahh. I'm sure he flaunts it to make everyone think his father willingly passed it to him during his last breaths." Fulric swayed a finger before standing up to meet me. "After King Crohl died, Alora went back to the palace. She couldn't bear to think of leaving not knowing what happened to—" Fulric coughed and held up a hand for me to wait.

"Sorry." He ran his hand through his beard. "She needed to know everyone else had been spared. So she traveled in her new form up to the king's quarters, through a window of the tall turret. It was there she saw the Prince. He snuck into the embalming chamber and ungloved his father's right hand. He tried slipping off the ring. It would not budge, as it was bound to his finger. The prince, becoming frustrated, and hearing footsteps, chopped off the finger. He stole the ring with the finger and placed the glove back on the hand. It was then that Alora made herself known."

"Known? How?"

"How'd she introduce herself to you?" Fulric asked.

The feeling of a presence. The movement of the mist. Her marks left in the ground.

"She stormed through the room, and Prince Ronin called out her name. He knew it was her, and he used every bit of his soul to ruin her.

"That night." Fulric pressed a knuckle to his lips. "That was the night of The Quake." He looked back up at me, eyes watery. "That is his power, Evella. He breaks what is unbroken. He snapped his father's insides. And he used all he had in him to destroy the rest of Alora."

"But it didn't touch her? Change her form in any way?"

"No. Her physical form had already perished. His power instead channeled through the castle deep into the ground, cracking the earth, shattering it into pieces to the ends of Elsinor. He'd discovered a more chilling, terrifying way to manifest his magic."

To have such strength in his power...how could one man's Soulmagic change the face of far-off lands? And how could that man ever be stopped?

Yet, he hadn't destroyed Alora.

"King Ronin never learned where Alora hides?" My eyes grew big at a new thought. "Is that why there are more quakes? Because he's trying to kill what's left of his sister?"

"Believe me, we thought as much. I think you could say at first that's why the quakes continued. But his search for Alora diminished quickly after that night. Too busy taking on his role as King. Seeking out those with Soulmagic to keep them under control, so that he'd never be stopped. Instilling fear in the people of Elsinor, so they'd believe anyone who stood up to the king was the cause of the quakes."

I thought it all over—the persecution of those with Soulmagic, the murder, the sister turning to mist. The quakes. The stories I had learned growing up made sense.

But so did the story Fulric told.

"Do you see what you must do if you doubt me? If you wish to know the truth?" Fulric stood near the cave mouth, and I stepped closer.

"I don't understand. What can I do?"

"Go to the palace. To the crypt. There you will find King Crohl's tomb. You will find all sorts of his belongings buried with him, to carry on to The Beyond. You'll also find he's missing a finger on his right hand."

The cave darkened despite the fire, a reminder of how late in the night it had become.

"And no Royal Ring?"

"No Royal Ring."

"But surely someone would have checked for it before burial? To see if he really had passed it down to Ronin?"

"Who was to argue? Alora?" Fulric kicked a broken branch out of the cave. Had it been there when I arrived?

"It was said the king knew he was ill and dying, and hastily gave the ring to his eldest son. If the ring was on Ronin's finger, that was all the proof anyone needed. That's why you must check."

I swallowed hard, the cool outside air mixing with the warm cave air. I needed rest, my body pleaded for it. But how was I to calm my thoughts after learning this?

"When you see what King Ronin had to do in order to get that ring, then you'll realize who your real enemy is."

The darkness made it nearly impossible to see. But the branch returned, elongating and wrapping around Fulric's leg.

"No!" I reached out for him but not soon enough. He rose in the air, head down to the ground. The vine moved closer to the fire.

"Stop, Ulda!"

The branch backed off the fire, but continued to hold Fulric in the air. Darvo helped Ulda up into the cave, then Merja and the twins, giving them a knee as a step. He grabbed Arek by the waist of his pants and hoisted him over the lip of the cave.

Arek stood, patting off the dirt on his pants. "Was that necessary?"

Darvo grinned as he entered the cave. "Necessary or not, it was fun."

"For one of us." Arek finished dusting off his sleeves and turned to me. "Are you all right?"

"Think you can give us our light back?" I stared down Jahel, whether he could see me doing it or not.

"Oh, sorry."

The ambient moonlight reentered the cave.

"What's going on here?" I asked.

Arek stepped forward. "When you didn't arrive back at camp, I got worried."

"He was a bit of a mess, if you ask me." Merja smirked. "Your scent was fresh on the lantern Arek brought back from the lake, so I tracked you here."

"You all came to find me?" I scanned the group of six Soulmagi. I hadn't felt as much a part of the group as I did in this moment.

"Of course," Ulda said. "Arek said you vanished in the mist, and I've always been suspicious of it."

"Not us." Merja lifted her elbow onto Darvo's shoulder, an awkward height for it. "But we came anyway."

"Didn't want to miss out on anything," Darvo said.

"This reunion is lovely." Fulric slightly swayed in the air, the beardless area of his face red as an apple.

"Ulda, could you put him down, please?"

"You mean this person who kidnapped you?" Arek pointed up at Fulric, and Darvo snarled at his upside-down face.

"He didn't kidnap me. I came willingly." It was about as willingly as I had gone with Arek that morning in Corallon, but no sense in mentioning that. I had forgiven Arek, therefore my actions needed to reflect that.

"This is Fulric," I said.

Ulda slowly lowered him to the ground.

"You're going to want to hear what he has to say."

CHAPTER

SEVENTEEN

"Evella!" Merja nimbly hopped from pillar to pillar. I raised a flat stone for her, between the last two. She jumped on it, continuing to the next station as the others followed—Ulda, the twins, Arek, then me and Darvo picking up the rear.

The newest version of the course had only been up for six days, but together we had conquered it. As an added challenge, we ran through it using only one person's Soulmagic. This round was for me.

I focused on loose branches on the ground, pulling at that core feeling I had grown to recognize within me. They raised up and with a flash of my hand, the branches spiked into the last wooden pole. Merja easily climbed down, the branches helping with footing.

The last obstacle was a metal sheet, three times the height of Darvo. Fulric had found it on the shore, as he had done most of his belongings during his time on the island. He reinforced the back end of it with stacks of wood, creating a slippery flat wall we had to climb over.

I looked around for more rocks I could use as floating stairs.

"No." Fulric had followed us on the ground by each obstacle. He stood with his arms crossed, shaking his head. "No more of the same tricks. This time, just them."

"What?" I asked.

Merja stood closest to the wall, catching her breath. I knew what Fulric wanted, despite my questioning reaction.

He wanted me to lift Merja over the wall, with my power.

"If you can support their weight with the objects you command, you can directly command them."

I shook my head, but Merja nodded. "Do it. Lift me up."

"I don't know how to connect with you." Or anything breathing for that matter. I couldn't move as much as a rodent that had visited us during dinner the other night, much to Darvo's dismay. That was Arek's gift, connecting with animals. Not mine.

If there were ever a reason to command a person, it was during the quake that took Reil's life. And I hadn't been able to do it then.

An idea struck me, and I raised my hand. I focused on Merja's boots. If I could lift her footwear, maybe I could lift the whole of her.

Merja fell forward, feet swept out from under her, face planting in the dirt. "I regret volunteering." The ground muffled her words.

I faced the shiny metal wall, a distorted version of myself reflecting back. A version trying to be more powerful than she was.

"Come on, Evella. Harness that power," Fulric said. "You can do it, and you will. Get up, Merja."

Merja reluctantly stood. "You want me to go through this again?"

Fulric put up a hand to shush her. His optimism went from encouraging to frustrating.

"Come on!" Fulric clapped his hands.

"Stop yelling at me." He threw the concentration I had left.

"Get mad at me for all I care! Just do it! Lift her!"

I summoned the connection. The pull, the weight of it, evoked a guttural groan from me. The wall behind Merja vibrated.

"What is she doing?" Jahel asked.

"She couldn't..." Joris answered.

A grumble and snap, and the top of the wall leaned back, the front pulling up from the ground. The entire structure fell to the ground with a giant thud, one that shook through my boots and kicked up a cloud of dirt.

"That was intense." Merja slowly turned to me, a big smile on her dirtied face. "Do that again." She walked around the wall and bent down to one corner. "Come on, help me get it back up. Or could you lift it back up, Evella?"

I sat down in the dirt, the strain overtaking me.

"I think that's enough for today," Fulric said. "It'll be getting dark soon." I couldn't read whether he was impressed or disappointed in my maneuver.

"But—"

"Fulric's right," Arek cut off Merja. "We need to get back." He glared at her, and Merja gave in.

Fulric leant me a hand and helped me off the ground. He leaned toward my ear for a whisper. "I'm sorry if I upset you, but it was on purpose. Your power—it's tuned in to your emotions. Alora can sense that in you. You just need to find out how, and harness it the right way."

I nodded. He had upset me with the yelling, but it did evoke moving a large object. The largest yet.

Fulric touched Ulda's elbow. "I'd like you to stay a little longer. See how it's been going with not seeing your target."

Ulda nodded as the rest of us headed back to camp. It was part of the plan, leaving her behind. We didn't want the surprise spoiled, after all.

And we trusted one of our own to be alone with him. Not when he first introduced himself, of course, nearly two months ago. At first, the others had the same hesitations and suspicions I had in listening to his story.

What if he works for the king and it's a trap?

Or if he works with the Raiders?

Why was it hard to believe King Ronin caused the quakes? When I posed the question, most came to realize what I had. Father said alchemists and theologians tried to explain the phenomena as natural when they first started, but tall tales of dark powers spread. If it was easy to believe Raiders caused the quakes, it wasn't far-fetched that other people, like King Ronin and his henchmen, were the cause.

It was Arek who had the toughest time. I told him of the way we could know for sure.

"We'll be going to the palace once King Ronin summons us. We can check the tomb of King Crohl, and if he's missing a finger, we'll know."

"I can't do it, Evella," he had said. "Not with what the king has done for my family. Not with The Oath."

"Think of the ration shortage, Arek. Think of the despair that puts everyone in, no matter the terrin. Add to that the threat of quakes, not knowing when and where they'll strike. When people are desperate, they'll believe anything. They *want* to believe there's a dark enemy out there. The king is using that fear to keep people at bay, to keep them suspicious of anyone other than himself."

Arek remained in staunch disagreement. "I've lived in the palace almost my entire life. If it weren't for him, Nera wouldn't have a home, nor I. I can't go along with this."

"He was going to throw the two of you out when he discovered you."

"Yet he negotiated a way for us to stay."

Some negotiation, an adult trapping a child. I had placed my hand on his chest, his heart beating fast. "Open your mind to the possibility things aren't what they seem. You said so yourself, that there's so much out there, out here, that we don't know. What if we are wrong about the Raiders?"

"What if we are wrong about Fulric?"

Fulric showing himself to us, giving us his story, put his life on the island in jeopardy. We could've captured him as an enemy of the king and brought him in for judgment. Why would Fulric put himself in such jeopardy if what he said were lies?

The others had seen the logic that landed me at the same conclusion, no matter how many times and different ways I looked at it. Fulric was telling the truth.

At the very least, Fulric helped us work better as a team. He hunted and put effort into running the camp as much as anyone else. It was hard now to think of us here in Spokizar without him.

And Alora. It wasn't until Alora spent more time around them and displayed her way of communicating—ripples in the pond, watermarks in the dirt and on their clothes—that they started to believe she was a soul of a person. What was most extraordinary was her ability to communicate with Fulric. Ulda said it was because of their union, regardless that it was unofficial, that he could interpret her whispers. It wasn't something his ears registered, but rather his soul.

As if she knew my running thoughts, Alora swirled at my ankles and darted ahead as we pressed back to camp.

The camp's appearance had changed with Fulric's presence as well. A temporary hut sat behind Darvo's and Merja's quarters. It wasn't well protected from wind and quakes, but it was large enough to hold all of us under when rain hit at mealtimes—an occurrence that became more frequent as we approached spring. Fulric had built it quickly shortly after meeting us, to have some place to stay instead of going back and forth between camp and his cave.

The morning's fire had left only ash by early evening. I walked around it to my shelter, a good bit evolved over the past two months. Darvo had helped me repack mud between twigs. "Rodents are the worst," he'd said, doubling the thickness of the mud mortar at the base where the walls met the dirt floor.

Ulda had helped me with the door, twisting branches and filling in gaps with leaves and flowers. As the flowers wilted over time, she'd replace them before I even had a chance to let her know. Both improvements better shielded me from the peak of winter we had crossed. Nowhere near the severity of Corallon's winter, but Spokizar kept a constant chill in my bones. Even now, with the promise of spring at our doorstep, the increased wetness put a damper on my hopes of warming up.

"We'd better get going before she gets back." Arek stood in the middle of camp, eyeing the others. I gave him a nod and reached for my sling hanging above my bed. The rule was no weaponry on the training course, and I stuck to it. My blade remained under my pillow at most times. But the sling was different. It was like an old friend, a comfort I needed in my pocket whenever we were off the course. Plus, I didn't want to lose my skills with it. It had taken years to achieve what I had.

I pocketed it and made way for the shore. Most of the goodies had been stashed there over the past few days in preparation. Today was Ulda's seventeenth dawning. I knew her father passed away close to her fourteenth dawning, and had wondered if it evoked sadness every year since. I wanted this year to be different, and convinced the others—which didn't take much cajoling in the least—to help with this surprise feast. Ulda was such a kind soul, it was more than easy to do something nice for her.

Jahel and Joris got a large fire going, while Merja brought down supplies from her makeshift seaside canopy cache.

"Let me give you a hand." I saw the string of a satchel overhead and connected with it, lifting it off the platform and lowering it to the ground.

"I got one!" Darvo stood in the waves, knee-deep, with a flopping fish in his hand.

I lost control of the satchel, and it free-fell to the ground.

"Watch it!" Merja snatched the satchel. "There's eggs in there for the cake."

I wanted to say Darvo had distracted me. That the anticipation of Ulda arriving at any second gave me too much anxiety. "Sorry." I swerved to the fire and lifted a pan above the flames. Merja held out two eggs and I focused intently on cracking them along the side of the pan. It was intense, delicate work that took a lot of focus and much of my mental energy. But I cracked them and they sizzled as I poured crumbled wheatmeal in with them.

Merja waved a dull pink flower for me. She registered my confusion. "Adds some sweetness to it."

She crumbled it in her hands, and I guided the pieces over the frying pan cake, the mush barely rising but smelling delicious. I gave room for the twins to cook the fish Darvo caught over the fire, and Arek busied himself with critters of the forest. I had no idea what he had planned but knew he was up to something.

"She's coming!" Darvo shouted, defeating the purpose of keeping a watchful eye in the first place.

I set the pan aside, the rocky ground cooling it with a sizzle. The fish remained on the crude spit as the twins joined me, Merja, and Darvo. Arek commanded the critters, some of which could've provided for tonight's celebratory dinner—especially the hedgemunk, to line up.

Alora swept across the shore, covering us in a cloak of mist.

"Hey, don't put out the fire," Jahel said.

A portion of mist concentrated in a tight ball over Jahel, dropping a handful of water on his head.

"That's what you get for doubting her," Merja said between her chuckles.

Jahel wiped the water off his face, and another bolus of mist hovered over Joris.

"Hey, I didn't say anything." Joris put his hands up in the air. The mist ball retreated.

Ulda's voice emanated from the direction of the pathway with Fulric's, laughing over something. Alora swept away, unveiling us in front of them.

"Delightful Dawning!" Darvo shouted it first, the rest of us together after him.

"Oh my goodness!" Ulda placed her hand over her heart. "I didn't even realize you all knew."

Arek swished his hands in the air, and his critters broke into a chorus. It was a chattering of squeaks, squeals, and the occasional snort from the hedgemunk that faintly resembled an old simple folk song, the lyrics long lost.

When they finished, Ulda clapped joyously. "That was perfection. Thank you, Arek." She wrapped her arms around him and held him tight.

I turned to the twins. "Fish ready?"

It was truly a feast for us. We had fish, smashed root vegetables, a surprise from the twins of wheatmeal ale, not to mention the rarity of a cake. It turned out more like a sweetened cracker, the fire having charred the edges, but it was too good of a time to care.

The twins, Darvo, and Merja had gone from food to drink, talking loudly and jibing each other around the fire. Ulda and Arek sat together, Ulda shaking a chunk of seaweed on the sand, while Arek guided a gully bird to chase it. I was genuinely happy to see Ulda cheerful on her dawning.

In watching them, there was a special bond between Ulda and Arek.

They had been the first two on the island. Of course they'd know each other better than anyone else here. But I couldn't dull the sting their connection brought me.

I walked away from the warmth of the fire down the shore, taking a seat on one of the larger rocks separating part of the shore from the forest. The coolness of the air brought me back to reality. Tonight was a party, but tomorrow would bring more training. Fulric pushing my power to its limit. How much more could I take? I had made enormous progress, but how would I know when I'm done? When can I return home? Ulda's dawning was a happy occasion, but it made me think of Wren and Tulla, their dawnings coming in the spring and summer. Would I still be here, trying to do the impossible?

"Hey." My heart skipped in surprise at Arek's voice. "Can I join you?"

I nodded as Arek walked over the large rocks, finding one near me to sit on.

"That was kind of you to do this for Ulda."

"I can only imagine how it would feel, being on this island as long as she has." I looked over at him. "As long as you have."

He sighed. "I've had my time off it, at least. Getting a certain other Soulmage to join us."

"You mean you didn't threaten—I mean, recruit the others?"

"Will never let that go." He leaned back propping his hands on a rock behind him, his smile glowing in the moonlight.

"I'm teasing."

"I know." His smile faded, his eyes focused and intent on me.

"Speaking of teasing, I saw you there with Ulda. Plant versus animal?"

"Just having some fun."

I cleared my throat. I didn't want to put Ulda in a compromising position, but he deserved to know. To at least consider. "You know she cares deeply for you, right?"

He turned his stare down to his feet.

"She told me, shortly after I first arrived, that she was quite enamored with you when she first came to the island. That since she discovered you're an Oather, she'd let it go." Down the coastline, Ulda danced seaweed over Darvo who lay in the sand, playing dead and resisting laughter from the tickling. "I'm not sure it's entirely gone."

Arek scooted nearer. "I'm aware of her feelings, whether she knows I am or not."

"And..." I didn't know how to put it. The words came out slowly, laboriously. Ever since the night of the lake, something had changed. But I hadn't been able to face it, not with all the training, with Fulric around, working on bettering our shelters, arguing about the king. It was the first quiet moment in a whirlwind of days, weeks, that I could address it head on. "Do you feel the same for her?"

Arek looked up at the stars, as if they held his answer. Maybe they did. Maybe someone's Soulmagic was to read them, interpret what they saw here from afar that we could not in the midst of it.

The rock beneath me rattled faintly, the trees behind us shaking a hair.

"Did you feel that?" I asked.

Arek nodded. "Must've been a quake farther away, off the island."

I bit my lip, the turn of conversation unpleasant. It only served as a reminder of why we were here, the training, being away from my family, trying to discover my full power. It was overwhelming.

"Hey." Arek crept closer, so close we were almost hip to hip. His hand grasped mine, the warmth comforting and aching. "I love Ulda. I do."

"I see."

"But not as you're picturing it. I love her as a friend loves a friend."

"Oh, right. Because that's all you can do, having taken The Oath."

He squeezed my hand lightly. "There's only one person that I've felt differently for. That I've connected with in a way I never thought possible."

He reached up, touching my cheek. I wanted to cry and laugh, to blurt out everything I was feeling. He leaned in close, the distance agonizing. My lips were drawn to his, ready for this moment, ready to be touched. To connect. For a second, my worries about the king, my family, The Oath, disappeared. There was a heat between us, a pull that tugged at my heart. I closed my eyes, waiting. Waiting...but he didn't reach me. I opened my eyes.

He backed off, face pained as if one of Merja's arrows hit him.

"What is it?" I asked.

"—un!"

I slipped out of the dizzying confusion of the moment.

"Run!" Joris waved his hands running along the beach. "Head to the woods!"

My heart flung in my throat. "What's going on?"

"He must see something in the dark we can't."

I heard it. A loud collection of noises, a rumbling, deafening, powerful roar.

"It's a wave!" Arek grabbed my hand and rushed to the woods. I turned around, the ocean looking no different.

But the stars. I couldn't see the stars. Or the faint glow of Elsinea across the water.

"Hurry!"

The rocks made it nearly impossible to run. I had to focus on each step, desperately wanting to see what was behind us.

The twins bolted with Fulric to the woods. Ulda swooped in the air above their heads, retreating to the trees.

"We need to get far in and high up."

I turned around, white foam rolling down a wall of water, sucking the sea in its pull, extending the beach.

A swath of gray enveloped the shore, stretching from rocks to sand.

"Alora!" I shouted at the foolish spirit, the words lost in the catastrophic splash of the wave, water flooding the beach, hitting my back. I lost grip of Arek, the breath knocked out of me as I turned in tumult underwater.

The swell crested and dropped me. I found footing in the rushing water, holding onto a tree trunk I had luckily missed hitting. Arek's head popped up, his arm waving he was unharmed. I scanned for the others and heard shouting far away, above me.

Ulda waved from a canopy and pointed to the twins on another tree. Fulric tipped his knife in salute near them.

That left Darvo and Merja. My heart sank at the thought. Had Darvo snapped out of his death in time to run?

But my worry was short-lived as Darvo waded through the slowing rush, the water up to his waist. He dunked his head in the water and came back up, taking a few more steps before repeating.

He was looking.

For Merja.

I let go of the tree trunk, the current slower but still carrying me landward. I pumped my arms hard, legs straining to walk through the water. I lowered to my shoulders, swimming giving me a better chance to make it to Darvo without being utterly exhausted.

"Where is she?" I yelled.

"I last saw her back there." Darvo pointed behind him. "But she would've been carried this way. Right?"

I nodded, while Darvo took another dunk underwater.

She would've been carried this way. If she had been free to float.

I pushed against the current, out toward the sea. My legs burned, boots struggling for grip. I lowered in the water, not able to see anything. I waved my arms around. Nothing.

Taking another breath at the surface, I lowered again, stepping a pace further out. My arms flailed about, hoping, wishing to hit something. This time they had.

A boot.

I clasped it, inching my hands up to an ankle, knee, to a body. I resurfaced for another breath and clung to Merja, lifting her up. Something held her down. I reached around her back. A fallen tree's limb hooked onto her shirt's quiver. I tried tearing the shirt, breaking the branch. I couldn't separate the two.

I arose again, Darvo pulling his way toward us, but making little progress. "Please, Evella!" he shouted.

The cold water numbed my body, my lungs. I took three quick breaths before taking a long inhale and dove down. I tugged on Merja but nothing. Either I was going to save her, or we'd both die—her from being stuck, me from exhaustion and cold blood.

The anger in me grew. Anger that this happened on Ulda's dawning.

Mad that another quake was ready to cause more deaths. It had been too long for her to hold her breath underwater. She wouldn't last much longer.

The rage multiplied, and I stuck out my hand.

For all the Spirits, and whatever nonsense out there, get up! Get up! Reil slipping away. King Ronin and his smug smile with his ring, lying to my face. The destruction on Corallon, Midmarea, Elsinea. The images flashed in my mind as I begged for Merja's life.

Get up! I let out a scream with the connection.

Merja's torso lifted, rising away from the bottom, creating a swell at the surface. She bobbed there, face above the water, as Darvo arrived and clasped her in his hands.

I gasped for air, breathing for dear, sweet life. One last look at Merja —was that branch still stuck to her?—before arms fell around me, lifting me out of the water. I was carried toward the trees, Arek's face a wet blur above me in the darkness, then jostling. He was running.

Dry land.

He set me down, hand on my face. "Evella? Can you breathe? Are you all right?"

I opened my eyes then closed them. A light smack on my cheek, and I opened them again. I blinked away the blurriness.

"Arek?"

"It's me." He let out a chuckle of relief.

"I'm fine. Just exhausted." I moved to sit up, and he helped me. "Where's Merja? Is she all right? And Alora?"

Alora lowered close to the ground, condensed yet clearly unharmed.

"Good," I said. I hadn't known if the wave would've broken her apart, dissipated her into nothingness.

She swerved out of the way, and behind stood Darvo, his back turned to us. Hard coughs were let out, and Darvo lowered himself over Merja.

Then her voice. "If I'm going to die, it won't be from drowning. It'll be from your crushing hugs."

I crawled my way to where she lay and scooted by Darvo.

"Evella saved you," Darvo said.

Merja looked up at me. "Is that right?"

"Her power did it." Fulric stood over us. "She lifted you with her power."

I shook my head. "I—"

"It doesn't matter how it happened." Arek placed his hand on my shoulder. "Just that you two are all right."

I barely had the energy to stand, let alone argue with Fulric. I could've connected with the tree branch, or even the water. There was no way of knowing how I did what I did.

"I'm just glad our magpie is all right," Ulda said.

Merja closed her eyes for a second and took a deep breath. "I'm going to let that one go, Ulda. Being your dawning and all."

Ulda smiled, content she won the small victory over Merja.

"Can you walk?" Darvo reached out a hand.

Merja swatted it. "I'm fine, really. Let's just move on from it, shall we?"

"Yes, Darvo," I said, making my own move to stand. "Don't make a fuss over it." I looked at Merja and smirked. "After all, we're the safest lot in Elsinor."

For the first time, I made Merja laugh with me.

CHAPTER
EIGHTEEN

"Are you sure we've been summoned?" I set my fork down on my empty breakfast plate and floated my mug up to my hand for a sip.

"Positive. King Ronin summons by way of pigeon, and there's been a red one up there all morning." He pointed up to the forest canopy, a red bird to the left of Merja's shelter sticking out against the dark rich colors of the brunsam fir.

"Kind of an annoying one if you ask me." Merja cleared her plate over the fire. "Been chirping up a storm all morning."

"Red means an immediate summons."

"Immediate? What do you think it is?"

Arek shrugged, the weight of the summons showing on his forlorn face. "He's never sent a red one before."

"Do you think it has to do with last night's quake? That it happened on Elsinea?"

"It for sure happened on Elsinea." Fulric spoke with a full mouth. "That wave was a direct consequence of a quake, and by the direction of it, it could've only been Elsinea. And a bad one at that."

"I hope no lives were lost." Ulda had been quiet all morning, perhaps recalling the anniversary of her father's death, now that a party didn't distract her.

Fulric stood, wiping his mouth with his hand. "You know what this means, don't you? This is your chance. To confirm the truth."

Arek's demeanor grew more morose, but Fulric was right. We needed the proof he swore we would find. Then we'd know for sure our true enemy.

We left camp as soon as I gathered my cloak, blade, and sling, heading for the western shoreline. The others followed, wanting to assess last night's damage and see what could be salvaged.

Everything was waterlogged—the stone shore, the rocks with their pools of seawater, the soggy forest floor. Thankfully the surge of water only made it halfway to camp. If the quake that caused it had been any bigger, the circumstances would've been different.

The most frightening aspect was seeing the debris carried over from Elsinea. Scores of wood used in buildings, an entire door, boots, a toy doll, a wagon wheel, even wreckage of a boat. And that was what they found within moments of arriving.

Arek spoke to the snowcats, reassuring them of the journey we were about to take across Mariner's Gauntlet to Elsinea.

Fulric grasped my wrist and I his in a congenial goodbye. "Don't worry about the others."

"She never worries about me." Merja winked as she carried wood Darvo had chopped. Several trees had fallen near the shore from the wave, and chopping them not only helped with shoreline cleanup but provided fuel for the camp's fire. Once it dried out.

Fulric put a hand on my shoulder and leaned closer. "Allow yourself to be proud of how far you've come. Trust yourself and your instincts, especially around the king."

I gave a faint smile and parted with him, joining Arek on the sled.

"The usual?" he asked, pointing to the back.

"Sure."

Arek positioned his feet in the harnesses and kneeled up front while I sat in the back. We didn't have the sack to bring with us. This was merely a trip to report back to King Ronin, hopefully to return by this evening.

Oh, and to prove the king caused The Quake, killed his own father and sister—her body, at least—and continued causing quakes to instill fear in his people.

I clasped my arms fully around Arek's waist. The ride in—or swim in —months ago hadn't been a pleasant one. At present the waves were roughest closer to Spokizar's shoreline, and we needed a great deal of energy from the snowcats to crest them.

Fulric sensed my thoughts. Was that his power? Did he possess Soulmagic in the sense he could listen to people's thoughts? Or was he just intuitive, as much as a human could be? He swore he was not a Soulmage, but the issue of completely trusting him remained.

"Alora will help you at the start. She won't wander too far off, but she can take you out to open water."

At this, the mist rolled by him, spreading around the sled. Alora moved ahead of the snowcats, the tail end of her density still enclosing us, as she somehow tamed the waves lapping on shore.

Arek commanded the snowcats, who swam furiously through the roughest patches. It wasn't nearly as bad as the way in, but it did shake and jostle the sled, forcing me to tighten my grip on Arek.

As the water calmed into softer rivulets, Alora backed off in goodbye before receding back to Spokizar.

"Are you all right?" Arek asked.

"Yes." The word betrayed me in its lack of strength out of my mouth. We were about to take the king's hospitality, use it against him and invade a tomb that all Elsinor would see as sacrilege, to implicate the king.

"It will be all right." His voice was almost as betraying as mine.

"I'm scared we're in danger just setting foot into the palace, knowing what we may know. I mean, what if we don't know all the Soulmagic capabilities the king's men possess? Or even the king himself? What if one of them can infiltrate our thoughts? Read what we now know?"

Arek's shoulders slumped. "We can't know for sure. The best thing to do is try not to think about it."

"Oh good. Try not to think about what we're doing as we're doing it. That's great."

Arek's chuckle flickered his stomach beneath my grip. "We can only help what we do know. And we do know that Haro remembers everything, so be careful what words you choose to say in front of him."

I nodded, perhaps something Arek could feel on his back as I rested my head on it. The memory of last night, before the wave, surfaced again. Heat flushed my cheeks, my hands gripping him, thinking of how close his lips had come to mine. I savored it for a second before remembering his reaction, near repulsion, and pushed it away.

"Speaking of Haro." I cleared my throat, taking in the cold air to bring my head back to harsh reality. "I thought I'd get him talking while you go to the crypt." We had already agreed Arek was the best to go, since he knew the palace grounds, especially the underground, better than me. Plus, someone needed to distract anyone from discovering him. "Maybe I can get him to share what he knows about King Crohl's death." How I would conjure that out of him, no idea.

A small wave smacked the sled, splashing over the sides. Arek made an adjustment with the snowcats, and we angled more to the south.

"It depends on how young he was when his powers appeared. I know he's old enough to have been around the king during that time, but did he have his memory powers then?" Arek shrugged beneath his cloak.

Soulmagic held many mysteries, including its origin. It seemed like something you either had or didn't, but in talking with the others, Soulmagic didn't always present itself clearly when born. Perhaps it took time for the soul to bond with something in the outside world, to make a connection. Or that for some powers, we're too young to realize what we can do, or have no trigger to alert us of the power until we're older.

For Merja, as a crawling baby, she couldn't get lost. Her parents stopped worrying about her when she roamed freely about the town in daylight and arrived back at her house before supper. But for the twins, they didn't discover their powers until they were walking toddlers. Jahel discovered his first, after learning Joris was deathly afraid of the dark at night. He taunted his brother during the day, darkening his room until

Joris cried or promised Jahel his dinner ration if he stopped it. The taunting didn't last long, for once Joris could control his reaction to the dark, he discovered his special vision. Much to Jahel's chagrin.

As for me, I was older than that. Perhaps six or seven. It was around the time I both got tired of relying on others for help and was asked by Father to contribute to the family with work. When my arms got tired of holding the water bucket, I let my mind do it. I could carry firewood in both arms and a few extra branches to reduce the times I had to go back to the wood pile.

Once Father discovered what I was doing, he was both in awe and worried. He said I had an amazing gift, but not everyone would think so. That I couldn't use it in public anymore. For the most part, I had listened. Until Reil convinced me otherwise.

What did Father think of me now? Did he imagine me living with a ragtag bunch of Soulmagi, openly practicing our magic? Or did he think I lived serving the king in the luxury of the palace—a scenario I had once foolishly envisioned?

"Wish we had Alora's help last time we crossed." Arek's voice carried cleanly through my thoughts.

I nodded. My fears of the journey on the sea were unwarranted. With Alora's help at the start, and with the low clouds and near lack of a breeze, the sea was unusually calm. It almost beckoned us to come back to Elsinea.

I didn't know what the king wished to learn about our training, nor did Arek. We quizzed each other on questions he might ask, and devised answers that would sound pleasing enough on our progress yet also show the need for more time. We wouldn't be lying. We did need more time, whether Fulric was telling the truth or not.

Instead of boarding the snowcats up on the far western shore across the terrin with Samish, Arek said we'd head for the closer, eastern shore. But as we approached, my jaw dropped, the breath taken out of me.

A large chunk of land had disappeared into the sea. It was as if an enormous beast took a bite as wide as an hour's walk across. Debris still fell into the water from the ramshackled huts and houses along the edge. It was hard to believe it didn't take several lives last night. The thought sickened me, the anger I had felt helping Merja returning, sending a tingle through my hands.

"I've never seen one so bad." It was all Arek managed to say as we turned south, finding stable ground to dock. We disembarked, and he tied the snowcats next to a group of horses by the entrance to the market. The few horses nearest them backed into each other, side stepping away from the scary beasts. It was laughable now, knowing how calm and tame the snowcats were under Arek's presence. Did they stay that way when we were out of their sight?

I followed him through the sea of people in the marketplace. The gray day with low wind made for a musty, muddy experience through the narrow dirt roads of the village. Was it ever empty there? Or did there need to be people pressing between one another, elbows jabbing into hips, for there to be enough business to keep the shops open? The chatter I did catch contained whispers and rumors about the quake—if so and so survived, how this person saved that person, and that poor family that lost everything. The mood turned somber when holy house bells chimed. By the third set of chimes I wanted off the island, away from death.

My heart quickened the nearer we came to the castle, the clamoring of people enclosing me. Arek grabbed my hand, and I didn't let go, letting him guide me through the densest part until we arrived at the palace gate. Again we took the turret to the right, and he stopped me before we entered the first courtyard.

He let go of my hand and touched my shoulder. "We need to be seen as strong. Confident. The king is very perceptive. We can tell him all we want about how we've improved, but he'll notice in our body language if we're scared or weak."

"Strong," I said, nodding my head. "Confident." I stood a little taller, and Arek tapped my shoulder in approval before we walked together through the first courtyard. Confident was not the word I'd use to describe my mental state, but maybe walking with my shoulders and chin up would help. That, or I looked like a fool.

We stepped beneath the walkway dividing the palace quarters in half. The open doorway to the basement let out the dizzying smell of lunch being prepared. My stomach growled but I ignored it, my head still processing the loss this terrin went through.

We walked briskly to the grand turret, two guardsmen nodding to Arek and eyeing me but letting me pass. The stained-glass windows were backlit in the walls of The Great Hall but the doors were closed. I had worried how I'd seek out Haro, separate him from the king, but there he was with his pointed chin and hooked nose, standing guard like a tall vulture.

He reached out his hand and placed it low on my collar. It felt poisoned, as if he were branding me, and I wanted to shake it off.

"His Greatness is in an important meeting right now. There's always quite a commotion after a quake." Had he rolled his eyes? Are quakes a pesky nuisance to him? "He wanted me to tell you he will see you shortly and hopes not to keep you waiting long."

I ignored the impulse of grabbing his wrist and twisting his arm, letting the hand burn through my cloak. I smiled politely. "Thank you, for the message."

He grinned, a slimy venomous grin that soured my stomach.

"In that case, I think I will pay Nera a little visit." Arek stared me down while smiling.

"Oh, yes, that's a great idea," I said. "I'm sure Haro here will keep me company until the k—His Greatness—can see us." I had casually called him the king and even the untitled Ronin the past several weeks. *His Greatness* hurt to escape my lips.

Haro hesitated, stumbling over his words. "Well—but—I wouldn't keep His Greatness waiting."

Arek had already turned around and walked a handful of paces. "Don't worry. I'll be back soon enough."

I met the seedy eyes of Haro and managed a chuckle. "Um, remind me, you are the one who can see through others' eyes?"

He looked around, the hallway empty save for two women of the court giggling about something as they strolled through, then met my stare. "No, that's Icad. If you had my power, you would've remembered that."

I grinned, feigning embarrassment. "I do apologize, you are right." I touched his elbow, holding back the bile sliding up my throat. "Maybe you can help me, since you obviously are an expert in Soulmagic."

Just when I suspected he saw through the false flattery, he softened. "How could I possibly help you?"

"Well, we've been practicing the art of our powers these past months. I'm not sure if His Greatness informed you, but I trust you'll keep that between us, Soulmage to Soulmage." I winked.

"Of course I knew." His voice cast doubt. Surely it stung to know the king didn't always share plans with him.

"Oh good. We can speak freely then." I ignored his sour reaction. "I was wondering if the strength of power depends on how soon you realized you had powers. For instance, if I discovered mine as a young girl, does that put me at an advantage or disadvantage? When did you discover your powers?" I stepped away from the double doors of The Great Hall, leading him in a slow stroll.

"I imagine for you to be so powerful, working alongside His Greatness, you had to have been quite young. And with the nature of your ability, how did you know that what you remembered actually happened? With a power like that I figure it'd be hard to know what was real versus what you imagined."

He waved his free hand in disdain. "No, no. I always knew what I remembered to be true. Of course, people around me didn't want to believe it."

"No! You had to convince them?"

"It's how I came about working at King Ronin's side."

"Do tell." I afforded a glance at the doorway to the basement as we passed by. No Arek. Hopefully he was already at the tomb. The crypt was two levels below our feet, one level below the knowledge of most people in and out of the castle. If Arek hadn't lived here as a child, and disobeyed Nera endless times, he wouldn't have known of it either.

"I saw something when I was no older than three," Haro said. "When I reported it back to my mother, she did not believe me, not in the least."

"Oh no! You poor thing." For a second, I tried to picture what he looked like as a kid. All I could see was a scrawny child dressed in the same clothes with the same bird face. "Was it that outrageous of an event to believe?"

He checked in front and behind us, then leaned closer. His breath could've smelled like the sweetest of lilybuds but his gnarled teeth were repulsive enough to scare it away. "I witnessed a soul separating from its body." He raised his eyebrows at revealing the world's most astonishing secret.

The irony was that despite knowing such a thing possible, I couldn't believe he revealed it to me. Who else could he have been talking about other than Alora herself?

Fulric was telling the truth. Or if it wasn't Alora, at least the act of soul separation was confirmed.

"That is quite a tale." I shook my head. "But I still don't understand how that grew favor with His Greatness?"

"Ah." He wagged his finger. "My mother did not believe me, but... King Ronin did. He realized the usefulness of my ability, recalling every minute detail, and kept me at his side ever since."

"What about your mother?" My pacing stopped, and I turned toward him.

"What about her?" He snapped, angry at the question. "She didn't believe me. If she had, maybe she wouldn't have died a few years later, still working as a servant."

"Well." I thought through my words carefully. *Where the heck was Arek? He should be back by now.* "I understand what it's like for people to want to...mute your abilities. People who do not see the potential good in them." I patted his elbow before I let go with my other hand. The hand had turned numb from touching his repulsive body. "That is why we need to help each other, support one another."

His lip curled up at this, as if that were the last thing on Elsinor he wanted to do. "Yes. I suppose so."

"Haro?" A chubby man with thin legs waddled over. "His Greatness has finished and would like a word with you, before he forgets the details."

Haro sighed. "Very well." He gave a slight bow in departure and went off with the portly man to The Great Hall.

After that discussion, I definitely needed a dip in the lake when I arrived back at Spokizar.

I retraced my steps slowly, glancing at the basement doorway. This was it. If Arek didn't make it back before we were summoned, the king would question his whereabouts. And if he did make it back but we didn't have time to discuss—

I heard his panting before seeing him through the doorway. He slowed down, catching his breath while nodding to a man passing by.

He made his way over to me, and I continued walking instead of shaking the information out of him like I wanted to.

"What took you so long?"

"I could've used a bit of help with the stone lid."

My breath became heavier as if I had been the one running around the underbelly of the palace. "I spoke with Haro. He told me about seeing a soul slip from someone's body, something he watched happen when he was just a little boy."

"Never mind that," Arek said.

"Never mind? You do realize it could've been Alora he saw?"

Arek grabbed a hold of my hand, stopping my feet and my mouth, and everything in between. He opened his other hand. A broken handle, like that of a paintbrush, sat in it.

I held it, slowly turning it around to catch all sides of it. "I don't understand."

Arek took it back. "King Crohl is indeed missing a finger, and this was in the glove in its place. Ronin must've gone back to the body before it was lowered to the crypt." The truth and his emotion slapped me in the face. "It's all true. Fulric was telling the truth. I didn't want to believe it." His words trailed off, his head shaking. Tears formed in his eyes.

I wrapped a hand over his clenched fist. "We'll figure this out." I nodded, convincing him and myself. "Together."

My vision turned dark, and everything in my body disconnected from me. I had no thought. I floated in a black abyss without breath, without heartbeat, without fear.

The light in my eyes grew into full circles until I registered Arek's concerned face. I heard and felt my breathing again. My heartbeat.

"Evella, you there?" Arek shook my shoulders.

"What do you mean?" I stared at his hands, shaking me. "What just happened?"

Arek glanced behind him. Footsteps pulled further away.

"I think Icad got you. Whenever he slips into someone else, they go blank."

Repulsion overwhelmed me, and I clutched my stomach. It was one thing to have touched and flirted with Haro. It was another to have Icad violate my mind.

I shot Arek a worried stare. "He didn't see the handle, did he?"

"As soon as I realized, I slipped it in my pocket. He may know I have something, but not what. Even if he did, we can't know if he knows what it's from."

"What if he gets the king to ask you to empty your pockets?"

"Why—"

"Evella Trapper and Arek Meranath." A man stood outside the entrance to The Great Hall. "His Greatness will see you now."

It was the first time I heard Arek's surname. Learning it meant something—that I knew a piece of him he kept protected all this time. That I was a little closer to him than seconds ago. He returned my gaze with a 'keep it together' look.

I was supposed to keep it together, despite the chance of being compromised. But it was too late to do anything now.

It was time to see the king.

CHAPTER
NINETEEN

We entered the double doors to The Great Hall. Several members of the court lurked about, as if taking a much-needed break from a days-long meeting. They sipped on their wine and cider and chatted about this servant sleeping with that one, or compared their garments.

That was, until they saw me. Who knew what the king may have said about me or Arek to any of them. But with their stares and hushed whispers, they had some idea of who I was. Or my power.

Yet the king hadn't seen my ability in action. Did he simply believe I wielded power? Or was that part of his ability? Ulda had said something about Soulmagi sensing the gift in other people, and Fulric swore Alora could, even in the condition she was in.

"Ah, there they are." King Ronin extended a hand in welcoming. He wore a long white robe with golden swirl accents, an outfit that opposed the simple attire at our last meeting. One tailor fidgeted with the hem at his feet and another at the end of his sleeve. Ronin looked more like a wintry wizard than a king. Maybe the description suited him better, knowing what powers he possessed.

"So you've made it there and back with no issues?" His face read surprise.

It didn't sit well with me. "Is that unexpected?"

His mouth curled into a half-grin, and he opened his eyes wide. "Oh, no. I had every confidence in you. In others..." He tipped his head side to side.

"What do you mean others?" My stomach twisted, dread spreading over my body. "Were there others sent to Spokizar that didn't make it?"

The king dismissed the tailors with the flap of his arms. He stepped toward me and wrapped his arm around my shoulders. Not a word he spoke was trusted, especially after the discussion with Haro, and Arek finding the fake ring. Arek had been the toughest to convince, having grown up under the protection of the king. But even he believed Fulric now.

Arek looked at the king in disgust. Whether it was in reaction to knowing the truth, or the repulsion he felt seeing the king's arm around me, I wasn't sure. Either way, he had to tone down the anger and resentment or else we would be compromised.

The king stopped me in the far corner of the room, Arek standing next to me. He faced us both.

"You have to understand what we're up against." He glanced at Haro and Icad who stood behind us, making it more difficult for others in the room to see or hear what was being said. "If we are to defeat the Raiders, we need the most able Soulmagi in the land. We don't know how many are working with the Raiders, nor their abilities. We need not only Soulmagi, but survivors. If they couldn't make it from Elsinea to Spokizar, then they'd have no chance defeating Raiders."

"You let Soulmagi die?" I couldn't hide the resentment. It was too difficult. But maybe Raiders got to them first, which still was a negative outcome. Why would he let his enemy gather Soulmagi?

Arek nudged me before speaking. "I understand." He turned to me. "He's right, Evella. We need the strongest Soulmagi out there, ones who know how to survive on their own. If they couldn't make it across Mariner's Gauntlet then they wouldn't have made it far in training, let alone actual combat."

I wanted to smack him. He couldn't possibly believe the words coming out of his mouth, but he was very convincing. Which unnerved me more.

"Which brings me to why we're here." He turned to the king. "Our training has progressed immensely. We've gotten further in the past two months than all the time prior to it."

The king grabbed his shoulders briskly. "What great news this is. That's exactly what I wanted to hear, given that I have your first assignment."

Arek looked at me, and my ears filled with fuzz.

"What I tell you now, you must keep a secret. Only those who need to know have been told."

The heat of Arek's hand sizzled close to mine. I wanted to grab it, to squeeze the hate I had for this man out of me. He had made Arek lie to get me to come here. He'd been lying to his people all along about the quakes. How much needless suffering occurred under his reign?

"In reaction to the devastating quake that occurred last night, it is time I get all the players in one place. I've invited all the delegates of the terrins to come tomorrow night for a dinner. I've had to organize special passage for some to make it here on such short notice, but we need to act fast. It is time we unite against the Raiders. I would like the both of you to be there. It will take some delegates more convincing than others to join in on the cause. If you were to display your abilities, talk about your training and what you can do, I think they'd be persuaded to unite."

"Surely if they have all seen the effects of the Raiders, they would jump at the chance to join with you?" Staying another night in this place was about as pleasing a thought as jumping naked in the Stohl River. I had seen enough of the palace, the facade of a world the king continued to hide behind.

"That's not the only reason I want you here." He touched my shoulder and Arek's, squishing us together in a huddle. "I want all the trained Soulmagi to come. I've made sure that the right people knew of this news and spread it, ensuring it reached Raiders." He tipped his head down and looked up at us with his lilted eyes. "Tomorrow serves as a diplomatic dinner, yes, but also a strategic play. Raiders will want their chance at the delegates, but they won't get it since your team will interfere."

"Interfere?" Arek's voice rang out, and the king hushed him. "You want us to take on a possible large party of Raiders tomorrow night?"

"We're not ready." I shook my head. It wasn't a lie. How were seven Soulmagi supposed to overpower an unknown number of Raiders? "There could be a hundred of them."

"And we don't know how many Soulmagi they have," Arek said. "If they do indeed have any."

The king pointed a finger. "That's the thing. They will be surprised with your presence. They don't know how many you number, after all. We can use their surprise to learn what we're up against, how many souls they have in the fight."

"It's too soon." I pressed the knot in my forehead developing over my eyes.

"It's too dangerous, Your Greatness. I don't mean to be contrarian, but—"

"Then don't be." His hands traveled down our arms, petting the defiance off us. All it did was infuriate the rage in my gut. "You will have the full support of my guards to back you up. I think you'll find you are stronger, more capable than you think."

He fixed his eyes on me. Again, he implied knowing something about me that I didn't. Or he was overconfident in my abilities. It didn't matter. We weren't going to follow along with his mission that would likely wind up with us killed. He only needed to *think* we were going along.

I nodded to Arek. "He's right," I said. Arek looked at me as if I had lost half of my brain. "I think under the circumstances, under the pressure of having to defend ourselves, we will end up being stronger than we know."

The king clapped his hands together, finally not touching either of us.

"Plus, we need to know the strength of the enemy." I hoped Arek understood my meaning through my stare. His face went from shock and disgust to acceptance.

"Right, then." He nodded slowly. "We accept your invitation. We'll gather the others."

The king held up a hand. "I want to make it clear. Just the two of you are officially invited to the dinner. I can't have an army of Soulmagi show up. It would be too conspicuous. The others should be stationed outside the palace."

The words I had planned caught in my throat. My mind busied with possible scenarios. We had to reveal the truth about the king, and the dinner provided a perfect opportunity. All the terrin leaders there? Would there ever be a better opportunity to convince the world of his corruption and deception?

"I agree that we can't have all of us at the dinner."

"You do?" Arek bit his lip, at least giving me a chance to explain myself.

"But I think it's wise to let them within the walls of the palace. They'd have a better vantage point to survey the coast. You know the Raiders will most likely attack by sea. Plus, it would be easier to communicate with your men once they are spotted."

Arek's shoulders relaxed, and he afforded a tiny grin. "Evella is right. They'd be safer inside and could act quickly when Raiders are spotted. Out there they'd have to fight the evening revelers, plus the darkness."

The king took a step back and stroked his beard. If he didn't approve, we'd have to devise a way for the others to enter the palace. If they had to sneak in, and Spirits forbid they got caught, any plans we'd make to expose the king would be ruined. I could almost kiss Arek for understanding my thinking.

"No." King Ronin stood tall. "It's too risky to have them here. I need them out there, beyond the palace walls, to protect us and protect the people. And on the off chance the Raiders attack by land, we'd be the better for it."

"But—"

The king held up a hand, shutting me up. "That is all. Haro here will give you a copy of the formal invitation. That will get you in the palace."

"The guards already know me," Arek said, side-eyeing me.

"My closest guards will be with me. All guests coming into the palace tomorrow night must have an official invitation and check their weapons at the gate. No exceptions. I look forward to seeing you tomorrow evening."

The king awaited our departure. Arek gave a stiff shallow bow, and I mimicked him, feeling stupid and dismayed.

Haro walked us out of The Great Hall and into the hallway surrounding it, stopping by the doors to the courtyard. He reached into his coat and pulled out an envelope, closed with the royal seal. "Do not lose this, or you will not be admitted." He looked at Arek, then me. "Even if I do know who you are."

"Ah, Haro. What happened to our kind sticking together?"

Arek elbowed me, and Haro sneered.

Arek accepted it, and Haro nodded to the doorway. I followed Arek out, happy to be out of the goon's presence and the king's, for that matter.

"I tried," I said low upon Arek's shoulder.

"I know." He walked swiftly toward the underpass. "I guess the good news is that we have an idea about the security for tomorrow."

"Is that good news?" My stomach rumbled, the smells from the basement kitchen reaching the courtyard. "What about Icad? Will he be able to plant himself in one of us, figure out what's going on?"

Arek took my elbow and led me to the underpass, stopping at the basement doorway. "As far as I can tell, he can only do it if you're in his sight. But we shouldn't take any chances. If either one of us sees the other glazed over, face frozen, stop what you're talking about and be rid of any evidence."

I nodded. "What are we going to do? How will we get the others in here?"

Arek shook his head. "I don't know. But we'll have to think of something. For now…"

He reached in his cloak pocket and took out the broken piece of wood. "Take this with you, to convince the others of the truth."

"What do you mean, take it with me? What about you?"

"I—" He looked behind him, at the doorway. "I have to get to Nera. She needs to know what's going to happen tomorrow night."

"What?" I held onto his sleeves. "You can't tell her anything, not a word about this. She can't know we're moving against the king."

"She needs to know. She needs a chance to leave here." Arek shook his head, eyes tearing up. Something worried him that I didn't grasp. "What if we do reveal the truth about the king, and he revolts? What if he executes every servant he has in retaliation?"

I hadn't thought of it. I hadn't had time to think a whole lot about what would happen after, when we had no plan for during.

"Please." He squeezed the handle in my hand, curling my fingers over it. "Tell the others and prepare. Do you remember where we left the sled and snowcats?"

I nodded. "Yes, but—"

"They'll listen to you."

"How do you know?" This was absurd. I had no idea how to guide the snowcats, let alone if they'd even get up off the ground when they saw me, or even bite me without Arek being around.

"Trust me."

"I do." It came out, and I realized I meant it. I did trust him, despite the deception at the start. If he had truly been wicked, he would've never told me the truth about any of it. "But that doesn't mean I can command the snowcats. How can you be so sure?"

He ran his hands through his hair, frustrated at arguing with him, or worried about the lack of a plan, or what would become of Nera. "Because they listen to anyone who has taken up space in my soul."

I had opened my mouth to argue with whatever he was going to say. It stayed open, the words hitting me, echoing in my head.

"Please, Evella. Do this for me."

I couldn't say no with the pleading in his eyes. But I couldn't leave him. I didn't want to leave him. We hadn't been apart for months. Not having him with me would feel empty, wrong. "How about I stay with you, help you speak to Nera?"

"No." He shook his head adamantly. "It's something I must do. She doesn't trust anyone but me, and…we've been a little family for so long. The truth must come from me."

I swallowed hard, eyes turning blurry. "I'll wait. I'll wait here, or outside the palace for you."

"Please." He pressed my hands together in his, the wood still in my grasp. "You need to get to the others so you can plan. You're wasting time arguing with me."

I shook my head. It wasn't right. At some point, during our journey to Elsinea, to Spokizar, during training, whenever it was—we formed a team. It wasn't right leaving him behind.

"Evella, I want you to know I wouldn't have been so cruel, to you or your family, if I had known the truth. If I had known the king was—"

"You couldn't have known." Despite my efforts, the tears rolled down my cheeks.

"I'm sorry for that. You and your family deserved better."

I slapped his shoulder, pushing away the tears. "I already forgave you for that, you big idiot."

It made him break his pitiful face, lifting his mouth into a smile.

"Why does this feel like goodbye?" I immediately regretted erasing his smile.

"It's a temporary one. You'll do great with the snowcats, and I have trusted friends in Elsinea who will help me get back. It will be alright."

We had come so far and faced so much, it was nearly silly to think we couldn't manage to get back to Spokizar safely.

Separately.

"I'll only be a half day's ride behind you." He lifted my hands and gave them a soft kiss.

It did feel like goodbye.

I suppressed my emotions and walked through the far courtyard, out the palace gates, and into the market.

Perhaps the snowcats would sense that Arek had taken up space in my soul.

CHAPTER

TWENTY

I pushed the sled to the edge of the water, the leading snowcats completely swimming. Arek was right—they had rattled with excitement when I arrived, and it took effort to settle them down. I wondered if they were awaiting Arek's arrival so I spoke to them.

I had no idea if they understood the words out of my mouth. But I used them anyway. "Arek will be coming after us. He wants you to take me safely to Spokizar."

Whether it was understanding or some soothing power of my voice, they calmed down and moved into formation in front of the sled.

I didn't know Arek's hand twists and flicks. Yet again I didn't have a soul connection with them, so I guessed it wouldn't have mattered.

But they swam northeast. They knew where to go and how to get there, and I left my trust in them. I secured my feet through the loops and sat on my knees like I'd seen Arek do so many times. It wasn't the most comfortable of positions. My feet grew numb and my knees ached to be straightened shortly after we reached open water.

There were times on the island I had been out of Arek's presence. Many times. But this was different. We were truly apart, separated by the sea. The further I ventured atop the waves the stronger the pull to retreat, to go back to him.

He was right, I had to let the others know the truth, and we needed to devise a plan fast. We had just over a day to come up with a trap for the king, a way he'd confess, or at least not deny allegations against him.

Yet it still pained me to leave Arek behind. I was alone on the water. I couldn't count how many times I had been alone on Corallon, hunting, trapping, off to trade. Just going on a walk. But I never felt lonely. After Reil's death, I didn't long for someone to be at my side. He was with me along the hunt, if only in spirit, when I wanted him to be. Knowing he was gone, I preferred to be alone.

But this loneliness, it clutched my heart. Scenarios crossed my mind in which Arek died, or was captured. Nera could turn him in after revealing the truth. I should've stayed behind. But this is what he asked of me and…I had to do it.

The wave crests formed white foam, playing tricks with my eyes—a bird bobbing on the water here, a silvery fish reflecting light there. But they were only ripples mixed with imagination.

Or were they? Something wasn't right. Water swelled nearby, and the snowcats grew antsy. I looked over my shoulder, sensing the disturbance.

A rusted brown vessel emerged from the water. It didn't rise completely, exposing only the top deck.

A dark figure emerged from a porthole. He wore black and crouched low on the surface of the ship. He stared at me while shouting commands below deck.

The craft gained on me.

"Faster. We may be in trouble." I didn't care how foolish it sounded to speak to the snowcats, especially with the water's lapping and splashing around our vessel. The wave conditions worsened as we drew nearer to Spokizar, threatening a repeat of the first trip there. Glancing over my shoulder, we needed to move faster.

"Come on!" I jostled the reins, unsure whether the snowcats could feel anything with the water drowning out most of the senses.

The vessel behind me had to be a Raider vessel. There was no other explanation. Ferries between terrins weren't submersibles, and no ferry existed between any terrin and Spokizar. The king said so himself—Raiders were alerted to his precious dinner party tomorrow evening. Why wouldn't they arrive early to go undetected? They could've watched our arrival and my departure today without anyone knowing.

My heart raced and stomach jumbled like a cork on the waves.

The man remained crouched low on the vessel, aimed right for me.

"Arrows," I said to anyone who would hear, which amounted to one person. *Me.* The man didn't shoot arrows this time or threaten with any weapon. Perhaps I could knock them out of his hands or guide them away if he had. What was his purpose? To catch up to me and then what? Kidnap me? Take me in the belly of that ship? Surely he had a knife or blade, something if he were planning on doing that. And why was there only one this time? Why not more if they wanted to overtake me?

I had the notion to slow down and let him catch me, just to sort out the questions running in my head. *Don't be foolish, Evella.*

I half-praised reaching the roughest part of the sea, closer to Spokizar. The spot Arek and I began to lose control of the sled and had tipped over.

"Not today." I held tight to the reins. The shoreline blurred, and I blinked. It wasn't my eyes playing tricks. Alora was coming.

She knew it was me, stretching out to protect me in her blanket of mist.

My quickened speed hadn't won much distance between me and the Raider. Would he also take advantage of the calmer seas Alora afforded me? Did the distance give enough time for Alora to retreat and the rough seas to return?

It didn't matter now. If he followed me onto shore, certainly the others would siege war on him. They did it for me and Arek, after all, despite being in jest.

"Come on, a little farther." The snowcats thrashed wildly, vigorously paddling me to shore. Alora formed a crescent around the back of me, pushing the seas into a flat calmness, fending off the roughness to meet the Raider. I understood now why she attempted to quell the wave last night. She was able to have an amazing amount of influence on the regular sea. And who knew, maybe without her presence the consequences would've been worse.

The first snowcats reached land, and I unharnessed my feet, leaping into the water which reached my calves, and pulling the sled up onto shore. Alora remained out over the water, too thick to see the Raider vessel.

Ulda rushed to greet me with a hug.

"That's a better welcome than tripping me with vines."

Ulda grinned bearing her small perfect white teeth. "I can do that too if you want."

I chuckled. "No thanks. Here, can you help me with them?"

I crouched to unharness the snowcats and with Soulmagic guided the sled completely out of the water. I had to confirm I could use Soulmagic when it counted, under siege. Otherwise, what was the point?

Ulda helped corral the cats, who didn't mind her gentle hands and demeanor.

"We need to get off the shore quickly. I was followed by a Raider."

"You sure?"

I nodded. "Alora calmed the seas for me, but I think she's trying to confuse him, get him lost in the fog."

Ulda put a hand over her brow, squinting to see through the dense mist.

"I don't see anything," she said.

"Me neither." I dismissed the snowcats, and they trampled through the stone shore to the forest, knowing their way to camp. "He could've gone back underwater."

"Then he wouldn't be able to get too close to shore," Ulda said. "Too shallow. He may get stuck."

"Maybe that was Alora's plan." I smiled at the thought. How could a mist think of a plan? It didn't matter the practicality, because this mist was the remnant of a living soul. I couldn't explain that, either.

Alora rolled closer, until she cut through me and Ulda, and floated into the forest.

"Thank you!" I looked at Ulda and shrugged. "Think she heard me?"

"I'm sure she knows you appreciated it."

The water's surface left only cycles of waves and swells. No rusted vessel. No dark figure.

Ulda put her hand on my shoulder. "If he did come back, we'd more than defend ourselves." She smiled, content with alleviating my worries.

"Wait." She looked behind me, then furled an eyebrow. "Where's Arek?"

I smashed the pocket of my cloak, feeling the wood safely inside. "We need to gather everyone. I'll tell you everything then."

We marched through the forest to the camp, my boots squishing in their wetness, slipping here and there on the smoother rocks. Cheering and hooting sounded ahead.

The camp was unrecognizable. A black cloud lingered over the shelters, the fire all but vanished.

"What's going on?" I grabbed the hilt of my blade, a security I wouldn't be able to have on me, nor my sling, tomorrow evening.

"Hold on." Ulda gently touched my elbow. "They're practicing."

"Practicing?"

Fulric stepped out of the darkness, grin on his face. He took no notice of me or Ulda and turned back around to the dark cloud, knife in each hand. He slung them through the blackness, and I heard the howl of Jahel, along with a deep whistle of amusement from Darvo.

The black cloud vanished in a breath, and Joris stood with both blades in his hands, holding the hilts. A giant grin stretched across his face.

"Well done, brother," Jahel said.

"Thanks for the cover." Joris nodded at his twin.

"Impressive," Fulric said. "You have improved immensely in such a short period of time."

"I think it was always in me," Joris said. "I never got to test it out this much."

Fulric slapped a hand on Joris' shoulder, congratulating him on a job well done.

"Fine tuning your skills?" I asked.

"Evella!" Darvo grinned such a happy grin that I nearly hugged the big oaf.

Merja crossed her arms in her usual stance. "Made it back in one piece, I see. What's the news? Where's Arek?"

Ulda nodded at me, wanting the answer to the last question as well.

"First of all." I scrambled through my pocket and pulled out the handle. "This was found on King Crohl's body."

The twins rushed over, and even Ulda wanted to see the broken wooden thing.

Merja eyed Fulric. "Oh look, she brought us a souvenir."

Fulric approached, examining the handle. "What does this mean?"

I took it back and held it out for the others to see. "Arek brought this up from the crypt. King Crohl indeed was missing a finger, and this was put in its place. He was buried with hands gloved, and no one was close enough to notice the missing finger hole had a wooden rod in it to fill it up."

"He deserves to die for what he did," Fulric said.

"And what he's still doing." I nodded at Fulric before looking at the others. "King Ronin told us of others—other Soulmagi that he found that did not make it here to the island. The journey here was a test of their strength, a test some did not pass."

"How many others?" Ulda asked.

"I don't know. I don't know if they were captured or perished. I don't know if I want to know. If he can nonchalantly let Soulmagi die under his service, we have no reason to think he'll ever stop with the quakes. And tomorrow night is our chance to do something about it."

"Tomorrow night?" Fulric stepped closer. "What's tomorrow night?"

"The king is hosting a dinner for the eight delegates of the other terrins. He's using the excuse of last night's quake on Elsinea to bring them together. Which, to put it simply, was awfully destructive."

"I knew it," Fulric said. "Had to be, to create such a wave."

"Destruction aside, the delegates will all be in one place—the palace —at the same time. He plans on uniting them to lead a campaign against the Raiders."

"But they're not the ones causing the quakes," Fulric said.

"Can't exactly say they're guardian spirits either, can we?" Joris said.

"It doesn't matter." I waved my hand to shush them. There was only so much time to prepare. "Arek and I are invited to the dinner party. You all are to be there too, but not inside the palace. The king wants you to look out for Raiders. Information about the evening has been purposely leaked to them. The king expects an attack, which would only fortify his false reason for hosting the thing in the first place."

I expected interruption but they listened attentively. "Now, I don't know the exact details of how we will do it, but—"

"You have a plan!" Jahel said.

"No. I have an idea of what we need to do. Not so much a plan of how to do it."

"Go on, Evella." Fulric nodded in encouragement.

"With all the delegates there, it's the perfect opportunity to get the truth about the king out to everyone. I don't think we can just invade the dinner party and tell them. It must come from the king, in either a slip-up, or tricked into confession." I shook my head. The more I spoke the dumber it sounded. "Somehow, we get him to confess what he has done and continues to do. The delegates won't stand for it, and it'll be the end of his reign for good."

"And then what?" Merja put her hands on her hips. "Who replaces him? Or what system? It'll be lawless all around. Or something worse."

"Like living on Tusinda," Darvo chimed in. Merja nodded her head at him in agreement.

Jahel's faced turned red. "It has to be better than what we have now. A leader who willingly kills his people?"

I stepped in between them. "If we are going to do this, we need to start planning now. We don't have much time until the dinner."

"What about Arek?" Ulda said. "You didn't answer about him."

I let out a breath and pressed my lips together. It wasn't my place to tell them about Nera, and how and why he wanted to tell her. "He stayed behind a little longer, but is on his way. You have to remember, he grew up in that palace. He has some personal…belongings to gather. You know, if we're going to do this, his home won't ever be the same again." Their faces were a mix of eagerness, worry and excitement. "We *are* going to do this, right?"

Fulric took a step. "Yes, we are."

"We?" I asked.

"I'm going with you. Count me in. Consider me the delegate for Spokizar."

"Uninvited delegate," Merja said.

"You have my vote," Jahel said.

"Second," Joris said.

"What about Alora?" I said. "Leaving her on the island?"

"I didn't say I wouldn't come back." Fulric smiled with a wink. "I always come back to her." Alora appeared, swooshing around him in a cyclone until she drew a low giggle out of him. "All right, enough."

"And you all?" I asked.

Jahel and Joris looked at each other. Darvo grinned, and Merja gave a firm nod with a huff.

"It's settled then," Ulda said. "I'll finish preparing dinner, while the rest of you plot the demise of King Ronin." She giggled. "That has a ring to it, doesn't it?"

"Not anymore," Jahel said. "At least not for old King Crohl."

Joris heartily laughed at his brother, and Merja rolled her eyes.

Fulric rushed to his chest of goodies. Having lived on the island so long, he had quite a collection of items in various hiding spots. Most were either found scouting the coastline or handmade from skins, pelts, and plants. He retrieved a quill, and ink made from dirt and crushed berries, and some thin shaven tree cuts as parchment.

"Perhaps first we need to draw out the palace grounds." He drew a triangle and added details to it.

"Not quite." I pointed at the grand turret. "It's part metal and part wood, from the damage of The Quake. And here." I pointed to the sides. "There's another floor built on these for the court up here, and for servants over here."

Fulric tapped the quill on the parchment in frustration. He conceded. "Maybe you are better off to draw it."

"I—" I shrugged, but supposed no one else had been there as much as

I had. At least not in the basement. But they all had met the king, hadn't they?

"I can give you some of the details, some of the changes since The Quake. But there's one of us who knows every corner and nook in the palace, and that's Arek."

"Who's not here right now," Merja said.

The grip around my heart tightened at the reminder. "He should be here soon. In the meantime, this is the best we've got, so what are your ideas?"

"Dinner is ready." Ulda appeared behind Darvo, a breakable twig compared to his stature.

"Oh good," Jahel said. "I didn't want to plan the king's death on an empty stomach."

"We're not going to kill him," I said.

"What?" Merja asked. "Why not?"

"Like I said, we're going to expose him." Of course some didn't find my idea as appealing as death. "Death would be too easy an out for him. He needs to be seen for who he is, and live in that shame for the rest of his life. In confinement."

Jahel looked at his brother and smirked, with a head nod back and forth. They were pleased with the answer, but I needed the others to understand.

"Besides, if we killed the king, the people of Elsinor would never know the truth about him. We'd be seen as enemies and forever have marks on our backs."

"Wonder what that's like," Jahel said. "Being forever marked for the world to see."

Joris nudged him and shook his head.

"What? It was a joke."

"A bad one at that."

"We're the ones with permanent scars on our faces. Doesn't that give us permission to joke about them?"

"Let's eat before I give you another scar," Joris said.

Ulda seemed at her happiest when serving others. She grinned as we sat by the fire and ate the dinner she prepared—hedgemunk and parsnip stew. I silently hoped it wasn't the hedgemunk that took part in her dawning song.

I managed to shuffle the food around my bowl and nibble on a few bites, my mind elsewhere.

"Are you worried?" Ulda plopped down beside me, and I scooted over a smidge to give her room.

"About how much time do we have?" The skimmed-over answer didn't satisfy her. Ulda was an honest, open person and didn't understand why anyone would be otherwise. "I'd be lying if I said no. I've never done anything like this before."

She dipped her head, staring at me with those big green eyes. "I meant about Arek."

I shook my head in defiance of my brain. "No. He said he'd be half a day behind me, and I believe him."

Ulda took my hand in hers. "You've barely eaten a thing. I can see when worry eats somebody up. And you're a worry buffet tonight."

I sighed and released my hand from her loose grip. "I just—it was hard to leave him. I still think maybe I should've stayed."

"Arek will be fine. You'll see." She smiled softly. "You did the right thing in coming when you did. Now we can have a plan, and if we get anything wrong with the palace, Arek can let us know."

I nodded, half tuning out and half not believing he'd be back tonight.

"He'll be fine," she continued. "I swear it."

"How can you be so sure?"

She set her plate on the ground and slapped her hands on her knees. "Because Arek somehow got Evella Trapper off that island of Corallon, to come train with a bunch of misfits on Ghost Island."

She managed to get a chuckle out of me. "It is a pretty amazing feat when you think about it."

Ulda nodded while grinning. "That's how I'm sure."

TWENTY-ONE

" I know with certainty this hallway leads out here." I pointed to the growingly detailed map of the palace, indicating the basement kitchen passageway's link to the hallways wrapping The Great Hall. "I know there are other hallways branching out from this main one, but I can't tell you where they go. If any of them lead near an entry point or even outside, then we could use them to our advantage."

We stood in Fulric's makeshift shelter, the sun gone beneath the horizon. The little heat it gave off during the day went unappreciated until night struck. The darkness worried me. It was difficult enough to get to Spokizar from Elisinea, but Arek would be doing it in the dark. What if Raiders still patrolled the waterway? Would he spot them before they spotted him?

"Evella?" Merja asked.

Ulda nudged me, and I snapped back to the conversation. "What?"

Merja was losing patience. "You're sure that's how you get to the crypt?"

I stared at the tip of Merja's finger. "Yes. I know Arek went down that corridor and returned from there. I can't imagine people would be roaming down there, so it's the best place I can think of for you all to lay low until it's time."

"That's assuming we can get in undetected," Jahil said.

"We can get in," Darvo said with authority.

Joris looked up at Darvo. "It's the undetected part he's not sure about, big guy."

Darvo curled his upper lip. "Merja and I have a plan for us."

"Oh really? And just when were you going to share that with us?"

Merja eyed Joris. "Sometimes plans rely on leaving others in the dark."

"No, that's my job." Jahil smiled smugly.

Fulric wedged in between Ulda and Jahil. "I think it'd be best that everyone knows what each person is doing, where they will be and when. We can't have any mistakes due to poor communication."

"We can't have any mistakes, period," I said. My unsettled nerves got the better of me, and despite the cold, I was breaking into a sweat. I stepped back from the group and out of the shelter.

"Evella?" Ulda followed. "Are you all right?"

"I just need time to think," I said. "I'm going to patrol the shore."

"Alora will help Arek once he's within her reach."

While I appreciated the help Alora gave, there was only so much she could do in her form. "I don't think it'll hurt adding a pair of eyes."

"Then let me go with you. It may not be safe out there by yourself, especially if Raiders return."

I held up a hand. "No, please. I'll be fine. You stay with the others. See if you can figure out what Merja has planned. I'm erring on the side of Fulric on that one. We can't keep each other in the dark on our movements. We have to work together."

Ulda nodded and reluctantly turned back to the shelter.

I roamed through the forest, to the pebbled beach on the western edge of Spokizar. The clouds were sporadic enough to see pockets of stars in between, the moon's glow sifting through the trees. The sea's horizon held a shimmering wave here and there. Were it not for the debris remaining after a days' worth of cleanup, no one would've known a giant wave had passed through here last night.

I had no idea how Arek had planned on getting back here, but I watched for him. For anything breaking up the surface of the water.

After a while I sat on the rocks, crossing my legs and wrapping my hands around my arms. My sweat dried, uncomfortably chilling me. I craved the camp's fire, but didn't want to leave my post.

Alora hung close, sprawled out in thin cover along the shore.

"I've got this."

A slight rise and fall of Alora in protest, but she drifted to the cover of trees.

I hadn't realized how much I came to rely on Arek's company. He had been around me every day since leaving Corallon. Exactly when did I go from not wanting to be around him to hating being away from him? He was my one constant on this trip, this phase of my life that still felt surreal yet more important than anything I'd ever done.

Our journey linked us together. He knew more about me in less than three months than most of my family knew in my lifetime. His life seemed so far from my own, growing up in the palace walls, never having to worry about his next meal. But he had some underlying understanding, as if he knew what it was like to starve, to have to work for anything and everything. He was low on the king's list of importance until recently, and judging by the conditions of the kitchen, no one could've called him spoiled.

He had lost his mother and hardly had anyone.

But he had me now.

It was only last night we had sat on the rocks together. I tried not to think about it again, but how could I not? A frozen blip in time, what he had all but told me before our lips nearly touched.

Branches cracked, and my hands leapt to action raising stones in the air, readying to defend myself if need be.

Footsteps approached.

I turned around, and a figure emerged from the woods.

Ulda. So much for her staying behind.

"I know you don't want me out here." Her words instilled a solid guilt for thinking them. "But I knew you had to be freezing with this weather."

She unveiled a cloak in her arms and wrapped it over my shoulders.

She really was a good person. "Thank you. I was getting chilled, to be honest. I've been looking forward to spring, but I'm starting to think it'll be more of the same."

Ulda smiled, content. "I'll leave you be."

I grabbed her hand. "You don't have to go."

She lifted her eyebrows, questioning me with a sideways glance.

"I promise. You were right. I could use some company out here."

"If you put it that way." She sat next to me. I took off the cloak and spread it over the both of us. She huddled closer to get warm.

"I didn't want to be around that lot anyway," she said. "Arguing over this and that. It's going to be amazing if we get anything accomplished tomorrow."

"I'm sure we can accomplish getting caught." I looked at her, and we both broke into laughter. "It's funny but it's not."

"No, it isn't," she said between giggles. "Not the least bit."

Our chuckling calmed down, and I caught my breath. The air cooled the lungs, our breath visible in the dark of night.

"I never had the chance to thank you for last night. The gang told me it was your idea."

I shrugged. "It was a team effort, and you're welcome. You deserved to have fun on your dawning, despite the circumstances. I think we all needed a little fun."

"It was fun." She placed her elbows on her knees.

"While it lasted."

Ulda sighed. "Can't control everything."

"Don't I know it." I gave her a wink, and we shared a soft chuckle. I still didn't know how I had freed Merja. Fulric wanted to chat about it, but being summoned by the king and focusing on tomorrow's task, he didn't have the chance. I was glad of it.

"Do you see that, over there?" Ulda pointed to the sea.

I squinted, scanning the horizon. "Is it—" Something thin and tall pierced where the sea met sky. "A mast?" I stood, gazing out over the sea, and Ulda met me at the new height.

"I think so," she said. "It's a boat."

"We have to get Alora."

"Let me." Ulda turned away and ran to the woods. Once near the trees, she grabbed branches and limbs, propelling herself faster through the thick forest.

I kept my eye on the small vessel. It could be Arek. It could be Raiders. Or someone else. I hoped it was Arek with every part of my being.

The wind howled and whooshed behind me, blowing my hair in front of my face. Alora thickened and wafted out to sea over the water. She blocked the line of vision to the small boat, too thick to see through.

"We just have to trust her," Ulda said.

I nodded. Alora helped me more than once today. Hopefully it was Arek who benefited from her help now and not Raiders.

A thought caught me off guard. I hadn't thought about the role of the Raiders since finding out the truth of the king. Now that we knew the king caused the quakes, what were the Raiders out there for? Were they still an enemy? The one who followed me across Mariner's Gauntlet here to Spokizar—was he chasing me for capture or did he have another motive?

The mist neared the shore and parted, the boat slicing through the middle. Seawater held flat around it, Alora keeping the waves calm. The figure was unrecognizable until he waved as the boat's bow hit the shore.

Arek hopped out, feet splashing in the water. He dragged the boat half out of the water before Ulda ran and wrapped her arms tightly around him.

"Oomph." His voice squeezed out of him. "Why couldn't I get this kind of greeting last time I arrived?"

"I said just as much this afternoon." I couldn't help but smile to see his face. I wanted to run to him, to hold him tightly in my arms. The faintest ping of jealousy sat deep in me. Ulda was comfortable enough with him to not hold back, and he comfortable enough with her to receive it wholeheartedly.

But I hesitated. I don't know what was more awkward. Longing to hug him, or me standing here not knowing how to act.

"I'll run and tell the others you've arrived. We've all been waiting for you." Ulda ran off again into the woods. Alora completed her journey back onto land, and Arek thanked her before she headed back to camp.

"You weren't out here on lookout for me, worried, were you?" Arek grinned, a flash of heat striking across my ears and chest. He tugged at the boat until the stern was out of the water onto the shore.

"I just happened to be taking a stroll on the beach."

"At this hour. In the cold?"

I tried coming up with something witty but all I could do was stare at him, happy he was safe. "How'd you manage getting a boat?"

"I told you, I have trusted friends in Elsinea."

I scowled in doubt.

He chuckled. "We can't fit all of us Soulmagi on the sled to tomorrow's event, now can we? King Ronin happened to agree."

"The king provided it?" My mouth stayed open in awe.

"I didn't say I trusted the friends, but they trust me."

"Not for long." Reality cast a somber veil over the banter. "Tell me, what happened with Nera?"

Arek sighed. "It was what I feared."

I looped my arm around his, the closest I got to a hug, and we walked to the trees.

"She's so devoted to the king. She didn't believe a word of it."

I bit my lip. "Maybe you should've kept the wooden handle to convince her?"

He looked down at his stepping wet feet. "It wouldn't have swayed her. It was more important that everyone here believed the truth."

"Well, it did work, if it brings you any consolation."

He tried for a smile, but it worked abysmally. "She wanted me to stay with her and not come back here. It's what took me so long. She pleaded I stay."

Now I was the one looking down at the ground. "I'm so sorry, Arek. That must've been hard."

"No harder than you having to leave your family for this." He turned to me, looking in my eyes. He did understand pain. His life, different from mine, didn't spare him that.

I yearned to tuck my head in his shoulder, have him hold me and I him.

"I really hope she doesn't say anything. I'd hate to think my actions today put any of you in danger tomorrow."

"There will be a level of danger no matter what."

"You know what I mean."

I nodded. "I haven't told the others why you really stayed behind. I said you were collecting some things of yours, since you may never return. I didn't feel it was my place to tell them."

"Thank you for that." He patted me on the hand.

I stopped and faced him. "I need to ask you something, before we get back to camp."

"What is it?" He made one step closer, and the moonlight peeked through the break in the clouds. The cast shadows chiseled his cheekbones and moonlight rolled off his skin, a dark statue of a man before me.

I caught my breath. "Are you going to be able to carry out our plans and leave her behind? Can you live with that?"

"I'm here, aren't I?" His voice carried a tinge of annoyance, but then his rigid shoulders loosened in an exasperated breath. "I feel like I've already lost her."

I wished to have the words to console him.

"Wait, does this mean you actually have plans to carry out?"

I huffed. "Supposedly. We could definitely use your help."

"Then we'd better get on it."

We plodded through the forest, Arek knowing the way in the dark better than I did.

I tripped on a root but caught myself. "Where's Joris when you need him?"

"Probably causing trouble with his brother," Arek said.

We arrived back at camp, the others arguing under the roof of Fulric's shelter. Merja pointed a finger at the twins. Jahel held up his hands in defense, while Joris scoffed, mouth ajar in defiance. Ulda had Darvo in an unrelated conversation, considering they both giggled. Fulric leaned on a post, arms crossed. He was more than relieved to see us approach.

"Finally. You can help us out with the schematics."

"Good to see you too, Fulric." Arek patted him on the shoulder and examined the drawing of the palace.

"Ah, you're missing over here." He sketched in the rest of the hallway tunnels I wasn't sure of, and added two aqueduct lines I hadn't known about at all.

"With that…" Fulric rubbed his beard. "I think that's how we get in."

"I'm not so sure," Arek said. "It's a tight squeeze through there, not to mention you'd reek. It's where the palace's waste washes out. Everyone in the palace would know where you've been."

"No, no." He wagged his finger in excitement. "It could be used as a diversion. Look, the nearest guards by that drain would be posted at the front western turret. They'd be the ones to react to a problem there."

"Unless the king has more stations than normal," I said.

"But that's where you two come in," Fulric said. "You will be openly welcome to enter. Do what you have to do to check out as much of the palace as you can. Report back to Ulda, who will be outside the eastern wall."

"There are rockwood trees growing through the rock crevices there," Arek said.

Ulda grinned. "Those should do to reach you."

"Once we hear back from you, we'll better know what we're dealing with. If there aren't other guards nearby, we'll use the aqueduct. If there are, we'll have to use Merja's plan with Darvo." Fulric looked at the two of them who were more than eager to execute whatever plan they had.

"What's that plan?" Arek asked.

Fulric's gaze jumped to the drawing. "I made the unfortunate mistake of getting it out of them. I'll catch you up later."

Arek eyed me with the same uncomfortableness I felt.

"What's important is that you two find out what we need to get us in. Once we're in, when the time is right, we'll corner the king in The Great Hall."

"Are you going to kill him?" Arek asked.

"Madam Forgiveness here won't let us," Merja said.

Arek looked at me, and I felt ashamed. Did Arek want him dead? Did I convince them of making the wrong decision?

"She's right," Jahel said. "It's more important if the king confesses to his crimes, in front of the delegates. Otherwise he dies a martyr."

Arek gave a strong nod. "He needs to pay for what he's done, that's for sure. But we have to make sure the world knows what he did before anything happens to him."

I briefly grinned. Of course Arek understood. It had to have taken a lot out of him to believe the king was the enemy after growing up under his protection. Then to not want to exact revenge through murder, but spare him?

Merja rolled her eyes. "You're both as bad as her. If it were up to me or Darvo…"

"But it's not," I chimed in. "We have to do what we agreed to, as a team, or this won't work." Had Merja actually killed someone before, or did she play the role of recluse? I didn't dare ask. For one, she'd never open up to me. And two, I was too afraid to know the truth about her. Some things were better kept secret.

"But how are you going to do it? How do we get the king to confess to everything in front of the delegates?"

Joris grinned. "That's the best part."

"It'll definitely be fun," Jahel said. "You have to admit that much, Merja."

She shrugged but revealed a tiny smirk. "Evella is good for some things, I guess." She winked at me.

Arek looked at me. "You came up with the plan?"

I shrugged. "Everyone helped. It was a team effort."

"She has a habit of saying that," Ulda chimed.

Merja laughed. "You can say team effort. But when it doesn't work, we'll be pointing at you."

My heart leapt in my chest. "We threw out several ideas, but decided this was our best chance."

Arek leaned over the parchment and stared up at the group encircled around him. "So? Tell me."

TWENTY-TWO

"They know we are all coming." I stood by the sled, the snowcats growing excited over the ensuing journey. It had only been a day since they led us to and from Elsinea, but it was like they got a taste for it again and longed for more. "I can't see why we all don't go in the boat."

Fulric and the others readied the boat Arek had arrived in last night. It would be cramped to fit all of us, but not impossible.

I didn't have fine clothes to wear to the dinner, but the king probably thought it best Arek and I looked different anyway. Soulmagi were supposed to be different from delegates. If we looked like vagabonds who lived in a forest for months, the better for it.

That didn't mean I wanted to risk getting wet on the journey. Plus, the boat seemed a safer bet over the sled. I petted one of the snowcats on the neck, the animal stretching his head up to receive it. I knew they were capable, but Arek couldn't deny the boat would be safer.

"The bigger the group we are, the more conspicuous." Arek didn't look up from harnessing the snowcats. "And arriving before the rest helps with the plan. It gives us time to assess security."

He stood, hands on his hips. "Plus, the more distance we have between us and the rest of the group, the more satisfied the king and the guards. They'll think we followed orders and left them out in the town to keep an eye out for Raiders."

It made sense but I didn't want to tell him that. I wanted a secure, dry mode of transportation on what very well may be my last night on Elsinor. Then again, if it was my last night, why bother being dry and comfortable?

"I know you don't want to hear this." He softened his demeanor. "The more ways we have to escape, the better. We very well could be split up, and I'd feel better knowing we had two vessels over one."

He sensed it too. The danger of the evening. The plan. That if things went wrong we could be doomed. It was hard to think what would happen afterward if things went right. It seemed an impossibility, and my mind didn't allow itself to go there.

"We'll be right behind you." Fulric stood ahead of the others, Darvo and Merja closest to the boat, eager to go. They showed no fear of death in them. I knew little about their circumstances leaving Tusinda, but whatever had happened, it hardened the both of them. People weren't born that way.

Ulda was more practical, hesitancy in her face and worry in her wringing hands. As for the twins, they had survived a deadly disease as babies, which gave them a sense of invincibility.

People without fear could do brave things, but they also could make poor, deadly decisions. These Soulmagi were a dangerous lot.

But they were my people. We only had each other.

"When we enter the eastern port, head to a slip opposite us," Arek said.

"We know the drill," Merja shouted from near the boat. "We're with you but we're not."

Arek nodded and gestured for me to board the sled. I turned to Fulric and gave him a nod.

"We're doing the right thing," he said.

Ulda looked to be near tears. I walked to her and wrapped my arms around her. "Thank you," I said. "No woman has ever been a friend to me as you have."

Ulda released from my grip and smiled, looking at me like I was crazy. "You talk like this is the end, when it's only the beginning."

I smiled back.

"I'll see you at the eastern wall."

I agreed and headed for the sled.

"We don't get a hug?" Jahel said, and Joris nudged him.

"Save it for after the victory," I said.

I glanced at Fulric one last time, his stance stalwart, eyes focused on me.

"See to us, Alora." He turned back, and Alora passed us, calming the way for us as Fulric and the others boarded their vessel.

I secured my place on the sled behind Arek. He guided us away from shore as Alora tamed the waves. The evening was one of the more peaceful ones we've had in a while, and beyond the wildest parts of the choppy water, there was calm. The lowering sun sent out a burst of color across the surface, a wedge of golden amber and flax zigzagging toward us.

We rode in silence, the heaviness of the mission weighing on the both of us. Talking about it wouldn't help, but staying silent only magnified thinking about it.

It was somewhere halfway between Spokizar and Elsinea that I couldn't take the silence anymore.

"You know, I could take over if you wanted to take a break."

Arek chuckled. "I don't doubt it. I was right about them listening to you, wasn't I?"

I nodded and tightened my grip around his torso, reminded of what he said about me having a place in his soul. How was it easy for him to say such things yet so difficult for me to say them back?

The dot on the horizon was barely visible behind us. Alora had long left us and made her way back to shore for Fulric's departure. There would be a good amount of time for us to arrive at the palace and survey the security. If we had a chance to roam before the king discovered our arrival.

Now was my chance to get out what I needed to say. Once we arrived on shore, we'd be weaving in and out of the business of Elsinea, keeping our eyes out for Raiders and trying not to bring attention to ourselves.

I didn't realize just how tight my grip had become around Arek until he tapped my hand. "Do you mind loosening up?"

"Sorry." I couldn't loosen up the knot in my stomach. "Can you slow down a bit?"

"Are you getting sick?"

"No, nothing like that."

The snowcats dropped their energy level a notch, propelling forward but nowhere near the pace we had been going.

Arek half-turned to me.

"I don't know if I'll get another chance to say it, so I'm just going to say it." *So do it, Evella. Say it.*

"Yesterday, when we split up." My voice turned hoarse. I was on my way to get the king to confess to his crimes, yet I couldn't divulge my feelings to Arek. "It made me realize how much time we've spent together."

He looked down at the sled, then up at me, waiting patiently for my bumbling words.

"And how awful it felt when you weren't coming back."

He placed a hand on my knee. "But I did come back."

"I know, I just—" I took a breath. The vessel behind us no doubt was growing into a larger dot on the horizon. "I didn't know I'd feel like this ever again, about someone."

The corner of his mouth curled up into a grin. "Feel like what?"

I shuffled, not a whole lot considering we were balancing on the water's surface on a sled.

"Hey, it's all right. Whatever you have to tell me. Because who knows what will be by the end of tonight."

I stared into his eyes, my own watering at the thought. "That's the thing." My voice broke, and a knot formed in my throat. "I've already lost someone dear to me. I don't want to go through that again." I looked up, the tears rolling down my cheeks, ignoring the cold air cooling them off. "I don't want to lose you too." If we exposed the king, people would come after those loyal to the king. Especially Oathers. And if we lost, and Arek was caught as a traitor...

He touched my chin, tilting my head up. "I don't want to lose you either." He moved his hands to my wet cheeks, holding my face as we bobbed on the water's surface.

A feeling swelled inside of me, an ache that grew the more I felt his touch. I wanted him closer, to feel him beneath the cloak, to feel his beating heart in his chest. "Kiss me." It left my lips and I didn't care. We could die tonight, and I'd rather die knowing his taste.

"I can't."

It hurt more than a slice of the knife. "Can't, or won't?"

"I can't put you in danger, any more than we're walking into tonight." His hand left my cheek, then squeezed my hand. He leaned in and touched my forehead with his.

It was a form of torture. Couldn't he see I didn't care about some promise made to a tyrant? "How would he even know? How could—"

"He used Soulmagic." Arek backed away, breathing hard. He couldn't even look at me. "During The Oath."

"No." I shook my head. "That can't be. He wouldn't."

"I guess a part of me always suspected it, but now that we know his capabilities, I'm sure of it."

Despite not wanting it to be true, it made sense. King Ronin had no moral compass. Of course he wouldn't simply take the word of someone swearing The Oath. He'd guarantee it, with Soulmagic.

I reached for Arek's chest, and he intercepted my hand, shaking his head. "I can feel it. Whenever you're close, whenever I think about doing...it hurts. Like a vice on my heart. I see these flashes in my head of you in pain. Dying. They haunt me."

The night at the shore, when he'd turned away. He'd had to bear something I didn't understand.

"You have no idea how much I want to..." His piercing gaze returned, the life bleeding out of me. "The things I want to do, to show you..." He blinked away the tears welling in his eyes. Tears of frustration. Anger.

Love.

The guilt of knowing he'd suffered, was suffering, eclipsed my selfish desires. I reached for him and kissed his forehead, letting my lips stay there, not letting him rip me away until I was ready. I slowly retreated, hands still clasping him. He gently tugged on my wrists, breaking the connection. It was all I was going to get.

"I don't know what will happen tonight." His low voice carried through the sound of the lapping rivulets around the sled. "But I'm glad to have had this moment with you."

Too many words came to mind, and I chose silence. A moment was what we had. Just one amidst the chaos. The sense of dread returned, the weight of death hanging over us, over this mission.

What was it Ulda had said? *You talk like this is the end, when it's only the beginning.*

Maybe it was the end for us. The end of something that could never truly begin. But it gave me hope, that there'd be a new version of us. The next phase of our lives knowing what could be and what couldn't. A new beginning. It added to the list of things to fight for—my family, the people of Elsinor. My purpose.

"As much as I don't want to say this, we'd better get going."

I cherished the calm for one more second before we parted, and he guided the snowcats back to speed.

We finished the ride in silence, the vessel behind us more distinguishable and closer, but enough of a distance to not raise suspicion we were together.

Arek secured the sled and snowcats, and we made our way through Elsinea. I didn't have to worry about the others finding the palace. For one, it was hard to miss sitting at the southern summit of the island, and two, they had Merja. You could spin her around twenty times blindfolded and she'd be able to point north.

I held on to Arek's elbow as we weaved amongst the people. How oblivious they were, carrying about their business, readying for supper, the taverns filling up with patrons. They had no idea what was going on in the palace that overlooked their mindless daily tasks. No idea what tonight would bring them. What it would mean for Elsinor.

The elbows and nudges, foul words from irritated people...if only they knew what Arek and I, and the rest of the gang were trying to do. To protect them. To save them from destruction. From death. Would everyone know who we were by tomorrow morning?

Or will we have evaded being identified, being named?

It was a possibility, not receiving credit. I wanted to make the Trapper name right again in Corallon. Mother and Father shouldn't have to live with the tarnish I had placed on the family. But what was more important, clearing the family name, or saving the world?

For all the noble intentions we had, it was ridiculous to think we would end up saving the world.

The palace lay before us, the widest part standing over the town, the posts of the gate like teeth, holding back whatever predator it held in its mouth to devour those below.

Even though the sunlight wasn't completely gone over the horizon, the palace was unusually well lit. Torches hung along the side walls and in the eyelets of the turret windows. Guards stood at a firmer attention.

"The king was right," Arek said. "These aren't the usual guards. I don't think I recognize any of them." He held a slight worry in his eyes. "You ready?" He patted my hand that clung to his arm.

I sighed. "Nope." I managed a small smile. "Shall we?"

I walked by his side to the guard, trying my hardest not to show fear and act like an invited guest would. We were invited, after all. So why was I stiffening up and holding my breath?

Because most of the guests weren't planning to rat out the king.

Minor detail.

We stopped at the hand of a guard. "Entry by invite only." The guard held a bow across his back, while the accompanying guard had no qualms about showing us the hilt of his sword, the tip of which reached his calves.

"Evella?" Arek asked.

"Oh yes. I have it right here." I perused my pockets under my cloak, my hands shaking and body uncomfortably hot.

"Here we are." I handed over the invite Haro gave us.

The guard examined the writing, as if analyzing the ink strokes and grains of the paper. For a second, I wondered if Haro deliberately gave us a false invitation. It wouldn't surprise me. I didn't trust him at all, and he had a particular disdain for me and Arek. Or anyone who wasn't the king.

It would be the perfect setup—a way to keep us out and humiliate us at the same time.

The guard with the sword patted down Arek and me, checking our boots, belts, cloak pockets, and anywhere else a weapon could be hidden.

"They're clean."

"You may enter." The other guard handed back the invitation. "Keep this on you at all times. There are several checkpoints before you reach The Great Hall."

"Thank you." I kept the invitation in my right hand, and we walked through the turret to the first courtyard. It was eerily quiet, no members of court or their gossiping liaisons across the yard. Only emptiness.

And guards.

"I see three," I whispered. Two stood near the entrances from the turrets and a third paced the eastern wall.

"There's a fourth." He nodded to the southwest corner, another guard standing watch before the underpass.

This wasn't good. Without the usual people roaming around, discussing, making noise and distractions, we were the main focus. How were we going to get anything by the guards? How was I supposed to inform Ulda over the wall?

Before I could consult with Arek, he was pulling me toward the fourth guard.

"What are you doing?" I whispered.

"Excuse me, sir." Arek held up a finger. "We were told we'd need an invitation to pass various checkpoints."

"That's right," the guard said, voice scruffy and stern.

"Would I be able to send Evella inside here, while I…" He leaned closer, raising his eyebrows. "Take care of business?"

The guard cleared his throat in annoyance. "She'll get in, but you'd be stuck out here. There's a checkpoint at the next entrance and before The Great Hall."

A stroke of genius, Arek's deviousness. "How about we go downstairs then?" I said. "I'm sure a servant could fetch a pot—"

The guard put up a hand. "The stairways are being patrolled. My advice? Find yourself a corner or hold it in."

The guard faced the front of the palace, finished with this conversation. We at least learned something about security.

"I think it's safe to assume that all entryways and exits have a guard," Arek said.

"Agreed." I scanned the walkway forming a triangle over the top of the palace. "I see one guard on each side up there. How will I let Ulda know? She can't scale the wall or send over a branch without them seeing. And we can't roam here for much longer without looking suspicious."

"Hurry up and write down what we know for Ulda."

"But—"

"Just do it."

I got the parchment and quill Fulric leant me out of my other pocket —luckily not viewed as weapons, despite the quill being questionable— and marked on the drawing of the palace where we knew guards were and where we expected them.

We stepped onto the pebbled outline of the yard, and Arek grabbed a sizable rock. "Here."

I stared at it in my hand, confused.

"Tie the drawing around it. When the guards aren't watching, get it over the wall quickly."

"I don't know if I can throw it that high."

"Really? You're a Soulmage, have a lightweight object to move and your mind goes to throwing it first?" Arek marched over to the corner of the outer wall and underpass and pulled his pants down. The guard we had talked to had a view diagonally across. He let out a grunt and turned his head away.

Two guards pacing the eastern walkway stopped, one guy tapping the other and pointing to Arek.

It was my chance. Arek relieving himself, as surprising and

humorous as it was, kept their attention. I stared at the rock in my hand and signaled the pull in the core of my being to connect with it.

The rock floated above my hand. I peaked at the guards again, their laughter ringing through the grounds at how long Arek was taking. Ulda had better be on the other side by now, paying attention and not trying to scale the wall. I let out a breath and pushed the force inside me hard. The rock hurled up, and I pushed it away, over the side of the palace. Without sight of it, the connection weakened.

It was going to freefall on the other side.

Then I felt a tugging. Someone had reached it. The rock disconnected from me right as Arek grabbed my elbow.

"You ready?" His question held more than one meaning.

"Yes, I think so." We faced the grand turret and began walking. I had been here but a moment and forgot I was a Soulmage. Months of training vanished from my mind in the stress of the task. "The question is, are *you* ready? That was impressive."

"I may have had a drink or two of Darvo's grog before coming."

I scoffed. "And I let you guide the snowcats."

"Oh, don't complain. It helped give me the courage to…" He met my gaze, the confession on the sled too fresh.

How much I wanted the evening to be over, with all of us safe. "Perhaps you should have a drink more often." The banter did little to ease the tension throughout my body.

We took a few more steps to the entrance, and I refocused on the task at hand. "I got it over," I whispered. "Someone noticed because it was taken from my grasp."

"Let's hope it was Ulda."

We were a handful of steps from the next guard at the entrance to the turret.

"Yes, let's hope." I spoke low and quickly. "Else they're on their own."

"And so are we."

TWENTY-THREE

I t didn't take long to have our answer.

A commotion broke out at the entrance gate.

"Get him off me!" one of the guards said.

"He's not breathing." It was Fulric's voice carrying through the courtyard. He said the words a little too unnaturally, too loudly. But the sight of Darvo flat on the ground probably shocked people enough not to notice. What a strange power to have, faking death, but Darvo promised it was useful beyond parlor tricks, and he proved that now.

"Well I can't breathe!" The guard shouted.

I eyed the walkway above, two guards keeping their post. It was to our advantage. As Darvo's dead body drew a crowd up front, Merja, Ulda and the twins slipped through the gate. They stood in the shadows, leaning up against the stone wall.

Now we had to worry about the inner guard at the underpass.

We stood near enough to the grand turret entrance that the guards posted there took notice. "Invitation?"

Arek patted his body. "You know what, I think I may have dropped it when I was…taking care of business."

I slipped the invite in my pocket beneath my cloak, going along with his plan without knowing what it was. There was only so much planning we could do from Spokizar, guessing what we'd encounter. There was bound to be a certain level of improvising.

"I'll just be a second." Arek headed to the corner near the underpass. The guards kept their eyes on me, each second an eternity. Darkness grew over the courtyard. Arek roamed around the corner, speaking to himself.

It didn't take long for the guard on the other side of the underpass to approach him.

And then I saw what he was doing.

The others had crept along the western wall, the shadows darker on that side of the palace. As Arek busied the nearby guard, the others made their way to the doorway of the basement.

One walkway guard above was drawn to the argument below between Arek and the other guard.

He'd spot the others sneaking in if I didn't do something.

"What are you doing, you fool?" I shouted across the courtyard, stomping away from the grand turret entrance.

Arek and the guard ceased their dispute. The guard above still looked at the two men.

"What did I tell you?" I said it louder. "I have the invite right here." I took it out from beneath my cloak and waved it in the air.

Now I had the attention of both guards.

"What are you talking about?" Arek paced toward me, the guard following him. "Do you see what I have to put up with?" he engaged the guard.

It was enough of a diversion. Four figures crossed beneath the underpass and disappeared into the basement doorway. Darvo and Fulric were to stay posted outside, near our exit point. Whoever they encountered from then on was their problem to deal with.

"I swear, I should cut you off from grog." I grabbed Arek's arm and tugged him along with me. I waved the invite at the guard and smiled. He wanted to punch us both, jaw tense, but growled under his breath instead, walking back to his post. The guard above turned back around, facing the outside of the palace.

"They're in," I said.

"Let's hope they let us in after all that."

I squeezed Arek's arm. We approached the guards at the grand turret again, and I handed over the invite, smiling unnaturally large. "I told him, it would be our luck to be so graciously invited by His Greatness, only to lose the invitation." I laughed nervously, and the guard snarled his upper lip. He gave the invitation back and waved us in.

A quick scan of the hallway showed the doorway from the basement was unguarded. What were the chances that held true for the entire basement? We'd been warned the stairways were patrolled, after all.

Arek nodded to the entrance of The Great Hall. "Are we the last ones to arrive?"

Peeking in the doorway, a massive table sat in the middle of the room. The delegates sat around the table, three women and five men representing the eight terrins outside of Elsinea, minus Spokizar. The king sat at the head of the table, facing the doorway.

"His Greatness couldn't have everyone enter the same way."

We turned around, and Icad gave a wicked smile. "He staggered the times and entrance points, just to be safe."

"How smart of him," I said, my voice wavy with nerves.

"Now if you don't mind, stop lingering and go inside. They've already begun the first course."

Something didn't feel right about this, outside the obvious uncomfortableness of the situation.

"He's definitely keeping us on our toes," Arek said.

Icad stood in front of us at the doorway. "Your Greatness, distinguished guests—"

The formal announcement never made it out, as the king shot up out of his chair. "Ah yes, my surprise guests of the evening. Please, welcome, and have a seat."

The eight delegates looked at each other as we hesitantly entered the room. The king had saved two chairs on the end of the table on either side of him. We walked a gauntlet, all eyes on us, burning my skin and boiling my insides with what we were about to do.

A bearded hefty man around Father's age caught my glance. His mouth opened slightly as he recognized me. I knew him as Rendok, and of course he was here. He was Corallon's delegate, and I should've expected to see him. Yet it came as a shock to see anyone from Corallon here. What would he report back to Corallon? To my family?

I sat to the king's left, hoping it offered view of the basement entrance through the clearer fragments of the stained-glass window. The seat was too angled to see anything in that direction. Arek sat across from me, his face blank. Perhaps he was better for it than whatever my face read—fear, apprehension, nausea.

At closer inspection, beads of sweat crossed King Ronin's forehead. He wore the newly fitted white robe with gold embellishments, the garment looking regal and unfortunately heavy. The grand fireplace was not alight, yet heat emanated from it, suggesting it had been lit until the king grew uncomfortable. Strands of green garland adorned the mantle, and potted shrubs lined the two long walls. Short candelabras on the table rounded out the evening's decorations, wax dripping onto the table.

Two servants placed a small plate in front of us. The delegates had nearly finished their first course. With the looks I was getting, eating was the last thing I wanted to do in front of them.

"Now that we are all here." The king smiled, his voice commanding over the room. "I think you know why I've called you out here tonight."

"You mean it isn't to show off your abundance of supplies on Elsinea?" It was the delegate from Tusinda, for he wore the same dark, fitted clothes as Merja and Darvo. His eyes were large and head bald and red, as if he spent his days aiming it at the sun.

Thankfully I hadn't taken a bite because I would've choked on it. Apparently not all delegates feared and respected King Ronin.

Those seated elsewhere would have missed the hairpin twitch in the king's eye. "No, Zaron, not for that. As you should know, we are affected by supply shortages as well. Fortunately our cooks have a gift of making the most of what we do have."

The delegate gave a quarter eye roll and looked back down at his plate.

"Shortages are only one of many issues we face. The quakes are worsening. And I hear word of terrins making alliances, cutting ties with others." He eyed a woman dressed in a flowy green fabric dress, and the man next to her, dressed in light brown garments too thin for the evening's weather. I guessed they were from Ulopra—Ulda's terrin —and Yobrol, the only two terrins south of Elsinea. Ulda had told me when united under Elsinor, their collective land thrived. After The Quake, Ulopra received all the rain from the west, which made their forests flourish—luckily for her ability—while Yobrol quickly turned into a droughted desert.

Father had spoken of alliances up north. Were other terrins doing the same?

"Everything plaguing our world leads to the same culprit," King Ronin said. "Raiders."

The delegates looked at each other, a few breaking into whispers.

"It is time we unify against our common enemy. Every terrin has its strengths, and I brought you here tonight to assess what you could bring to this war for our lives."

"It's a war you want, against The Raiders?" It was a short, stout man halfway down the table.

The king held up his hands. "It may not have to come to that. My hope is that we show such an enormous amount of strength that they cower in it. They'll stop their heinous cruelty."

It was I who wanted to roll my eyes. While it was unclear how Raiders fit into this new reality, I was absolutely certain the enemy was sitting next to me.

"That is why I have brought these very special guests." He smiled at me, then Arek. "Meet Evella Trapper, and Arek Meranath. Wielders of Soulmagic."

The shock reverberated through the delegates, and this time whispers turned to shouts. Rendok, the Corallon delegate, remained silent. Maybe it made sense to him, that I had Soulmagic, based on the rumors around our island. His face did not read surprise. Rather, understanding.

"They have been training secretly with like-minded people."

"You mean other Soulmagi?" A tall woman asked.

"You must understand that Raiders have been kidnapping our young men and women. Is it a coincidence that those missing were suspected of possessing Soulmagic?"

The table fell silent.

"We can't fight Soulmagic with our hands and pride." King Ronin shook his fist in the air. "The only way to defeat it is using it against itself."

A cacophony of voices permeated the room. Outside The Great Hall, guards shuffled about, their words indistinguishable from my seat.

Then Fulric's face flashed amongst them, before disappearing.

I turned to Arek. Fulric wasn't supposed to be inside. How did he get in? It wasn't with the others—I counted four bodies in the courtyard. Unless he swapped with someone. And had he left Darvo?

Arek's eyes grew wide. He had the same bad feeling.

"What's going on?" The king looked at Icad, keeping guard to The Great Hall alongside Haro.

His eyes closed for a few seconds before opening again. "Someone killed the guards up front."

The wind knocked out of me. Killing guards was not a part of the plan. Well, not unless absolutely necessary.

Could it be Raiders? The king had lured them here. Were they attacking?

If the others didn't make their move right now, surely the king would lock down the room or move us to another location. It would be too late for our plan.

And if any of the others were discovered, who was to say Arek and I wouldn't suffer the consequences? We were one in the same. We were all Soulmagi working together. The king would never believe Arek and I had nothing to do with this.

The table's candles extinguished and the room went dark, blacker than night. One of the women delegates screamed.

"Everyone stay calm!" a man shouted. "Must've been a breeze, blowing everything out."

Or Jahel.

"King Ronin, are you all right?" someone asked.

"I am fine." The king remained in his seat next to me. Arek kicked my feet under the table. He was still there.

"Is this a demonstration?" another asked. "A display of your guests' powers?"

Despite the utter lack of light in the room, Merja had reached her position. How I could be certain I couldn't say—the warmth of another body close by, or sensing the space being taken up in the room. But Joris had successfully guided her with his dark vision to the king.

"This is no joke," Merja said, her voice deeper than natural.

The king startled. "Who are you?"

"It is your sister." She spoke with conviction. "Alora."

"Impossible. Guards, where are my guards?"

But Jahel's darkness wrapped around them too. Funny the power darkness had over movement, speaking, breathing.

"You may have killed my body, but you know my soul lives on," Merja said. "You've seen it with your own eyes. The night you killed me. And our father."

The delegates in the room gasped.

"What do you want?" Fear laced the king's voice.

"You don't deny it then, killing your family?" It was Joris who said it.

"He doesn't deny it," a delegate said. Whispers picked up amongst them.

"Of course I deny it." His fist pounded on the table. He tried to stand, but Ulda wrapped the garland's thick stems around him, the leaves rustling in the blackness.

"Tell them the truth!" Merja commanded. "You only wanted the crown for yourself. You murderer! It was you who caused The Quake. You're a Soulmage!"

The strand of foliage tightened around him.

"The king has Soulmagic?" a delegate said.

"It makes sense, doesn't it?" said another. "This lavish dinner, how prosperous his terrin is over the rest of us."

"Don't be silly," the king eked out of a compressed chest. "If I had Soulmagic don't you think I'd use it now!"

He was stalling. We knew he'd consider using Soulmagic to stop us.

If he did, his secret would be revealed. If we couldn't get him to voice his truth, we'd get him to use it.

"You could destroy the palace, and everyone in here, couldn't you? Don't deny it!" Merja yelled. "Say it! The truth!"

Ulda's grip on his chest and neck threatened to be too tight for too long. We were going to lose him.

"Just tell us the truth," I pleaded. "If you have Soulmagic, that would strengthen our forces against Raiders. We'd be under the service of a great Soulmage. Who wouldn't want that for Elsinor? Please, Your Greatness. I can't help defend you if I can't see you. Listen to what they ask of you. You'll be of no service dead."

"Enough," the king squeezed out the words. Perhaps his life flashed before him, being so close to death. Or had I convinced him?

"It's true, I'm a Soulmage."

I gasped in fake surprise, overpowered by the others' reactions in the room.

"Please...loosen..."

The branch rustled for a second, and the king coughed. "More," he begged.

"You can speak just fine like that," Merja said. "Tell them what you've done, Brother. Or will they be offering you up to The Beyond tomorrow?"

The garland tightened once again.

"Fine! Fine, I admit it. What she says is all true, about my father, and my sister and brother."

A brick dropped in my chest. I had forgotten the king had a brother. And here he confessed to killing him, too.

"Why? Why did you do it?"

"It was time I had the crown."

This couldn't have been happening but it was—the words flowed out of his mouth.

"My father was a coward with no cunning. No insight. He couldn't see the enemy if they were standing on top of him."

"But why me? Why kill me and Erlin?"

"Because you knew the truth. You knew I had powers. And Erlin was just as stupid as Father. There. You've got what you wanted, now let me go!"

The darkness vanished in a flash. Jahel and Joris stood near the entrance, and Merja behind the king. Ulda released her botanical grip on him and backed away. The king clung to his neck, coughing and wheezing.

Ulda's face froze. The strand of garland rose from the floor and wrapped around her neck. A snap rung in the air, and her face turned bloody red.

"No!" Merja grabbed a blade from her boot and sliced through the branch. Ulda fell to the ground, eyes closed and arms splayed out.

"It was him!" Arek pointed to Icad, whose eyes opened back to awareness. "He possessed her!"

No. NO!

Merja screamed, Ulda's lifeless head in her lap.

"You fools!" The king's voice was hoarse as he stood and pounded the table. "Seize them all!"

The delegates looked at each other, Haro making for Merja, and Icad for the twins.

"Wait!" I bursted from the chair. "You heard what he said." I pointed to the king. "He killed his own father for the crown. *He* is the cause of the quakes. *He* is why we are all suffering!"

Arek rushed to his feet. "I trusted him as you all have done. But even I know when it's time to believe the truth. It's time we end this, and that means seizing him!"

The delegates hesitated, looking at each other. Could no one make a decision? They heard what he had said. How could they not act? I threw Rendok a pleading look. If anyone, he should understand.

"Haro will tell you!" I didn't know what else they needed in order to believe. "He remembers. He saw Alora's spirit leave her body that night, as the king murdered her."

"How dare you!" Haro leapt for me. I guided what I could connect with on the table and flung it at him, a plate and silverware colliding with his face and chest. It was enough for Merja to wrap her arms around him, locking him still. The twins jumped to seize Icad.

"I said what I had to say to stay alive!" The king shouted. "Of course I didn't do those things."

The confusion in the room was debilitating. This was not how it was supposed to go. "No, he's lying." I turned to King Ronin. "You're a liar." I hadn't felt hatred for anyone as much as I did for him. Starvation. Devastation. Outright murdering his people. And he could care less. My fingertips tingled with rage.

"If anyone's been lied to, it's me," he snarled. "Guards!"

Fulric appeared in the doorway, stepping over something on the ground. I squinted, my eyes still adjusting to the light.

I held my hand over my mouth.

Bodies.

He stepped over bodies.

Fulric marched through the room, a man possessed, taking note of no one but King Ronin.

"Arek?" I asked.

His wide eyes matched my bewilderment.

"Fulric, what—"

It was too fast.

"Don't!" Merja screamed, torn between reacting and not wanting to let go of Haro.

Fulric pushed the seat into Arek's knees, buckling him down.

It wasn't until the blade flashed silver that his intentions were clear.

But Fulric wouldn't attack, would he? He couldn't take down the king like that. Had he not learned from Alora, the love of his life? The king would split his body in pieces.

King Ronin reached out a hand, aimed at Fulric.

Fulric leapt in the air, blade at King Ronin's chest.

I reached out, the rage releasing.

CHAPTER

TWENTY-FOUR

King Ronin let out a cry. Blood bubbled in his throat, splashing out his mouth.

My hands shook, my mind finding it impossible. *No. I couldn't have. It wasn't me.* But I knew the truth. I felt the connection with his beating heart and pulled, and hadn't let go until the incessant beating, the vile wickedness of that man, ceased.

What have I done?

My knees weakened, and I stumbled on the chair, straining to stay on my two feet.

The room swarmed with a wind, one that whipped my hair in my face. I closed my eyes, the current too powerful, nearly knocking me over. The wind subsided, all of us looking at each other, not knowing what just happened.

A rumbling grew. The stone walls rattled, dust drifting down to the ground. I held onto the table as the ground beneath my feet shook. Cups and earthenware knocked over, rolling off the table and shattering.

"Take cover!" One of the delegates scrambled underneath the table.

The room filled with shouts and screams, muffled by the growing rumbling and rattling of the palace.

I ducked beneath the table, along with Arek and Fulric. I wanted to yell, to hit, to make Fulric understand my anger.

"It had to be done," Fulric shouted. "Now you need to go!"

Stones fell from the ceiling, the table catching them on their way down.

"You betrayed us!" I grabbed his collar and pulled him closer. "You used us to get to him."

"He deserved to die years ago. Time has shown us that." He pressed a hand between my fists and his clothes, pushing me off. "I meant to do it myself. I never imagined this would happen. Right now you need to go before his guards reach you. Go!"

Fulric wormed his way out from underneath the table. His boots disappeared in the dusty rubble.

I looked at Arek. "I didn't mean—I had to stop—"

"It doesn't matter now. Fulric's right, we must go!" Arek grabbed my hand and pulled me out. The shaking interfered with my balance as I stood. The king sat lifeless in his chair, mouth and eyes agape, blood rolling down his chin.

"Come on!" Merja and the twins stood by the bodies of the dead guards at the entrance to The Great Hall.

Arek dragged me across the room, the delegates unmoving from cover. Only two of them remained out from under the table—the delegates from Tusinda and Corallon. I met the eyes of Rendok.

"I didn't mean for this—"

He nodded. "Go." Whether it was in approval of what I had done, or support for my escape, he was on our side. At least one of the delegates was convinced of the truth.

Merja and the twins broke into a run as soon as we met up with them.

"Stop!" I grabbed Merja's arm. "What about Ulda? We need to go back for her."

Merja laid her hand atop mine in a tight grip, then released me from her. "She's gone, Evella."

"What do you mean—" But I knew. I had seen Icad take over her body, seen the branches squeeze out her last breath.

"We can't just leave her body there."

"We have no choice." Merja locked eyes with me, a determined stance I had no chance in changing.

Jahel and Joris began their retreat, heading to the hallway leading to the basement.

For a second, I wanted to stay, to be with Ulda, not caring if the palace collapsed over me.

"We need to survive," Arek said. "For her."

Whether he believed the words or not, he knew they'd get to me. All of this would be for nothing if we didn't survive. A dead king and a group of dead Soulmagi who knew the truth about him wouldn't solve Elsinor's problems.

I reached out in connection with the garland next to her. I couldn't make it budge, the connection as weak as my body.

"Come on!" Merja beckoned.

I stumbled to Ulda, covering her body with the strands of garland like a blanket. If there was such a thing as The Beyond, she'd at least have a bit of nature to bring with her.

I turned to the others, and the room spun in my weakness. Arek clutched my hand, and we took off running to the basement hallway, my feet heavy as lead, each step draining what little energy I had left. Jahel and Joris waited in the narrow corridor, the quake splitting the walls with fine cracks and crevices.

"We're going to be crushed alive," Merja said, urging the twins onward.

Not knowing where Fulric vanished off to, I pictured him crushed beneath rubble. It didn't matter, in this moment, if he escaped or died. I saved his life by killing the one person we needed alive.

We rounded a corner, and two guards stopped the twins. Jahel darkened the tunnel. Two powerful punches on flesh sounded, and the darkness vanished. The guards lay on the ground, noses bloodied and eyes closed.

"Nicely done." Merja stepped over the bodies and took the lead. She stopped when we reached the straightaway leading to the kitchen.

"What is it?" Arek asked.

"This way is blocked."

"How can you tell?" Joris strained his neck, looking over Merja.

"I sense it. The corridor has collapsed, at the next doorway."

Arek stepped forward. "That's the kitchen." He looked back at me.

"No," I shook my head. "Arek, we have to leave now. You said so yourself."

The ground erupted in another wave of shakes.

"We can still get to the meeting point with Darvo through the cross tunnel." Merja walked ten paces then vanished off to the left. Jahel and Joris looked at each other, then ran off after her.

"I have to check if she's all right," Arek said.

"There's no time."

"Go without me." He squeezed my hands, the wall dust thickening on my hair and in the air, making it hard to see.

"I'm going with you." I stepped over the guards and rushed to the kitchen doorway.

"Evella." Arek lapped behind me.

I spun around on my heels. "If you're going to die over this, then so am I."

He fought for a counterargument, stuttered words not coming out of his mouth. His eyes wandered, as if an alternate plan floated in the air and he just had to see it.

"You heard Merja. We'll take the cross tunnel and meet up with them in no time." The words were easier said than believed.

I rushed toward the kitchen. Merja was right—the ceiling on the further side of the kitchen doorway had collapsed, blocking the hallway. If we had come from the other direction we wouldn't have accessed the kitchen. Inside the room, the fire had spilled over from the quakes, setting the hung tapestries ablaze.

"Nobody's here." I held up a hand, shielding my face from the brightness and heat.

"We need to be sure."

"Arek!"

He hurried off, entering the backroom. The heat intensified, the light almost unbearable.

"We have to go!" The deep breath cost me, filling my lungs with smoke. I coughed in my sleeve, not able to catch my breath in all the smoky air. A ringing grew in my ears, and I fell to my knees. My body cooked in the hot air.

I felt a tug on my sleeve, and Arek lifted me to my feet. He slipped his head beneath my arm and walked me out. We stopped around the wall, the stones warm on my back.

"Are you all right?"

Sleep could've taken me right then. What I had done to the king, it had taken nearly every bit of energy. The heat and smoke sapped the rest. I managed a weak nod.

"Let's go." His urgent steps compelled me to move. I stepped where he did, until my head cleared from the smoky fog. We had entered the cross tunnel, cutting beneath the courtyard.

"Any signs of the others?"

"Not yet." Arek's arm stopped me across my chest. Three guards rushed us, two arrows and a spear tip in our faces.

"Who are you and where are you going?" The shortest one in the front asked.

My hands clenched Arek's shoulder and elbow across me as he showed his unarmed hands. The guards wouldn't know who we were unless they had been stationed by The Great Hall, and those guards were dead. For all they knew we were guests of the king, which we were.

"Hold on," I said. It seemed trivial as the ground continued to erupt in waves of trembles. We could all die down here, arguing over our identities. I pulled out the invitation. "We were dinner guests of the king, and now—"

"Wait!" The two nearest guards separated and the third, tallest guard stepped forward. The same one who saw Arek relieving himself. "I know these two. They were acting suspicious coming into the palace."

I eyed the loose bricks above their heads, feeling for the connection. I knew I needed rest, that my power was drained. But I connected, feeling that hole fill up with matter. Just as I was about to break bricks down, I stopped myself.

Fear had overtaken me. Fear that I couldn't control it, that it would be out of my hands. Fear that I'd kill everyone standing around me.

A pebble broke loose and drifted down one man's face, a tiny remnant of what I tried to do. I wanted to cry and scream, yet didn't have the energy for either.

Arek's mouth waved open and closed until he managed words. "I—I don't see how we were—"

"They're with me." A woman's voice rang out from behind them. The guards turned, creating an open divide leading straight to a figure with disheveled hair, sooted face, and dirtied apron. Nera.

"He grew up in the palace, you nitwit." She slapped one of the guards on the head. "His Greatness will have you hung for laying a hand on him."

The tall guard stepped to her. "No, he won't. The king is dead."

How had he received word of it? How had it traveled so fast? No one had left the room before us, outside of Fulric. And it wouldn't make sense for him to go announcing it as he escaped.

Nera's jaw dropped. She covered her mouth, then took her hand away, patting her apron. "All the more reason to protect those who serve the king." She reached out her hand to Arek. "Come now."

Arek took Nera's hand, and I walked behind him.

"Now you'd better find the culprits who did this before they escape." She wrapped her arm around Arek's chest.

The two guards looked at the third, who nodded. They continued on down the tunnel.

"Thank you," Arek said.

She took her arm away. "Now get out of here."

"Come with us," Arek pleaded.

"Go, before I turn you in myself." She stared me down.

She blamed me. In her eyes, I was the one who tainted Arek's beliefs, who convinced him of the king's wrongdoing. I destroyed her only family.

"I love you, Nera. No matter what."

I touched Arek's shoulder but he took off in a run down the

corridor. Another section had caved in from the side, minorly slowing us down. He turned left, then right, and I soon lost track of where we were, how we were oriented beneath the palace. I had to trust Arek, who moved through the maze of corridors with confidence.

I did trust him.

Footsteps grew behind us, and a scrawny man with shreds for clothes approached us. His eyes were wide, face covered with soot and dirt, wrists in shackles. He took one look at us, then behind him, and carried on running.

Heavier footsteps followed. Arek pulled me closer to the crumbling wall and a larger man appeared in the dust. He looked familiar, with a long dark beard parted into braids. His eyes were maniacal, and he stopped in front of us.

"Where'd he go?" His spit foamed in anger with his words.

Arek pointed down the side hallway, and the guard took off.

"The dungeon," I said.

Arek nodded. "The quake must've compromised it. There could be any number of dungeon guards and prisoners roaming around."

"But you pointed him in the wrong direction."

"Did I?" Arek smirked. "Who's to say which one is the enemy?"

I simply nodded, and he took my hand. We continued through the labyrinth of corridors for a short while longer. He stopped at an old door, heavy and rusted, but open.

"That's a good sign, right?" I asked.

He nodded. "They must've made it through here, at least."

The corridor narrowed. We knew it would be a tight fit, but not as uncomfortable as the aqueduct we had considered that ran parallel to here. Darvo would be waiting for us with the boat. Arek had given him permission to retrieve the snowcats, but conceded if they didn't listen to untie them and let them be. We could all squeeze onto the boat. With Fulric out of the picture, it wouldn't be so tight, and we could move faster across the water.

Light crept in from a pinhole straight ahead. Its softness grew and opened wider the further we walked. Even though the night grew dark outside, it was shades lighter than down here. The walls dripped water, and the air smelled of sea salt.

We were almost there.

Arek stepped through the exit onto a landing outside, and I stood next to him.

"Stop!"

It was Merja, halfway down the cliffside to the shore. She had stopped with the twins. I squinted, eyes adjusting to the night's darkness. More figures stood near her.

Guards.

"They're cornered," Arek said.

Above, the sound of footprints and clanging metal alerted us to our own scenario.

"I believe we are, too." I tapped his shoulder and pointed up. A dozen guards stood at the top of the cliff, five body-lengths above us.

"We could turn around," Arek said.

"You could." A man's voice sounded behind us. He and four other guards positioned themselves at the tunnel exit.

Arek and I reached for each other.

Above, the guards pulled back their bow strings. The guards at our level threatened with blades. The only way was down, and the others were caught in the same dilemma there.

The air exploded in whistles. A guard yelled in pain as he plummeted from above, down the cliff. A second and third followed. And a fourth.

"What's going on?" asked one guard wielding a sword in front of me.

Three more whistling of arrows. Three more men dead.

Two of the guards by Merja below lay on the ground. She and the twins took advantage, fighting the remaining guards.

"Evella!" Merja threw something in the air with one hand, her other hand busy clashing with a guard.

As it separated in the sky, I recognized the string, the pocket. My sling.

It wasn't going to reach us, and I tried connecting with it, but it simply arced in the sky and began its descent to the ground.

A bird cawed, catching the string with its beak. It flew overhead, dropping the sling above me.

I caught it and glanced at Arek. "Thanks."

"Shall we?" He placed a rock in my hand, and I faced the guard nearest me. I flung the rock with a single swing, landing it between his eyes. His stance broke, and I reached for the sword, his grip on the hilt released. I pounded his helmet with the hilt as hard as I could, the guard falling back. It was too fast for the guard behind him, whose knife accidentally pierced his shoulder from behind.

Arek kicked the guard in front of him in the chest, knocking the other two down fully to the ground in succession. I reached for Arek's arm, and we took off without a word.

We scaled the cliff downward, inching our way to Merja and the twins. I slung rocks at the archers above, managing to knock two over the cliff. Several whistles rang through the air again, arrows arching toward the guards above, downing another handful of them.

"What do we do now?" I asked as we met the rest of the group halfway down the cliff.

"Still no Darvo," Merja said.

"Do you think he's hurt, or captured?"

"Hurt, who's to say. But Darvo doesn't get captured."

I doubted Merja was capable of being captured, but there she was a second ago, on the wrong side of the guards' weapons.

Metal clashed above us, echoing off the cliff. The remaining guards fled the cliffside, their attention taken by something else.

"Look!" Joris said. "Over there." He pointed down to the sea. "It's a ship. No—several ships."

The blackness of the sea afforded little contrast.

"We don't all have night vision," Merja said.

"It's where the arrows are coming from," he said.

"Raiders." Arek agreed with my intuition.

"Is that?" Joris took two steps down toward the shore. "Darvo? It's Darvo on one of them."

"They must've intercepted our boat," Merja said. "I swear I'll kill every last one of them if they hurt him."

Joris waved, and a large figure on the water's surface waved back. The longer I fixated on the point in the sea, the more figures appeared in the darkness, standing atop vessels. "I don't think he's that unhappy about it."

"Or he's too stupid to realize," Jahel said.

Merja cupped Jahel's neck, planting her face in front of his. "Never insult his intelligence again, you hear me? Or you'll be the one with an arrow in you."

"Fine, mercy," he choked through.

"Come on, we can't be fighting with each other," I said.

The echoed clattering above stopped, the silence eerie. At the clifftop, a dark figure appeared. He held a short blade, shimmering in the moonlight.

Fulric.

"I've held them off as long as I can," he shouted. "Go with them!" He pointed to the Raiders.

"Are you crazy?" Merja said, more to herself than to Fulric.

"They're the ones saving your lives right now," he shouted. "Hurry! More of the king's men are coming!"

Fulric turned his back to us then ran off.

The Raiders down below yelled and waved.

Merja, Jahel, Joris, Arek and I looked at each other.

"What do we do?" I asked. Someone had to speak up first.

"What can we do?" Arek said. "I think we have to go with them."

"If for anything, they have Darvo," Merja said.

"And he did bring up a good point," Jahel said.

"Yes, they shot the guards, not us," Joris said.

I took a deep breath. An arrow whizzed by my ear and landed in the middle of our circle.

"The guards are shooting," Jahel said.

"Run!" Joris nearly threw Merja down the cliffside. Joris followed her, and Arek protected my back as we crouched low, slipping down the wet rocks. My legs shook, unsteady on the loose rocks. It didn't help that the tremors continued to sprawl out from the palace. My feet slipped and it took every effort with my hands to hold onto the side of the cliff. More arrows came our way, but the cliffside was too angled for any to hit us from above.

We made it to the shore and crouched low.

"Now what?" Jahel said. "Just board a ship?"

"Come on!" A Raider urged us. He stood in front of other Raiders, his stance commanding and stalwart. "We'll cover you!"

"Why?" I stood from my crouch, Arek tugging at my sleeve. The arrows whooshed by, one, two, three landing on the beach around me. I stepped closer to the water's edge. "What do you want with us?"

"We came here to help," he shouted.

"How did you know we would need it? That we'd be here?"

"Get back here!" Arek shout-whispered. Another arrow landed next to my foot. A Raider behind the leader fired one up at the clifftop.

The water's small waves lapped over the toes of my boots. The lead Raider's vessel sat close enough that I could make out some of the features on his face—nothing unique, just the darkness of his eyes, his nose. His lips pushed up into a smile.

"I knew because my sister told me."

I stood frozen on the shore, completely vulnerable to either enemy. The thing was, I no longer knew who was an enemy. If anything, the citizens of Elisinor would think me and the other Soulmagi were the enemy. The gang that killed their king. "Your sister?"

"Yes," he smiled wider. "Alora warned me you wouldn't accept help so easily."

Even though I couldn't tell if his nose was narrow or wide, eyebrows thick or thin, chin square or round, I knew his words told the truth.

"Everyone." I turned back to the others and waved them over. "We're going with them."

"What?" Arek led the others over to me. "How do you know we'll be safe?"

"Come on!" Darvo waved again at us, grinning. He obviously was not harmed by Raiders, and that was good enough for now.

I turned to Arek, to the others, meeting their eyes as they stood in confusion.

"Because any enemy of the king is our friend," I said. "And that man right there is Erlin."

Merja blinked hard, shaking her head. Jahel and Joris furled their eyebrows in unison.

"Alora's brother."

TWENTY-FIVE

"Is everyone all right? Anyone hurt?"

We sat on the deck of the Raider ship, an enormous clunk of metal that defied logic as it floated on the sea. Even in the dark I could sense most of the ship lay underwater. I hadn't paid attention to my body during the rush of escape. My right elbow was scraped up, probably hitting the narrow corridor walls at some point beneath the courtyard. Besides that and my dirtied clothes and skin, I came out relatively unblemished. At least on the outside.

I tried standing on the bobbing metal cork, but my legs were weak, and every bone and muscle fought against it.

Merja and the twins had more hand-to-hand combat with the guards. Jahel had a cut near his eye and Joris swelling on one cheek. Merja's knuckles were bloodied but it was hard to tell if the blood came from her or her victims. Darvo gave her a tight squeeze despite her resistance. Eventually she relaxed and accepted it before tapping his arm to cut it out.

"Ulda." My eyes watered, trying to focus on Erlin. I had no idea how much he knew about us. How much could Alora express to him, after all? "She was one of us. She didn't make it out."

"Icad killed her." Arek's lips pressed into a firm line of anger before he looked down at his boots.

Merja pounded her bloodied fist into her hand.

Darvo shook his head over and over in denial. "Not Ulda."

"Sorry, big guy." Merja laid her head on his chest, and he lowered his head. It took every effort not to lose it, not to break down in sobs.

"I'm very sorry," Erlin said. "I know this provides little consolation, but you are lucky to have lost only one of your own."

Arek grabbed my wrist, knowing it was going to swing in the air to hit Erlin's face. I didn't care if he saved us. "Losing Ulda was not *lucky*."

Erlin huffed. "I'm not the best with words, I do apologize. I meant to say we are lucky so many of you survived. When I heard about the plan, I knew it'd be dangerous. My brother has no sense of loyalty, or respect for life for that matter. He would've killed me had it not been for Alora. When she escaped her body, Ronin was so shocked that it gave me the few moments I needed to escape."

He reminded me of the multiple questions that needed answers. If I imagined Ulda's lifeless body for another second, I might go mad.

"How did Alora contact you about this?" My equilibrium didn't allow me to stand yet. Instead I placed my feet in front of me, arms around my knees. "I didn't think Alora could leave Spokizar for long, or travel far."

"She can't," he said. "That doesn't mean I can't visit her. Besides, we are connected. Always have been. I can sense her emotions as well as she can sense mine. I sensed something had changed on that island, and once we began surveilling the waters, it was obvious something was brewing."

"That was you, tailing Evella in the boat the other day." Arek's anger gave room for his curiosity.

"We try to keep an eye on the comings and goings of the terrins, to learn all we can about what's going on. We're not exactly in the best position to scour the land, as it is."

"And that was you, shooting at us, around Midmarea?" I could still hear the arrows whizzing by us on the sled, Arek urging the snowcats to swim harder, faster. "If you were on our side, why would you try to kill us?"

"First of all," he held up a finger, "we didn't know who you were nor what side you belonged to. Second, I wasn't on the ship that fired at you. And third—"

"We weren't trying to kill you. Just slow you down," the Raider standing past Erlin's shoulder said. He was tall and lanky, dressed in their uniform of dark garb adorned with a multitude of weapons. He had a perfectly straight scar across his left cheek. The original cut had to have reached bone with how wide and perpetually red it was.

"This is Kaleb. He was in command of that ship. You must understand most of the information we obtain comes from those who travel by sea. We intercept them on their way, question them, and let them go."

Not sure if I believed the letting them go part.

"We were on the lookout for a young woman that fit your description," Kaleb said. "I'm sorry if we scared you. Gave us a good tumbling, though."

I half-grinned, recalling how one of them struggled in the water. But his words lingered. A woman who fit my description? Why would they be looking for someone—

"That'll be different now," Kaleb said, "having to rely on the seafarers. I imagine we'd be more welcome on land now more than ever."

"I'm not so sure," Erlin said. "We know some will see the death of the king as a blessing. Others will want revenge."

"We weren't supposed to kill him," I said. "Fulric. It wasn't part of the plan. I realized it too late, what he was going to do. If I hadn't done something, Fulric was going to die." The flash of the blade, King Ronin's hands in the air, the release of my power to stop him. I closed my eyes but that only made the image clearer.

"We can't change it now." Arek patted my elbow.

"If I ever see that lying selfish bastard again..." Merja spoke the words through clenched teeth. "Ulda's dead because of Fulric. He threw us in there, just so he could have a way to get to the king. I swear I'll gut him worse."

"Don't want to get on your bad side," Kaleb said.

Merja gave him a killer stare.

"Noted."

"I know you're upset, Merja," Arek said. "We all are. But we don't know what Fulric was thinking. He did help us outside the palace, fending off guards."

"I can't believe you're defending him."

Erlin took a step and raised a hand. "Again, I am sorry for your friend. It's most unfortunate. And the death of the king does complicate things, though it's not entirely bad. Not everyone was in support of the king, and it's those men and women we will have to seek out when the time is right."

"When the time is right?" Jahel asked. "What is that supposed to mean? What exactly are you suggesting we do now?"

"We lay low. Let the word spread through the terrins." He crouched to our level, demanding our attention. "I want to make this clear, to each and every one of you. Tonight marks the beginning of change, something we've tried to achieve but never could. We knew what the king was up to. How do you think we've acquired so many men and women to join us?"

"And here we thought it was kidnapping," Merja said, the venom unhidden in her voice.

"I've—none of us—have ever held anyone against their will. It's true, we did seek out Soulmagi, and whoever else we could muster to join us. But everyone is free to leave whenever they choose to do so. You see, we haven't been able to penetrate the minds of most citizens, past their blindness to the king, past their conceptions of us being the enemy. But now, you have. All of you."

I surrendered to the pleadings of my body and lay on my back on the deck. It was too much to process in a short time. Ulda's death. The king's death. What may or may not happen from here. What spin the delegates will put on tonight's events to their people. I didn't want to have to think about it. The past or the future.

"You rest, Evella. After what I heard you did, you need it." Erlin stood over me, blocking out my view of the stars. Doubts lingered as to whether to trust the man, but at this point I didn't care. If he wanted me dead, he could've smashed his boot in my face right then and there. If he wanted to use me or the rest of us in some elaborate plot of his, we'd figure it out eventually. Although we figured out Fulric's plans a bit too late. Maybe we'd be better at it this time around.

"All of you, rest. We'll make way to meet up with the others." He nodded to someone out of sight, and something shifted in the vessel. Metal vibrated beneath my back, clanging and creaking into a new formation. Two slits in the middle of the deck opened and poles emerged, lifting diagonally until they stood vertical to the deck. Overlapping sheets of shiny material slid open, like a deck of cards splayed out on a table.

"It's amazing." Arek slid next to me, propped up on an elbow. "What are the sails made of?"

Indeed they were sails, the little bit of wind managing to fill up the material and push the vessel.

"Isn't that?" I squinted, the metal familiar.

"What Fulric used on our training course wall. I wonder—"

But I didn't care to think about it right now. I lowered my head to the cold metal.

"Here." Arek stretched out his arm, and I complied. Who cared what the others might have thought about us like this. Or what I thought about it. I tucked my head onto his chest as his arm wrapped around me. He was the very opposite of the metal, soft and warm and the best thing I had felt against my flesh in ages.

"How did you do it?"

I looked up at Arek, overlooking me.

"Kill King Ronin? How were you able to do that?"

I closed my eyes, the scene replaying once again in my head. The urgency to save Fulric. The rage for Ronin. The fear and anxiety coursing through me all evening. "I don't know."

Arek stroked the hair off my forehead, leaving it for another time.

As tired as I was, I couldn't fall asleep. The vessel sailed smoothly along the water, and the other Soulmagi, even the rest of the Raider crew, kept silent as we sailed.

"Where do you think we are headed?" I whispered.

Arek's shoulder raised slightly before receding again. "I sense it's northward. Probably best to get our distance from Elsinea."

I wanted to ask what we do from here, as if Arek held all the answers to the future. No matter the uncertainty, I wanted my future to coincide with his. How could we diverge on different paths from here, after all we had been through? This young man was a part of my life now, as I hoped I was a part of his. But did that mean we stayed with the Raiders? Did we go with the others elsewhere? Or off on our own? Would Corallon even accept me with the news? Rendok and I had an unspoken understanding, but maybe I had read too much into that. And if I hadn't, who knew what that meant for me and my family. Would he defend my actions when it came down to it?

We sailed on for quite some time, enough that lying on the hard metal deck was no longer an option. The others obviously couldn't sleep either. Merja stood near the starboard railing, which only reached to thigh level, perhaps to streamline the vessel as much as possible. Jahel and Joris investigated one of the sails, discussing with a Raider how they managed to make such an invention. Darvo took sips out of a flask that he passed back and forth with two other Raiders, his eyes heavy with grief.

Arek tapped my shoulder and pointed across the portside. "I think we've reached the others."

I squinted, looking out over the water. The reflection of the moon's ambient light broke on the water ahead. Two masts. Four masts. As we got closer I lost count.

"It's a whole fleet."

Arek nodded. "No wonder Raiders seem to be everywhere." He clenched his hand around mine as we approached the vessels. It was one thing for the six of us to be on one ship, with half a dozen Raiders. It was another to enter into their world, their territory—if they could claim any as such—completely outnumbered.

"What if we're wrong in trusting them?"

Arek looked at me, a smirk growing over his lips. "Then we jump."

I chuckled. "I'm sure you could secure us a few sea turtles to grab onto, take us to shore."

He winked at me, but I knew deep down he could do something like that. It was amusing and comforting at the same time.

The vessels were similar in design to one another. Most were attached together port to starboard, forming a floating platform that could easily fill the town square in Corallon.

"I'd ask you don't wander off too far," Erlin said. "We'll need to descend before daylight. But you may find better food and drink amongst these men and women than on this ship right now."

He nodded at the other Soulmagi. "Go ahead. They know enough about you all to welcome you and share supplies."

"Come on." Darvo urged Merja away from the railing. "You need to eat."

"Don't tell me what I need or don't need," she said, as they stepped onto the vessel connected to us.

As our crew slowly sprawled away, I turned to Arek, glancing at my hand in his. "The Oath." I hadn't thought about it until now. Was he seeing visions of me? Did King Ronin's death break the Soulmagic binding him?

Arek grazed my cheek with his free hand, his fingers cold. I wouldn't have cared if they were covered in Corallon snow. "There's only one way—"

Two Raiders ran toward us, their boots pounding on the metal. Arek closed his eyes. Had he seen something? Or was he as frustrated as I was with the interruption?

"Where is she?" The young man huffed, out of breath from running.

"I'm sorry." Another man, a hair shorter than the first, caught up and bent over, hands on his knees. "I told him to wait until you were settled but he wouldn't listen."

"Where is she?" The young man grabbed Kaleb, who pointed at me.

Arek squeezed my hand tighter and stepped in front of me.

But then I saw the man's face. The moonlight was just enough to make out the pinched nose and round eyes. His hair was longer, hanging over his ears and disheveled, but not long enough to pull back. It was the facial hair, the shaggy beard, that had thrown me off at first, why I hadn't recognized the shape of his face.

Reil's face.

My lungs froze. My heart trembled. My voice disappeared.

I hadn't had anything to eat at the palace dinner. Yet I ran, ran to the rail, doubled over, and vomited.

TWENTY-SIX

A hand touched my back.

"Doesn't matter how many times you've gutted otari or stomached gunnel. Seasickness gets the best of us."

I took two breaths and wiped my mouth on my sleeve. Seasickness had nothing to do with it. Or perhaps it helped contribute to it, along with my hollow stomach. I turned around, not awakened from the dream.

Reil's eagerness turned to apprehension. "Are you all right?"

"Is this some sort of magic? Is this a trick?" I reached my hand to his face, but pulled it back. I wasn't ready to feel the realness of him in front of me.

"No," he chuckled, the smile giving him a glow. "It's really me."

"Evella?" Arek offered a cup, and I took a sip. The smell hit before the taste, a strong acrid odor that opened my breathing. It stung going down my throat, then turned warm, an odd comfort. Darvo's grog.

"Thank you."

"Do you need anything else?" He briefly scurried his eyes to Reil and back. What was I going to tell him? He knew about my past. My history with Reil.

"I think I'm going to need a moment."

"You sure you're feeling all right?"

I nodded. I wasn't sure how I felt, but right wasn't the word for it. "Arek, this is Reil." I let the words hang in the air, seeing how long it took Arek to register them. His mouth opened a crack, and he carefully scanned Reil head to toe.

"I see," he said.

I stepped closer to him and touched his arm. "I just need some time to speak with him." I wanted him to know this didn't change anything. Or did it change everything? My stomach churned again, and I blinked it away, pushing the craziness down. I didn't want Arek to leave but I had too many questions to ask Reil. He had some explaining to do, and it was best we were alone.

Arek pressed his lips together and nodded. He turned away, and I wanted to grab him, bring him back. But Reil stood before me. The man I was going to be unioned with. The father of…

"How is it you're alive?" I asked.

"Come with me," he said. "Let's sit." He grabbed my hand, overjoyed to be holding it. It was numb along with the rest of my body. I walked with him unfeeling, confused, not knowing whether to embrace him or slap him.

He led me to the end of the vessel, the metal tapering off to a near point. Conversations were picking up volume across the conjoined ships. Torches and candles were lit, men and women clanging cups and imbibing and telling long tales of their seafaring.

But Reil and I, we sat at the edge of the world.

He let go of my hand and faced me. "That day, the last day we were together, when the quake struck— I fell amongst the breaking land."

I could see him reaching up to the sky, to me, as if it were happening right now in front of me.

"The thing is, I landed in the sea. I somehow managed to avoid the debris falling around me. I screamed but the breaking of land, the crashing of dirt and rocks into the water, it was too loud. By the time the noise died down the current had taken me east. I had nothing but my quiver to hold onto. It held a pocket of air, as long as I clenched down on the open side. I don't know how long I was in the water. All I remember is being colder than I had ever been before. I thought my muscles and bones had frozen, that the only thing working was my mind. That I had died but was cursed with my thoughts. But then, Raiders traveling from Tusinda picked me up."

I pictured him floating in the water, body frozen, all alone. It incited pity for him but not enough to overpower anger. "Why didn't you come back? Send word?"

"The Raiders offered to take me back to Corallon. But in getting to know them, they had a lot to say about the king, about the quakes. I didn't want to believe them at first. Who wants to believe their king means them ill-will? That their king values destruction and fear over peace and prosperity? But after some time, I saw the truth for myself. I wanted to help, I wanted to do whatever I could to stop the king. So I joined them."

He scooted a little closer and grabbed my hands in his. "I did come back for you, Evella. It's why the Raiders bothered to land on Corallon. But no one other than me knew what you looked like, and it was hard to travel without people recognizing me."

I thought of the Raiders landing on the shore, the same night I met Arek. Had that been Reil?

"But your parents, your sister—they all think you're dead." I shook my head. "How could you do that to them?"

"It's a sacrifice I had to make to keep them safe until our mission is complete."

I closed my eyes, picturing their house, the pure hatred his mother held for me.

"Evella." He shook my hands in his. "I've waited for this day for over a year. I actually can't believe you're sitting in front of me now." He broke his hold and opened his arms, leaning in to hug me.

My torso held stiff, the shock he was alive too debilitating. I caught the faint scent of him beneath the beard and long hair, the salt on his skin and the pulse of his neck so near me. I couldn't help but soften, despite my muddled emotions.

He let go and backed up. "The bracelet, do you still wear it?" He pushed up my sleeves and examined my wrists.

"You were gone," I managed. "For over a year." It didn't matter how long he was gone. I didn't want to wear a constant reminder of him, the love of my life that I couldn't save.

"It's no matter," he said. "I understand." He pulled my sleeves down gently over my wrists. "But now we're together again. I can make you a new one."

The pure joy he emanated was unsettling. How could he be away for over a year, *alive*, without a word to me or his family, and want to pick up right where we left off? I had loved him once. With every part of my being. If he truly was who I was meant to be with, then it would be easy to love him again, wouldn't it? Would I grow into that love again?

Sitting in front of him, I did love him. I loved that he was alive and that he found his purpose. But the kind of love that connected me with him, to spend our lifetimes together, was that kind of love there?

He jolted back and grinned. "My goodness, here I am shocking you that I'm alive, and asking you about a bracelet. As if that matters." His eyes were wide with wonderment, and his words came out with an eagerness, as if they'd been in his mouth for a year. "Tell me, the baby— is he or she well? I had pictured a girl but it doesn't matter."

There it was, the churning. My breathing quickened, the pounding in my chest hardening. The starry sky spun overhead as Reil's face neared.

"Evella." Reil braced my shoulders, holding me up.

I wanted to lie. I wanted to make up the happy world, happy family he had pictured for the last year. I wanted to give him that at least, but I couldn't. I couldn't keep it a secret. Not from him.

"The baby…" I closed my mouth and pressed my hand to my lips. I couldn't keep the nothingness in my stomach down. I shook my head and closed my eyes.

"Oh Evella." He leaned his forehead against mine. Suddenly I was taken back to the sled, on the water, Arek doing the same gesture. I had to throw it away. That memory. For Reil's sake. "It's all right, Evella." He wrapped his arms around me again. "I'm so sorry you had to go through that alone."

I hadn't gone through it alone, as much as I tried. I had involved my parents, and tainted the town against them, and made enemies with Reil's family. Nothing had gone to plan, and it was here, sitting before Reil, that I realized nothing ever went to plan.

Erlin approached us, steps sturdy and fast. "We are going to descend soon."

Reil looked up at him, the pain in his face slowly fading. "It's not close to sunrise yet."

"I know. But scouts report that word is traveling fast. I think it's safest if we go into hiding now before anyone else comes out on the water."

Reil nodded, and Erlin walked off, sending word along the connected ships.

"There's something I have to tell you, about the baby." I couldn't let him think I had lost the baby by nature, by some accident that couldn't have been avoided. He'd find out, if he ever set foot on Corallon again, if he ever returned to his family. He needed to hear it from me.

"The good news is, we'll have plenty of time to catch up." He stood and leant me a hand, and I rose to his level. "Time to reconnect." He searched my eyes for something—hope, happiness, love. Who knew if any emotion registered back.

"Honestly, Reil, I don't know what to think right now. This whole night, the past months, have been—"

He held up a hand. "Take your time."

More crew returned to the ship, including Arek, who slowly stepped our way, as if one of us would pounce on him if he didn't take his time.

Reil looked at Arek, then back at me. "We just need time, that's all." He looked back at Arek, and a new emotion took over his lips, curling them down with his angled eyebrows.

Suspicion.

"I'd better help Erlin prepare the ship." He clasped my hands and kissed them before slipping away. Arek kept his head down until Reil was long behind him.

I had no clear words to say to Arek. Everyone wanted to know how I felt while I had yet to discover it for myself.

"We're descending," he said.

"Appears so."

He walked with me to a porthole, a round squeaking hatch that opened into a black abyss below. The thought of being holed up in this clump of metal, beneath the water's surface, tightened my muscles.

Arek crouched next to the hole. "Are you ready?" He held out a hand to help me onto the ladder.

I hesitated, the other Raiders shuffling on their decks, disconnecting their vessels. The horizon was all but hidden, the night still dark, the sun a ways off from showing itself.

"No," I said, breathing in the salty cool air. I wasn't ready to leave my family, I wasn't ready to travel off Corallon to see the king, or train at Spokizar, or do what we had done tonight. It never mattered if I was ready because it all happened anyway. What's going to happen will not wait for my readiness.

Arek gave a wan smile, his face close to mine. "Are you all right?"

My body threatened to break down—my knees to buckle, my chest to heave, my eyes to flow tears. But by some miracle it didn't.

I shrugged. It was the best answer I could give.

"All right." Arek touched my shoulder. His eyes darted behind me and his hand retracted. "We can work with…" He shrugged, mimicking me.

I urged him to descend the ladder first, then I followed. I stood in the belly of the ship, the clunky metal that was to be my home.

Where we would wait in hiding, in safety, until the world was ready to be a better place.

Thank you for reading! Did you enjoy? Please add your review because nothing helps an author more and encourages readers to take a chance on a book than a review.

And don't miss more from M.E. Shotwell coming soon. Be sure to sign up for her newsletter at maryshotwell.com

Until then, discover THE IMRATI TRIALS, by City Owl Author, Lizzy Gayle. Turn the page for a sneak peek!

You can also sign up for the City Owl Press newsletter to receive notice of all book releases!

SNEAK PEEK THE IMRATI TRIALS

BY LIZZY GAYLE

Alone in his chambers, the king paused, sneering at the room's ostentatious finery, for none of it compared to his greatest treasure securely hidden from all but him. It was the very prize which called to him now, deep in the marrow of his being. Ready, he knelt beside the enormous fireplace laden with ash. The harsh weather of the Night Kingdom often called for keeping the hearths lit, but for the present, reaching inside and tapping the right place with his scepter was far more vital.

Rising, he waited as the marble slid aside almost soundlessly, revealing the spiral staircase down to his private dungeon. He trusted no one with the knowledge of this chamber's existence, for what he possessed was too powerful, too tempting not to turn even his most loyal subjects against him. Certainly, his daughter would never find out. Not until it was her time to join his collection, and that he hoped would be far in the future. Not because he carried a soft spot for her—she was too weak to deserve his admiration. He ignored the knowledge that this was by his own design as he snapped, igniting the single torch on the wall, and flooding the small round room with light.

His gaze roved over the set of gilded doors. Each one was fitted with a stone of power spelled to keep its occupant in a dream state. Only one of the three sat open, and the sudden memory played in his mind of the day his queen gave the last of her power. She'd opened her big golden eyes like she hadn't done in so many years—though only for moments— before the light slipped from them forever. Despite what she'd thought, despite it not being enough, he'd cared for her in his own way. Perhaps that was why he'd made sure never to grow too attached to their child. No need to torture himself with useless regrets again.

The king's attention shifted to the door at the opposite end of the row. He raised his scepter with the powerstone inside. Violet light erupted from the nucleus of the crystal, surging into the similar stone that sat behind a magical force-field on the room's center podium. When the light hit, the stone glowed as well, and he mentally directed the beam to the correct space. Unlike the center door, which had yet a third stone embedded and forever lit in its center, this one was unadorned. Its occupant was important, but not worthy or in need of extra protection. The center door would remain sealed until he had all the stones. Only then would he be strong enough to face Her without fear of wrath.

The woman inside the now open chamber blinked as she woke, eyes fluttering like tiny wings. She was attractive for an elf, but that wasn't his purpose in keeping her. When she saw him, she thrust her arms forward, meeting only the restraint of the iron chains that bound her to the wall. Unable to attack, she focused all her anger into her gaze, wishing she could hurt him back. But wishes were made of dust, and only those who seized power could mold the future.

He chuckled softly as she spit out a trail of colorful language in a raspy, rarely used voice. He lifted his scepter, and the sound stopped, though her lips kept moving. It took her a good while to realize he'd silenced her. She threw her head back against the stone, causing her long wild hair to slip back and reveal the points of her ears.

"I trust you've had a good nap, Miyal." He said it to irk her as he enjoyed watching her struggle. Knowing it was futile to fight against her bonds, that once he'd gotten what he needed, she'd be back asleep until the time came for clarification once again.

She curled her lip in a silent growl, daring him to try to make her. He smiled.

"I felt the shift in energy. The gods awaken." He stepped forward until he could reach out and lift some of her hair just to make her strain against her bonds again. "What must I do in order to collect the final two stones before it is too late?"

The fight drained out of her as he set the surface of the crystal in his scepter against her stomach. The remainder of her dress had long since burned away from the first of these sessions. He watched with fascination as her body arched against it, the pale purple light traveling up her chest to her throat and then over her head like a glowing hood. He'd have to recharge his magic when he was done here, and that meant a visit to his daughter sooner than expected. It couldn't be helped, though.

"And while you're at it, how long will my current energy source last?"

With one last tiny shove against Miyal, he released her voice so the deeper one with little affect could answer his query. She was poorly behaved, but she made a good personal seer. Quite accurate.

"The Imrati must be called. It is time to meet your destiny, Balram of Centos." He liked the sound of that, although he wished whatever spirits spoke through the woman would address him as king.

"The Imrati? You're sure?" He'd avoided the sacred tournament designed by the gods since he'd won the last one as a young man. Even the divine beings had been too shortsighted to envision someone like him could manipulate the balance of power they'd designed. He smirked, stroking his dark beard as he considered the fact that he'd outsmarted the gods.

"It is imperative to your destiny," the voice repeated, then continued, "Your source fades as she expends too much magic. She is like a star— bright but burning too quickly."

"How do I prevent this?" he hissed.

"You cannot. Though if she marries the Astrodonian combatant, you will receive the next stone. And if they provide an heir, a new source will be born with even more magic."

He nodded, calmer. Sooner than he'd have liked, the princess would be part of his collection, but it couldn't be helped. "And what of the other two stones?"

"One resides in the sky palace. But you will not access it until the princess' betrothal, though you will try."

"And the other?" he asked, tamping down the anger simmering below the surface. He knew the answer would be the same as always.

"The other is in the possession of your nemesis. Beware, for your foe is closer than you realize."

"As always, I will ask you again then, who do you name my nemesis?" The oracle had never given the name, and he often took his rage out on the useless bitch it spoke through. But he'd keep trying until he found the one she spoke of, or at least a new receptacle for the oracle. One that could answer *all* his questions. At least she'd added the warning this time. Whether the news was welcome or not, only time would tell. He would have to tighten his security, though he couldn't imagine anyone able to penetrate the fortress he'd created of Centos.

"His name must not be spoken," the seer proclaimed.

Rage broke free and flooded the king's system as his hand clenched around the scepter, trembling. "Speak it!" he demanded.

"I cannot."

"So be it," he whispered, then drew back the staff to swing.

Don't stop now. Keep reading with your copy of THE IMRATI TRIALS, by City Owl Author, Lizzy Gayle.

Don't miss more from M.E. Shotwell coming soon, and find out more at maryshotwell.com

Until then, discover THE IMRATI TRIALS, by City Owl Author, Lizzy Gayle

Forbidden Magic, a Dangerous Tournament, and a Choice that Could Destroy Her World.

Nyah, the illegitimate daughter of a sorcerer king, has always lived in the shadows. With only a touch of magic and no real power to call her own, she's accustomed to being overlooked—especially when compared to her full-blooded sister, Leuruna, the princess who suffers at the hands of their cruel father.

But when Leuruna transfers her magic to Nyah to protect it from their father's tyranny, Nyah is forced to flee the kingdom. Her escape takes an unexpected turn when she's saved—and kidnapped—by

Rivven, a mysterious and charismatic warrior with dangerous secrets of his own. His mission? To assassinate Nyah's father. But Rivven's plans come with a risk Nyah isn't willing to take: he wants to enter the Imrati, a tournament where the victor can claim the legendary powerstone and the hand of the princess.

It's the perfect opportunity to get close to the king and strike. But the stakes are higher than Nyah could have ever imagined. As she's pulled deeper into the trials—and into a scorching attraction for Rivven—she finds herself torn between her duty to her sister and the growing desire to stand by the man who's risking everything for a better world.

In a contest where betrayal runs as deep as the magic that fuels it, Nyah must decide: will she embrace the power inside her and take the chance to change everything? Or will she risk losing herself, and the people she loves, to a king whose cruelty knows no bounds?

Enter the Imrati—where only the strongest will survive, and the prize may cost more than anyone is willing to pay.

ACKNOWLEDGMENTS

It has been an incredibly long journey, releasing *Mist and Divide* out into the world. To cut a long story short, it didn't start out as an adult fantasy! After some two years of writing, rewriting, rewriting a thousand more times, here it is, and I am so honored City Owl Press again was willing to work with me to get it published. Sincerest thanks to Tina and Yelena for allowing me to fulfill my writing dream to include fantasy, and always keeping me in the loop of the latest happenings, and doing their best to support writers.

Luckily for me, this book found a home with my editor Tee Tate. What can I say? Our minds mesh, and you always know what I'm trying to accomplish and how to best make it happen.

My gratitude to Miblart for designing the wonderful cover, Agustina for the map in an incredible time crunch, and those at City Owl for the gorgeous interior.

Lastly, to my husband Matt, and three children. I had a seed of an idea for a fantasy story we shared around a fire one autumn night, and took turns adding to it. Some of those family additions developed into the bones of this novel. I hope you all enjoy seeing whispers of some of those pieces in this.

About the Author

M.E. Shotwell is the author of dark fantasy and horror for adults and teens. Several of her short stories have been published, including "A Sailor's Curse," featured as the finale in *Under the Full Moon's Light* Anthology (Owl Hollow Press, 2018). Her debut Adult Fantasy novel *Mist and Divide*, the first in the Soulquake series, releases Fall 2025 (City Owl Press). She loves incorporating her science and nature background into her fiction. When adulting, she's a wife to husband Matt and mother to three children. She currently resides in Tennessee. For more about her writing endeavors, visit…

maryshotwell.com

 instagram.com/authormaryshotwell
facebook.com/AuthorMaryShotwell
tiktok.com/@authormaryshotwell

About the Publisher

City Owl Press is a cutting edge indie publishing company, bringing the world of romance and speculative fiction to discerning readers.

Escape Your World. Get Lost in Ours!

www.cityowlpress.com

facebook.com/CityOwlPress
x.com/cityowlpress
instagram.com/cityowlbooks
pinterest.com/cityowlpress
tiktok.com/@cityowlpress

www.ingramcontent.com/pod-product-compliance
Lightning Source LLC
Jackson TN
JSHW082016100825
88918JS00001B/1